MONSTER PARTY

EDITED BY
ANTHONY GIANGREGORIO

OTHER LIVING DEAD PRESS BOOKS

MONSTER PARTY

Table of Contents

RIDE, MONSTERS, RIDE!

KELLY M. HUSDON

Nobody really knows how it came about that the tiny town of Waddy Peytona, in the great Commonwealth of Kentucky, was sealed off from the rest of the world. One day, a swirling fog encompassed the borders of the town, standing as tall as a pine tree and so thick nothing could be seen through it. Only a circle of the sky was visible, but it was enough to allow sunshine down and the stars to glitter at night. All of the electronic equipment stopped working, from the TV's and radios to computers and telephones. Search parties were sent out, but none returned.

People had their theories about the mist and where it came from. Some thought it was a government experiment, others an act of God. A few said it was space aliens, but there were always nuts like that in every town.

For Tom Baker, life-long resident of Waddy Peytona, a young man in his twenties with gangly legs, skinny arms and a thick head of black hair to match his eyes, none of that talk mattered because his life hadn't changed much. He still worked at the feed store and went about as he always had.

The day the monsters rode in through the mist, though, everything changed.

It was midnight and Tom couldn't sleep again. Insomnia was his newest friend, and to fight it, he often took long strolls while the town slept.

He stepped out of his house, locked the door, and slid the key into his pocket when something rumbled far away. It struck him as odd because it sounded like a motorcycle, but nobody in town that he knew of had one, and if they did, they wouldn't be riding it at this time of night. The other thing that bothered him was that the sound seemed to be coming from the mist, which stood about thirty yards out back of the store.

The sound grew louder and in number. He stood there on the porch and stared out into the haze, his mouth hanging open. Even though it was night, the mist always stayed a bright white; so white, in fact, it kept the entire town pretty well lit up.

The noise drew closer and the fog parted. Thirty men riding motorcycles poured into town, revving their engines and barking madly. But these were not ordinary men. They had the bodies of men but the heads of wolves and furry, clawed hands. As they rolled through the mist, they howled as one, their bikes pointed towards downtown.

Each of them wore black leather jackets and blue jeans with motorcycle boots. The backs of their jackets were decorated with a pattern of interweaving green roots with a bloody full moon in the middle. Across the bloody moon was embroidered in blood-red the words, *'The Pack.'*

Tom fell against the door, unable to tear his eyes away from what he was seeing. Those were honest to God werewolves on motorcycles riding towards the middle of town.

He grabbed his keys, opened the door, and ran inside, locking it behind him. He hid, peering out a pair of parted curtains. The werewolves rode on by, only slowing down to sniff the air occasionally, none having apparently seen him. And then they were gone.

Tom kept watch until he fell asleep, curling into a little ball by the window. He woke near dawn, the roar of the motorcycles jarring him out of his stupor. They rumbled past and howled, their leathers smeared with blood. One of them held the severed head of his old high school principal, Mr. Carpenter, by the hair of his head. The werewolf snarled and licked blood from the dripping stump before mounting it between his handlebars.

And off they rode into the mist, disappearing. They would return the next night, and they would not be alone.

Mr. Carpenter wasn't the only one they killed, as it turned out. A good half-dozen Peytonians were murdered that night, although butchered might be a better description. There wasn't much left in the way of bodies, just a few pieces here and there, scattered and bloody. A bunch more folks were injured. Darrell Goins, one of the best mechanics in town, got bit by a werewolf and in a fit of fear, his own father drove a stake into his son's heart, afraid Darrell would turn into a werewolf. Nobody gave him any grief over it, though, because everyone was scared, and it seemed a logical thing to do.

Skip Nichols, the new Mayor, called a town meeting. He stood on the steps of the courthouse and addressed the town. Nearly all of the one hundred residents of Waddy Peytona were out on the lawn that day, all of them scared out of their minds.

"Ladies and gentlemen," he began, like he was hosting some awards show. "It seems that trouble has come to our little town."

"No shit!" yelled someone in the crowd. Under any other circumstances, most folks would have laughed, but that day was a dire day, the first of many to come, and no one was in a giggly mood.

"The question is; what do we do about it?" Mayor Skip asked. Nobody spoke up. For a long, uncomfortable moment, the silence was so loud that Tom feared his ears would pop.

Unable to stand it any longer, Tom blurted out an answer. "We kill the bastards." All eyes turned to him.

"Just like in the movies," Tom said. "We know what they are. They're werewolves. I know it sounds crazy, but you all saw the same thing I did, and those bastards are monsters. We have to kill them."

A mumbling of agreement rippled through the crowd.

"But how?" someone asked.

"Well, I suppose just like Tom said. We do it like they do in the movies," Mayor Skip said.

"We need silver!" a woman screeched. And just like that, with the snap of a finger, the town went to work, everyone raiding their homes, finding all the silver they could. In the matter of an hour, everyone spilled into the streets and brought their goodies to City Hall and dumped them on the lawn. Mayor Skip looked at the piles of forks, spoons, trays and ornaments that dotted the lawn and nodded like King Solomon himself.

"Now, we need to melt these and make ourselves some goddamn bullets," Mayor Skip said.

And it was done.

That night, every able body hid in the shadows, armed to the teeth with their weapons made from silver. Tom waited at the store with a shotgun full of silver buckshot and an old silver sword that his Papaw said was honest-to-God from the Civil War. It was an old heirloom that had served as a wall decoration but now was once again a weapon of war.

Just after midnight, a rumble tore from the swirling mists. The Pack was back and ready to feast.

The plan was to let the werewolves get into the middle of town. Once there, the Peytonians would sweep in and attack. If any got away, then Tom and some boys that worked at the nearby gas station would pick them off.

He watched as the gang rode by and counted to five once they disappeared around the corner before stepping outside. Across the road, the Union gas station workers, four in all, came out, led by old Aaron McCoy, owner and stubborn old man. Tom met them in the middle of the road and they crept towards downtown.

Gunfire and screams shrieked into the night air. Up ahead, a din was raised and a cacophony of roaring engines and human cries mixed, filling Tom's ears with their dreadful cries. He and the gas station boys froze, unsure whether to proceed or not.

The motorcycles revved and headed their way. Tom's heart leapt, sure the townsfolk had turned away the awful creatures. But as the engines drew closer, they seemed louder and more numerous than before.

A member of the pack zoomed down the street, his eyes filled with panic and his snout sneering with anger. He took one look at Tom and the gas station boys and gunned his engine, barreling towards them. The gas station boys panicked and ran off but old Aaron, he spat a wad of tobacco juice on the ground, raised his rifle, sighted his target, and blew the werewolf's head clean off. When the boys saw this, they got religion and ran out into the street, whooping and hollering like they were at a tent revival.

They stopped dead when the rest of the pack roared their way. The boys raised their guns but the pack was too quick, zooming in on them. They jumped from their bikes and tore the boys apart, ripping flesh from bone and bone from body. Within moments, the boys were dead, a pile of skin, blood and jagged, broken limbs.

"There's too many of them!" Tom yelled. He grabbed Aaron and hauled him out of the street and around the corner of a building.

Just then, more motorcycles zipped into the fray, riding up behind the werewolves. The bikes were all choppers, ridden by a dozen pale men, gaunt and dressed in black tuxedos with short capes. It was another gang of bikers and each of them had the name 'The Fangs' etched in fancy red script on the backs of their capes.

Tom stepped from hiding to look on the scene. He would be goddamned if he didn't just stand there and watch a gang of vampires chasing after a gang of werewolves through downtown Waddy Peytona. He had seen a lot of sights in his day, but none like this.

Old Aaron yanked him back out of harm's way, and they crouched low and watched as things played out on the street before them.

The 'Pack' circled their cycles and made a line blocking the street. The 'Fangs' slid their choppers to a stop about twenty yards away, forming their own line. The leader of each gang got off their bikes and strode to the center of the space between the two groups.

"Count," growled the leader of the Pack.

"Luke," smiled the Count.

"We got here first," Luke said.

"We got here best," the Count countered.

"No way you'll back off?" Luke asked.

"No way, no how, no thanks," the Count said.

"We rumble then, tomorrow night. Right here, same time," Luke said. As the Count nodded, all heads turned to the swirling mists behind the Pack as another large rumble of engines came thundering along the road.

"Oh, no," the Count said.

Tom watched, fascinated and frightened, as what had seemed at first unbelievable now reached new heights of hysterical madness.

Riding out of the mists whizzed a dozen funny cars, all souped-up with fancy chrome pipes, bright colors, and flames. Each vehicle had the words '*Sons of Osiris*' painted on their sides. Tom hadn't seen cars that cool and retro since he went to one of those classic car shows when he was a kid. Driving each of these funny cars was an honest to God mummy, the kind that gets up and walks around in those movies about Egypt. They drove past the Pack, who snarled and howled at them, and parked in a line so that they were caddy-corner to the Fangs.

Their leader, a mummy with a fancy headdress that reminded Tom of some Egyptian king, got out of his car and shambled over to join Luke and the Count.

"Tut," the Count smiled. His fangs gleamed in the moonlight. Luke didn't say a word, he nodded to acknowledge Tut and that was all.

"Did someone call a meeting and I wasn't invited?" Tut asked, his voice like sandpaper being rubbed together. He laughed, and as he did, dust coughed from his mouth.

"I guess you want a piece of this town, too," Luke said.

"Indubitably," Tut said, more dust puffing from his mouth.

"Then it shall be a Royal Rumble tomorrow night," the Count said, with a flourish of his hands. Barely were the words out of his mouth when from behind them, growling through the middle of town in the direction the Fangs had come from, thundered another group of vehicles. They were monster trucks, all tall and fat and full of redneck pride, and driving each of the dozen trucks were identical-looking green men so large they filled the entire cab of each vehicle.

"And here I thought the party was already full," the Count said, rolling his eyes.

The monster trucks, painted green and purple, rumbled past the Fangs and stopped opposite of the Sons of Osiris so that now all the creature gangs formed a giant square. A big green fellow who wore a vest made of sheepskin with the words '*The Monsters*' etched in the back, got out of his truck and stalked towards the other gang leaders. He stood eight feet tall and was all muscle and brawn. He wore a trucker hat with a big confederate flag on the front and had a bolt jutting out of each side of his neck. He stomped over to the leaders, a big grin on his face.

"Frankie," Luke said.

"We all Frankies," Frankie said, waving back at his gang. They hit their air horns and screamed with delight. "We Frankies come to eat peoples, but then we Frankies see you guys all here."

"We were just discussing that, Frankie," the Count said. "We're going to have a rumble tomorrow night, and it looks like you're invited."

"A monster party?" Frankie laughed. "Frankie likes monster party!"

"Yes," Tut said, spitting out a few pebbles with his dust this time.

"It good," Frankie said.

The leaders stared at each other for a moment then they each extended a palm, spat into their own hands, and shook on it. A few seconds later and the groups were back on the move, each of them leaving town by a different route.

Minutes later and Waddy Peytona sat alone in such a silence it was like nothing had even happened.

Slowly, what was left of the Peytonians made their way out to the center of town where all the monsters had met. They looked at each other in a daze, uncertain of what to do. The crowd parted as Mayor Skip waded through them and stopped before Tom. He eyed the storekeeper with equal parts anger and fear.

"Well, smart guy," Mayor Skip said. "What should we do now?"

Tom thought on it a moment and came up with the only answer he could think of. "We do the same thing. We fight."

A murmur went through the crowd.

"Think about it. We got the silver already made up. Now all we got to do is fashion up some stakes for the vampires and get some torches ready to burn up the mummies and the monsters. We'll show these sonsabitches what real Fighting Kentuckians can do!"

The crowd cheered.

The next day, the town went to work, and by the time night descended, dozens of stakes and pots of burning fire were ready to roll. The townsfolk looked each other over, grim and determined. No monsters were going to drive them off their God-given land.

They hid, and when midnight came, so too, did the gangs. The Pack rode in first, followed by the Sons of Osiris, and then the Fangs and finally, tooting their air horns, the Monsters.

Everyone in town held their breath as the gangs circled each other, revving their engines, roaring and taunting each other. Finally, after about ten minutes of this, one of the Pack dove off his bike and tackled a vampire.

The fight was on.

Never had Tom seen such a sight in his life. He'd watched a lot of scary movies in his time, but none of them were as real or bloody or crazy as what he saw this night. Frankies ran over werewolves and mummies choked vampires with their bandages.

It was a free for all, screams and howls and cries mixing in the air and floating off into the mists that swirled around the town. No one gang was winning, but they were all fighting hard and vicious. In the meantime, the Peytonians waited, biding their time.

Then all hell broke loose.

Something loud roared in the mists and every creature and human looked up as the snarl thundered again. The entire town shook as something enormous moved through the mists, stomping the ground and crushing trees like empty cans of soda pop.

Tom glanced over at old Aaron who was standing next to him and watched as his ancient face turned whiter than a virgin's wedding gown.

A giant reptilian foot loomed out of the mists and smashed down into the middle of the Monster Party, crushing half the gangs. Then another reptilian foot came down demolishing an entire block.

A massive dinosaur walked into town, spitting bits of fire from between its teeth. It had a long tail with big bones jutting out and two tiny arms like those of a Tyrannosaurus Rex. Its eyes were blood red and its enormous teeth glittered in the reflected light of the mist. The dinosaur roared again, fire whooshed from its mouth, and four houses were engulfed in flames to burn to the ground almost instantly.

No one moved. Everyone, man and creature alike, stood rooted in fear. That's when the other one came.

Another cry split the air, this one a shout of hot rage. The cry was followed by a thumping, as if giant conga drums were being bashed by an epileptic drummer. Tom turned and stared as a colossal gorilla hopped out of the mists, almost as tall as the lizard, beating its chest and bellowing, fit for a fight.

The big lizard and the giant gorilla froze, measuring each other.

In the middle of what was left of the surviving gangs, Luke, the leader of the Pack, hollered out, "Screw this! I'm gone!"

His mob of werewolves hopped onto their bikes and fled the town, kicking up great clouds of dust and exhaust. As they rode away, so did the other surviving gang members, all hot on the werewolves' tails like dogs running after a bone.

The gorilla jumped on the lizard and they came crashing down, rolling around, and splintering all of Waddy Peytona beneath them. The remaining Peytonians ran for their lives.

Tom dashed over and grabbed one of the discarded choppers. He kicked it into life and drove it to the edge of town where the mists swirled.

He glanced over his shoulder and watched the lizard and monkey fight and knew there would be nothing left of his hometown. And if there was, it would always be a target for the monsters.

Tom said goodbye to his birthplace, put the bike in gear, and drove off into the mists to whatever fate awaited him.

MONSTER DETECTIVES

ANTHONY GIANGREGORIO

My name is Frank but everyone calls me Frankie.

Frank N. Stein, get it?

I'm the leader of the monster detectives.

My partners are a vampire and a zombie.

Strange you say?

Perhaps, but what most people don't realize, is that deep within our society, under the dark underbelly of humanity, lies a world the average citizen would never believe existed.

Monsters, demons, the supernatural, its all true, and it's up to me and my two partners to ferret it out and destroy it.

The hard part is doing our job while remaining anonymous.

It's not that hard for Vinnie to do. With the exception of disliking garlic and an aversion to wooden stakes and daylight, not to mention his pale complexion, he's basically normal looking. He can work at night with ease and with the exception of his fangs, no one would ever assume he's anything but human.

Even Zack the zombie has an easier time of it than me. Zack may be a rotting pile of meat, but with some dark sunglasses, a hat, and half a dozen cans of Lysol, he at least doesn't smell like week old road kill. He can usually wrap his face in bandages, put on some gloves and a heavy jacket, and get away as a burn victim as well.

And me?

Well, it becomes a little difficult to hide a seven foot tall man with green skin and bolts coming out of the left and right side of his neck. Though I should point out that in a few circles, I actually do blend right in and my bolts are considered a 'fashion statement.'

Together, we're the Monster Detectives, and if you experience something that doesn't make sense, that logic can't explain, then we're your *men*, so to speak.

The only thing we ask beside payment is that you don't ask too may questions.

I was sitting at my desk reading the newspaper when Zack and Vinnie came into the office. We rented half the floor of a rundown building on the south side of town.

"You read today's headline yet?" Vinnie asked me as he sat down in one of the two chairs in front of my desk. He was wearing a dark cloak to protect his pale skin from the sunlight and he threw the hood back to expose his handsome visage.

Zack merely stumbled in and plopped down in the other chair. I could smell him the moment he entered my office, but after all the years of working with him, I was used to it.

"Yeah, I just finished it, why?" I asked.

Vinnie nodded to the paper. "And the headline didn't sound a little, oh I don't know...off?"

"Off how?"

"Well, the cops said that a couple of teenagers were up on Overlook Point necking, right?"

I nodded.

"And that they were attacked by some kind of wild animal, probably a bear?"

"Yes," I said.

Vinnie smiled, showing his fangs. "Well, if that was the case, since when do bears rip off car doors and shred people into lunch-meat?"

I nodded, considering what Vinnie was telling me. "You think it's something that we might want to get involved in?"

"Sounds like a Lycan to me, Frankie," Zack said as he pulled out a plastic Tupperware bowl with a cover and popped off the top. Inside was something bloody, a liver or a pancreas. Without hesitation, he reached in and began shoveling it into his mouth. Zack was what you would call a 'messy eater' and he ignored the blood dripping off his chin and onto his shirt.

"Do you have to do that here?" I asked him.

Zack shrugged. "Sorry, Frankie, I missed breakfast. I may be dead but I'm still a growing boy." He let out a burp filled with the stench of rot and I fanned my hand in front of my face. I was technically dead, too, but the difference was my insides worked. My heart beat and my organs did what they do in any human, the only thing was mine came from different people.

I ignored Zack, or tried to, and looked back to Vinnie. "Is that what you think, too, Vinnie? That this was a Lycan attack?"

"I'd bet my left fang on it." He smiled, showing both fangs. "I say we find the next of kin and see if any of them want us to investigate, to find out what really happened to their loved ones."

I rubbed my chin as I considered it and finally nodded. "All right, I'll call my contact at the police station and see what I can find out."

"Good," Vinnie said and stood up. "You can reach me on my cell. Till then I'm gonna grab some shuteye." He yawned. "It's been a long night and I could use a few hours rest."

Vinnie walked out of my office. He was heading to his own office at the end of the hall. Once inside, he would go to his desk, open the lid to expose the hidden compartment inside that looked like a coffin, and climb in. The desk/coffin was custom made by a family of wood elves and Vinnie had said every penny he'd spent was worth it.

It was lined with purple velvet, had a mirror on the inside of the lid, and a small five inch television with a satellite uplink. That way Vinnie could watch TV before he drifted off to sleep.

I looked at Zack as he finished his breakfast. "Thanks for eating that in here. You got blood all over the floor."

Zack shrugged. "The maid will clean it. It's not like it's the first time she's found blood on the floors of our offices." He stood up, his limbs creaking like an old sailboat too long at sea. "I'll be in my office, too, let me know when you have something." He turned, and without so much as an apology, shambled out the door the way zombies often do.

I leaned back in my chair and sighed, wondering if it was all worth it sometimes. Then I decided I really didn't have much choice in the matter. For better or worse, I was stuck with a vampire and a zombie for partners.

Reaching for the phone, I called the local precinct and my contact to see what dirt I could 'dig' up on the young couple's death.

Later that night, a little after the sun had gone down, the three of us stood by the police impound lot, by the south fence, and out of sight of the security monitors. My contact had told me this was where the car of the dead couple was taken when the CSI team was through with it.

Vinnie was dressed in black, and with the sun down, he looked relaxed and confident.

"Okay, Vinnie," I said to him. "This is all you. Neither me or Zack can climb well, so go on in there, check out the car, and get back here before you're spotted."

Vinnie flashed his fangs at me. "Piece of cake." He looked at Zack with a grin. "Sorry you can't come, too, deadhead."

"I'll get over it," Zack said as he munched on a severed hand.

I never asked Zack where he got his body parts for snacking and he never offered.

Vinnie spun around and ran to the fence. As quick as a cat, he was up and over, landing lightly on the ground. He turned and waved to me and Zack through the chain-link fence. Then he was gone, a wraith lost in the falling shadows of the night.

While Zack and I waited, we chatted a little. We didn't have a lot in common and to tell you the truth, Zack wasn't much of a conversationalist. Maybe it was his rotting brain, but he just wasn't one for chit-chat.

Ten minutes later, Vinnie was back, and after scaling the fence, he dropped down between me and Zack and held up a digital camera he'd had on his person.

"Wait till you see what I got on this," he said as he handed me the camera. I took it from him and then pointed to our car parked ten feet away. "Later, once we're away from here."

They both agreed and we headed to the car. It was a black limousine, more than ten years old, and it was one of the only vehicles I can sit in comfortably. Vinnie drove, and Zack and I sat in the back.

I began studying the pictures in the camera.

Most looked like what you'd expect if a car was attacked by a bear. The windshield was smashed, the mirrors broken and hanging by their wires that powered them. The side of the car the 'bear' had attacked was dented and scratched, but as I looked at one picture in particular, my eyes creased in thought.

"Did you find the one I zoomed in on yet?" Vinnie asked from the driver's seat as he wove through the city traffic.

"You mean the one with the claw marks?" I asked.

"That's the one. Notice anything different about it from say…a bear's claws?"

Zack looked over my shoulder and said, "There's five claw marks instead of four."

I looked at Zack, then at the camera, and nodded in agreement. "He's right," I said. "A bear would have probably left four marks, but if it really was a werewolf, there would be five."

"Bingo," he said from the driver's seat as he cut off a cab and laughed when the cabbie honked at him.

"Okay," I said. "So we definitely have a werewolf on our hands and this one is hunting for human prey." I glanced out the window at the full moon. "Chances are it's gonna be on the prowl tonight as well. We'll need to act fast if we're going to find it."

"But what about the family of the couple? Don't we need to get a client first?"

I shook my head. "There's no time and we can't let this monster keep killing. We made an oath to protect humanity. You remember that, Vinnie?"

"Yeah, yeah, don't go getting all high and mighty with me, Frankie, I remember just fine."

"Good, so get going to Overlook Point. Werewolves stake out their territory like regular wolves do. If it's going to attack again it'll be in the same place."

Vinnie shook his head. "But the cops cordoned off the area with tape and signs; there won't be anyone up there."

I chuckled. "You think so? Vinnie, my boy, you've been undead for far too long if you don't remember what its like to be a teenager. Trust me; there'll be someone parked up there, maybe even more than that."

"Huh, I guess we'll see," he said and turned off the main road to a side street that would take us through the west side of the city to Overlook Point.

* * *

Overlook Point was in the middle of nowhere. By chance, a fifty foot section was devoid of trees or shrubbery. If you drove to the edge of the road, you had a grand view of the city below.

The Point had been active with teenagers looking to get hot and horny for more than twenty years and I knew even a bear attack—or an assumed bear attack—wouldn't stop sex-starved teenagers from coming here. The attitude of it always happening to someone else was prevalent in teens, and as we approached the Point, my hunch was correct.

Three cars sat at the edge of the Point, two cars and a pickup truck to be exact. The police tape that had cordoned off the area was on the ground, blowing in the wind, thanks to the first car that had driven through it and snapped it.

As we slowed down and stopped, Vinnie put the limo's transmission into park. I smiled when I saw the shocks of the pickup truck moving up and down slowly.

"So what's the plan?" Vinnie asked me as he turned around in his seat.

"We wait for the werewolf to show up and then do what we do best."

"Are we going to kill it?" Zack asked.

I shrugged. "No, we need information from it, but if the beast leaves us no choice, then yes, we'll have to kill it."

Vinnie patted his chest as if he was searching for something. "And I'm fresh out of silver stakes," he said with a sly grin.

I patted my chest. "Don't worry about that. If it comes to it, I'll deal with the killing."

"So were just going to sit here and wait for it to show up? We're just going to use those kids over there necking as bait?" Vinnie asked.

I nodded. "Yeah, I'm afraid so. Nothing works better than live bait."

Zack shifted in his seat beside me and pulled something raw and bloody out of a Ziploc bag he'd had hidden in a pocket. "Well, if we're gonna wait, I might as well have a little snack." He began tearing into the bloody object, his pale lips smacking as he sucked in the crimson gruel. Once more I wondered where he got his body parts.

I rolled my eyes at the sight of Zack eating, and Vinnie laughed and turned around. He turned on the radio, put his feet up on the dash, and we all got comfortable for the stake out.

I checked my watch for the tenth time in as many minutes. It was a little past midnight and I was growing impatient.

Out at the Point there were three new cars, each with fogged windows and bouncing shocks.

In the driver's seat, Vinnie was playing solitaire, and beside me, Zack was sleeping, his grunts and groans reminding me of a zombie from the movies. See, Zack was dead and he was a zombie, but his bite wasn't infectious and he could think as well as talk. Still, he did love to eat humans, though he didn't actually kill them for sustenance. Like I said before, I often wondered where he got the body parts he was always snacking on. I made a mental note to ask him when this case was over.

I was so lost in thought that at first I didn't hear the scream that rent the air, coming from one of the cars, but as the second shriek filled the night, I snapped back to reality.

"Looks like he's back," Vinnie said as he sat up straight, the cards he'd been playing with falling to the floorboards.

"Come on, let's go before he kills someone else," I said and kicked my door open and heaved my seven foot frame out of the limo. I made sure to slap Zack on the right cheek on my way out, and with a few grunts and groans, he snapped awake.

Zack's white eyes took in the inside of the limo, and when he heard the next scream shatter the night, he realized what was happening.

Vinnie was right beside me as he jumped from the driver's seat and we ran across the gravel to the three cars which weren't shaking anymore.

As we reached the cars, two of them put on their headlights and then backup lights lit the night. With screeching tires, the pair backed up and tore off down the road, leaving the one car behind.

This was the one being attacked, and as the overhead clouds parted and allowed the moonlight to bathe the area, I saw a large, hairy back as the werewolf leaned into the broken side window of the car, trying to get at the frightened couple trapped within.

"You go left and I'll go right," I told Vinnie, who nodded and sprinted around the car to come at the werewolf from behind. I could hear Zack's feet crunching on the gravel as he tried to catch up to us. Zombies don't run very well.

I ran to the driver's side of the car, and when I reached it, I didn't like what I found.

The once fogged windows had been wiped clean thanks to the terrified teenager trying to break free of the werewolf, the boy's hands pounding on the glass in terror. As I studied the scene, I wasn't pleased with what I found.

The werewolf had killed the girl in the passenger seat immediately after reaching inside and her throat was torn out, her blood still sputtering to cover the front seat and dashboard of the car. The teenage boy was still trying to fend off the werewolf, but the same time I reached the car and was grabbing the door handle to open it, the claws of the beast lashed out and basically tore the teenager's face clean off. The teen's arms and legs were waving and kicking as blood shot out to splatter the interior glass.

Meanwhile, the werewolf was gutting the girl, ripping out her organs to feed like the carnivore it was.

That's when Vinnie reached the werewolf, and with superhuman speed and strength, he grabbed the beast by its shoulders and yanked it free of the car.

It rolled across the ground and came up in a fighting crouch amid a cloud of dust.

Zack caught up to Vinnie and the two stood side by side, ready for what the werewolf did next.

As for me, I opened the driver's door to see if I could help the couple.

The door was locked so I used my strength and tore it off the frame. As the door popped off and I tossed it aside, the teenage boy rolled out and landed heavily in a heap of arms and legs. He was dead, there was no question of that, and when I peered into the car, the girl was already cooling, her torso ripped wide open from the claws of the beast.

There was nothing I could do for these two poor souls so I stood up and went to join the fight with my partners.

Just as I stood and turned to see what was going on, the werewolf lunged like a charging bull and ran at Vinnie.

Being a vampire, Vinnie was safe from being killed—unless he was beheaded by the beast—and he ran at the werewolf also, the two meeting in a loud slap of flesh and fur.

The werewolf tried to rake Vinnie's face with its claws and the vampire darted to the left and used his own fingernails to claw the back of the beast. He scored a hit and the werewolf howled in anger and pain.

Vinnie laughed, but in his overconfidence, failed to see the claw that swung around to tear open his throat.

Only his supernatural speed saved him from a beheading, but he still received a nasty cut to his left cheek and lower jaw. He jumped back and rolled away as the werewolf snarled and growled.

Zack had pulled a knife and he slashed at the beast's back while it was busy with Vinnie, the blade sinking in more than two inches before the werewolf spun around, knocking Zack to the ground.

I heard bones crack as Zack fell, but the zombie's face was as placid as ever. When you're dead, you don't feel pain.

The beast would have finished Zack off, or tried to, but Vinnie was back in the fight and jumped onto the werewolf's back, his fingernails trying to gouge out the beast's eyes.

By this time I was only a few feet from the fight and as Vinnie fought not to be thrown off the werewolf like it was a bucking bronco, I ran up and punched the beast in the gut, causing it to let out a *woof* that had all the air from its lungs spewing forth in one mighty gush of an exhale.

I was about to send an uppercut to its hairy chin when it spun around, causing me to sucker punch Vinnie in the side. The vampire yelped in pain, and I heard ribs crack, and he gave me a look filled with acid. I smiled, trying to relay my regret, but then Vinnie was flying through the air as the werewolf finally freed itself from him.

I was about to reach out and grab the beast when it dropped to all fours, spun around and took off into the woods bordering the Point.

It was gone in less than a second, swallowed up by the treeline. I watched the leaves shake from its passing, and was about to let out a curse that we'd lost it when I looked down, and there in the moonlight, I saw the bright crimson drops of blood.

It seemed that Zack had caused a deep enough wound with his knife that the beast was bleeding profusely and the blood was an easy trail to follow.

I went to Vinnie and helped him up. He shook me off as he wiped his clothing free of dirt and dust.

"I got it, Frankie, don't touch me," he snapped as he took a step away from me.

I held out my hands in apology. "Hey, I'm really sorry about that punch. I didn't think it was going to turn like that." I tried to rationalize it. "And besides, you'll heal fine. By tomorrow night you'll be good as new."

"That's beside the point," Vinnie said and winced slightly from his cracked ribs.

"Fine, we can talk about how sorry I am later, but right now we need to follow that werewolf. It's bleeding and there's a blood tail. We can follow it right to its lair and end this tonight."

Vinnie nodded. "Okay, let's do it, but you're right, were not done talking. You owe me, Frankie."

I was about to reply when I realized Zack wasn't where he'd fallen. I looked left and right and was about to call out to him, when I heard slurping sounds coming from near the car. I began to walk back to it, and as I rounded the rear bumper, I saw Zack leaning over the dead teenager, his face deep inside the boy's chest. He was tearing into the corpse's heart, his face and hands covered in blood and viscera. As he chewed and swallowed, the slurping grew louder and though I was a monster, I have to tell you, I tasted a little bile as I watched Zack feed.

"Zack, what in the Creator's name are you doing?" I asked.

Zack looked up, blood dripping off his chin. His mouth was full of meat as he chewed and swallowed. "What? Why let it go to waste? He's dead, right? And I'm hungry."

I sighed. I had to admit that Zack had a point. He needed to eat human meat and the boy was definitely dead. I turned to Vinnie. "Go move the limo so it can't be found, then get back here pronto. The cops are sure to be here soon. One of the cars that left had to have called for help, and with everything that's already happened around here, the police won't be long in coming."

"Got it," Vinnie said and limped away. He flashed me an annoyed look and I knew he was limping for my benefit. Vampires are tough, and though I can punch as hard as a mule's kick, I knew Vinnie could handle it.

Three minutes later and Vinnie was back. He had hidden the limo about a half mile down the road in a small cutoff. No one would find it there, especially not with the cover of darkness.

Together, the three of us headed into the woods.

Vinnie was first. With his heightened vampire senses, he could detect the faint scent of spilled blood. Next came me, trying my best to be stealthy, but my large form seemed to crash through the underbrush like a bull, or so it sounded to my ears.

Last was Zack. He had a coil of slimy intestine in his pocket and was holding a bloody organ in his hand, as he munched on it happily while bringing up the rear. Luckily, the wind was blowing away from him or else his bloody clothes—thanks to his feeding— may have confused Vinnie's olfactory glands. But as it was, the vampire was having no problem following the werewolf's trail.

Vinnie led us deep into the forest, and when we were about a half mile in, I could hear the faint sound of police sirens from behind us. It seemed the police had arrived at Overlook Point to investigate another 'bear' attack.

We walked for almost two miles until Vinnie held up his right hand and made a fist, signaling us to stop. Behind me, Zack was silent. He had finished his meal more than half a mile ago and had done his best to wipe his face clean of blood. He didn't do a very good job and even in the almost complete darkness of the forest— only what little moonlight penetrating the canopy to see by—I could see blood splatter was still on his face.

I waited to see what Vinnie had discovered, and then I began to hear grunts and snarls. Vinnie pointed to a copse of trees ten yards ahead of us and signaled that he was going to investigate. I nodded for him to go, and no sooner did my head bob up and down, then Vinnie was moving, a shadow lost amongst thicker shadows.

Zack and I stood together, looking at one another, me over a foot taller than him, when Vinnie appeared behind us a few minutes later.

I was so startled that I had my right arm raised and my hand curled into a fist, ready to smash whatever had popped up. When I saw it was Vinnie, I pulled my punch, feeling slightly embarrassed at being startled. I mean, I was a seven foot tall monster. What did I have to be afraid of?

"So, what did you find?" I asked Vinnie in a whisper.

He shook his head and said, "It's not good."

"What do you mean it's not good?" I asked. "Did you find the werewolf or not?"

"Oh yeah, I found him, and then some."

I was about to ask what he meant, and to tell him to stop being so cryptic, when he gestured for me and Zack to follow him.

Taking a wide berth of the area directly in front of us, Vinnie led us around in a wide circle. Five minutes later, he told us to stop and pointed to another copse of shrubs in front of us.

Doing my best to be silent, which isn't easy when you're my size, I crept up to the shrubs and reached out a hand to part them.

As I peered through the branches, I saw a glade, and frowned deeply, the sight before me not at all what I expected. The snarls and growls were louder now, too.

"I see what you mean," I said. "This complicates things."

The wind shifted, blowing the scent of myself, Vinnie and worst of all, a blood-covered Zack, into the glade.

In the small clearing beyond the shrubs, were five werewolves. In the middle of the group was the werewolf we had previously fought. The others were administering to his wounds, and when the wind shifted, all five heads perked up at the smell of intruders—namely us.

The pack snarled and spread out, and like someone had fired a starting pistol, they charged me first.

"Oh shit!" I yelled and that was enough to let Vinnie and Zack know we had a problem.

As the first werewolf came at me, I jumped forward to get free of the shrubs and we collided in the air. I was heavier than the beast, but it was solidly built.

We fell to the ground and began to roll around, as Vinnie and Zack fought battles of their own, the other four werewolves attacking en masse.

The werewolf clamped its jaws on my right wrist and I roared in pain. I used my free hand to punch the beast in the side. I felt bones break under my blow and the grip on my wrist weakened.

I took this opportunity and moved to my knees, then using all the strength in my seven foot frame, I threw the beast off me. It landed ten feet away and rolled end over end before coming up in a crouch. Its ears were lowered against its head and I could see blood on its fangs. It was my blood.

Then the moon went behind some clouds and the glade was all but lost in darkness.

I could hear Zack and Vinnie fighting behind me and I wanted to help them, as the odds were against them, but as I turned to assist my partners, the werewolf I was fighting came at me again.

I had no warning in the darkness.

Its dark fur blended into the night and I knew it was upon me when I felt its front paws hit my chest, knocking me onto my back.

Once more I was in a battle for my life. Science had created me but being rent from head to toe would still kill me. Though I didn't age—thanks to the formula of my creation—I could still die from bodily harm, fire being the worst.

As we rolled around on the ground, the werewolf tried to snap at the side of my neck, but each time all the beast got for its trouble was a mouthful of steel bolt. Luckily, the bolts in my neck were protecting me from harm.

Once more I began to pummel the werewolf with my ham-sized fists, and each time I landed a blow, I felt bones crack and snap.

Finally, I got my arms under it enough to push it off and the beast rolled away to come up fighting.

Then, thankfully, the moon broke through the clouds and I could see once more.

The werewolf was five feet away and was already preparing to lunge at me.

Acting fast, I reached into my jacket and pulled out a six shot revolver. The bullets had silver tips, made for just such an occasion. I didn't use it before at the Point because I was hoping to take the werewolf alive.

As the beast lunged into the air, its muzzle aimed at the front of my throat where the bolts couldn't stop its attack, I fired, my aim perfect.

The round caught the beast in the chest, and with a yell and an all-too-human scream, it dropped to the ground and remained still.

I was already turning to aid my partners, while behind me, the werewolf began to transform back to a human man.

Zack and Vinnie had managed to fight their way into the glade so they had some room to move. Vinnie was trapped beneath three of the beasts while the fourth—the original werewolf—had Zack's right arm locked in its maw.

No sooner did it bite Zack then it let go, making a face as it tasted the foul and rancid meat of the zombie. Zack used this moment to punch the werewolf in the face, his undead strength enough to knock a few of its teeth loose.

I raised my gun and was firing the second I had the first beast locked in my sights. The round hit the werewolf in the head, penetrating the left ear and blowing out the right side of its head in a spray of blood and brain matter.

As it fell to the ground, I shot the next one, the round striking it high on its shoulder. It fell away yelping in pain, and Vinnie dispatched the last one attacking him by gutting it from crotch to neck, his fingernails digging in deep and tearing into the fur and flesh as if it was paper.

Blood and organs spilled out, viscera coating Vinnie in a soupy mess as the werewolf slumped on top of him. It began changing back to human form almost immediately.

I turned to shoot the werewolf attacking Zack but found that my undead partner had things well under control.

He had both his hands inside the beast's mouth—one on the upper and one on the lower jaw—and with a low growl, he pulled up and down, prying open the mouth until the jaws snapped. The beast yelped once and went still, collapsing to the ground in a puff of dust. Zack never slowed. He released the dead beast and flipped it over. As the werewolf returned to human form, Zack tore into the deceased man's ribcage, quickly shoving the warm organs into his mouth like a starving dog at dinner time.

I didn't say anything. It was dead anyway. Man or werewolf, it didn't matter. Zack had to feed, it was his nature. If he didn't eat his daily requirement of human flesh, he would wither and rot away.

I vaguely thought how since this case began, Zack had been eating quite well.

Vinnie was on his feet again and trying to wipe the worst of the gore off him. He wasn't succeeding.

"If you had a gun with silver bullets all along, Frankie, why the hell didn't you use it before?" Vinnie asked me.

"Because I wanted to take that first one alive, that's why. But when I saw we were outnumbered, then all bets were off." I walked over and put a hand on Vinnie's shoulder where there was a clean spot devoid of gore. "Just be glad I had the foresight to bring the gun in the first place."

Vinnie had to give me that one. "Fair enough, but still, it would have been nice if me and Zack had known about your little ace in the hole."

I merely grunted in reply. I turned to see Zack gorging himself on human meat. I looked away, not wanting to see anymore. I may be a monster but even I had my limits.

I scanned the glade and the bodies strewn about. Four were male and one was female. They were all very dead.

I knew I couldn't leave the bodies like this, but what to do? Shallow graves were an option but then if these people had been here, it was possible they had clothing or vehicles somewhere nearby. Even graves wouldn't stop cadaver-sniffing dogs. No, I needed a better way to dispose of the evidence.

And then I had it.

I looked to Vinnie and said, "Grab as much dry brush and leaves as you can and put it over the bodies."

"What for?" he asked.

"A funeral pyre," I said. "This area is dry as a bone. We can set it ablaze and when the fire is out and they find the burnt bodies, the authorities will figure they were campers who got trapped in the wildfire."

Vinnie nodded. "Not bad, Frankie, that just might work."

"I hope it does," I said. "If the humans find out about werewolves, then they may look deeper into where they came from. The only reason we can survive in this world is that no one believes we truly exist." I looked over at Zack and said, "Hey, Zack, stop eating for a minute and help Vinnie get kindling."

Zack looked as if he was going to protest but I stomped my right foot, shaking the ground. Zack knew this wasn't the time to argue, and with reluctance, he left the corpse he was feeding on and began helping Vinnie gather brush.

Fifteen minutes later the three of us stood on the edge of the glade as the fire began to spread from body to body, the darkness pushed back by the crackling flames. It was just like I said. One match to a pile of brush, and in no time the blaze was going strong.

Already the flesh on the bodies was bubbling, the fat popping as it sizzled in the fire. The odor of roasting meat began to fill the glade, sweet and sour smelling.

Zack looked disgusted and I realized the redolence of cooking flesh was probably distasteful to him. He liked his meat raw.

We turned and began our two mile trek back to the limo. Vinnie led the way and he constantly had to fan away the flies that were hovering around him, thanks to his gore-covered clothing.

He glanced over his shoulder at me and frowned. "You owe me a new suit, Frankie, this one is ruined."

"Send me a bill," I said with a grin.

Zack caught up to me, let out a loud burp, and said, "You do know we made nothing on this job, right? We didn't have a client."

"Yes, Zack, I know that all too well. Let's just wrap this case up to protecting our secret. Like I said, if the humans find out monsters are real, then we're all in trouble."

Vinnie grunted. "Still, Frankie, it would have been nice to make at least a few bucks."

I shrugged my wide shoulders. "Hey, you win some, you lose some. Maybe our next case will pay better."

For the next twenty minutes no one spoke, we merely concentrated on walking.

Behind us, a glow lit the sky as the fire grew out of control, the smell of smoke tickling my nose.

Finally, Zack was the one to break the silence. "I'm hungry."

I couldn't help it, I chuckled at that. At least some things never changed.

SKYSCRAPER

ALAN SPENCER

"Stay in line formation. No sniveling, crying, or begging for your lives. You've been captured, and you will be processed accordingly."

Bryan Carter sloughed on, hearing these words issued from the line leader, a vampire. He kept a medium pace as they trudged through the business district of a decimated New York City. Walking down avenues eclipsed by the shadows of overbearing skyscrapers, he viewed the numerous tankers and military vehicles that had exploded, blowing up entire city blocks; the battle vehicles were rendered useless in a war that had raged on for less than a month.

Machine gun fire reduced walls into Swiss cheese, and the way was slippery with spent bullet casings. A wrecking ball had smashed through a local bank, where many humans had holed up in the safety of the vaults. Fires roared in vacant hotels, apartment buildings and businesses, as humans continued to be forced out of hiding.

Where they were being led to, Bryan remained uncertain, though they were moving deeper into the city. All that could be seen was ruined buildings, broken mortar and the occasional shape of human bones or piles of smashed entrails; what hadn't been picked clean by the zombies and the sewer rats the size of dogs.

"You're a lucky bunch. It's the truth, folks, so ready yourselves. Be prepared to fight. You people are the recipients of a fine offer, indeed."

The vampire talking to them was a ghoul. Talcum white skin. Mouth like a vaginal slit lined with teeth the size of a puppy's canines, yet sharp enough to snag skin and break open arteries and veins. Its leathery lips were shaped into a hideous smile as if drawn in black crayon by a deviant child. And the eloquent way it spoke, it lent the creature an even more unsettling presence.

Ten vampires up front, and ten in the back of the line, each monster helmed automatic weapons ranging from M-16's, AK-47's, M-60's, and a variety of low caliber assault rifles. The vampires used the props to convey that they were in charge; they were the military, the government, and any lawful authority.

Beyond the vampires, the walking dead flanked the left and right sides of them. Ripe husks of bodies melting in the sun, Bryan could hear their liquid meat slap onto the street with each new stride. He'd counted roughly twenty of the undead at each side of them, yet he knew there were many more in the ranks.

Then there were the misfires. Abominations nicknamed 'Hell's Abortions' and 'Throwaways.' Most were walking globs of human muscle and tissue; faces rendered sideways, organs grown on the outside of their bodies. Stump arms where mouths chomped and masticated for sustenance, torsos covered in eyeballs, their sinew visible as each orb flexed and studied its surroundings. Stomach churning and nauseating to study, Bryan averted his gaze and kept on moving.

He'd be seeing new abominations very soon.

"Halt and stand tall. Observe this building in front of you. It's twenty stories high and full of places for things—like us—to hide. This used to be the offices of the most prestigious and richest businessmen the world has ever known, and now they've been digested and shit out our asses, or they've become one of us. This will be our battleground."

As Bryan listened to the vampire address the group—what he gathered to be a hundred humans captured—he recalled what had brought him to this point.

There were no blurred facts about the ultimate cause. The media covered it in the first five days of the outbreak. The evidence was stacked high, pictures of the initial site, video feeds of the bent and warped steel bunker beneath the Red Desert where they'd fled and later slaughtered the human race. Reporters covered the staggering deaths and the attempted evacuations into other countries, but the ports were already infested with 'Hell's Abominations.' Other countries were overrun in a matter of weeks and any human intervention was easily subverted.

That bunker in the Red Desert had harbored the abominations; what had cropped up during nuclear testing—pre and post A-bomb testing and deployment. Birth deformities unknown to medical science inspired the mass captivity of each family affected by said nuclear testing that dated back to the 1950's. Within the impenetrable bunker, they'd thrived, conspired, and eventually, grew powerful enough to escape.

"Not all of you will survive this test. We only want one of you to live; the best of the lot. In this skyscraper, enemies will await you. All you have to do is make it to the top, or be the last to survive. Weapons have been placed in rooms and sections of the property, though your skill of fleet-of-foot and quick thinking will ultimately be your best fighting tool. Once you enter the building, you'll be given a few moments to collect yourselves—and then the battle begins!"

Vampires urged the group into the entrance of the building, a hulking skyscraper, which had been destroyed by a crude bomb. The front lobby had been incinerated, everything covered in a crispy black film. The zombies stood near the building to fortify any escape attempt.

They were trapped from within.

Bryan overheard whimpering and words of defeat, as other humans turned over table legs and ripped them off to turn them into bludgeons. A few had discovered the said 'weapons' the vampire at the head of the group had talked up. Samurai swords, grenades, 9mm pistols, a blow torch, hatchets, axe, maces, body armor, and even a motorcycle. The weapons kept cropping up the further the group spread out, including Bryan, who located a machete.

It wasn't much longer before the first abominations entered the scene.

Then things got deadly interesting.

The day the outbreak had spread to where he lived, Bryan had been driving home from a day working as a divorce liaison—a job that entailed sorting out people's property and finances in divorce cases without a law suit or taking a single step into the court room—and had picked up his wife, Karen, from work.

This was a habit he'd acquired because he did it one day when her car was in the shop, and she enjoyed being chauffeured so much, that he decided to make it a daily ritual. They were nearing home when a winged creature smashed through the passenger side window. A pronged reptilian hand seized her head, yanked her out so hard the seatbelt snapped, and his screaming wife was carried into the sky. That was the last he'd seen of her, or any semblance of a normal life.

Up from the high-rising ceiling, the white surface suddenly broke apart into living, breathing sections. Arms, legs, talon-tipped fingers and widening, shrieking mouths—those dreadful slits—descended upon them.

Vampires!

Machine guns blasted, pegging them from on high, as bloody rain cascaded down upon them. Bodies that weren't hit or fatally struck, touched down upon many, landing on top of their prey. Cloaking their leathery wings around their victims, the naked, fleshy things inspired shrills and screams of hysteria within the cocoon. When the vampires released their hold, and removed their wings, a flensed skeleton would drop to the floor. Sucked completely of worth, not a drop of blood or bolt of skin remained on the corpse.

Clutching his machete, one attempted to fly down upon Bryan and strip him of his flesh, when he closed his eyes and shouted in terror, *"Baaaaaaaaaaaaaaaaaah!"*

The edge of fingernails touched the back of his neck, so icy cold, the sensation like wet putty on his burning hot skin. The vampire was attempting to pull him into its wings and have him suffer in the skin vacuum.

Slicing, swinging, hacking, and slashing, the vampire-thing was rendered immobile. Somehow it still stood up, though headless and spurting blood from the stump. Crimson jets splattered him, and Bryan, shivering in its icy coldness, fled the thing he'd slaughtered.

He kicked aside a variety of human and monster pieces on the way up the stairs to the next floor.

A motorcycle chugged by him on the stairs, spitting out a cloud of fumes. One hand of the rider steered, and the other swung a samurai sword. Other people swarmed the stairs, kicking, shoving and punching their way through each other to 'safety.' Then the bullets rang off the staircase, pinging and ricocheting, the wall of gunfire unending.

Bryan ducked, as many others did. Some weren't fast enough and they were riddled with holes, murdered on sight. The gunner, who appeared to be a horror-stricken woman that could've passed as a lawyer in her business suit, kept sending M-16 gunfire at them from the top of the stairs, screaming, "I will be the last one alive!

Then the staircase itself shifted, uprooting itself from the wall. The guardrail was alive, the wood changing to something wet and slimy. A snake! A shape shifter! The head was at the top of the stairs, and the anaconda creature's head struck the woman, wrapping its green reptilian muscle-bound body around hers and snapping every bone in her body, the last being her neck, which snapped like a dry twig!

With the snake squeezing her from feet to head, guts and foamy blood spewed out her mouth. The pressure was so great that her head popped off her neck, and she became a human tube of toothpaste.

Rushing up the stairs, Bryan made it to the second floor, avoiding the snake that threatened to strike like a cobra. Dodging the threat, another danger unrolled from the ceiling. Falling like fleshy ropes, coils of what resembled intestines unrolled themselves and sucked the eyeballs out of unlucky victims' eye sockets. The vacuum suction was so powerful that the eyeless screamers' skulls would collapse inwards like a cranial cave-in. Hundreds of these creatures unwound themselves, latching onto whoever was close enough to exploit. Bryan dropped to the floor, out of reach of the suckers, and he crawled through puddles of blood and spent shell casings to evade them.

Getting back up, he continued on, and had made it a matter of yards, when an explosion behind him lifted him up off the floor. He tilted forward, almost spinning upside down. Soaring, he managed to stay in a position as if he was flying, and then he crashed into a hallway of offices. Head ringing, mind reeling, his shoulder blades aching from the impact against the wall, he laid still a moment and collected himself, for he couldn't will his body to move.

The undead surrounded the highway, stumbling after any living thing in a pack of hundreds. Bryan walked on the same stretch of highway, sticking to the area where his wife had been ripped from their car and taken away. He had to find her, alive or dead, he didn't care. He wouldn't leave her until he knew exactly what happened to her.

He gripped the cane tighter. He'd pried it off a dead man's hands; the man had been hit by a jeep after being mistaken for a zombie and was sadly struck down.

Continuing the search for Karen, an armored car pulled up beside Bryan, and the door opened. A woman dressed in army fatigues shouted, "Get in before they get you! You're crazy for walking in this area alone. You'll get yourself killed!"

"I can't go with you," was all he said, then moved on, striking a walking dead mailman across the head until his skullcap imploded on itself, and then added, "Best of luck to you, though."

Bryan kept on moving, weaving through the stalled and destroyed cars, dodging the undead, as he continued searching for Karen.

Able to get his body working again, Bryan was up and moving when he caught the pungent aroma of the anaconda burning; a blow torch had rendered the snake into a burning pyre. It writhed and thrashed its thick body, smashing through walls and glass windows, unable to alleviate its excruciating pain.

But the snake didn't matter so much when the next creature sprang out of the office beside Bryan, a red-eyed goblin whose flesh comprised of bolts of brown reptilian skin and a single bone-horn protruding through its apish skull. As it leapt onto him, Bryan pivoted to avoid the infernal thing, and it miraculously impaled itself on the tip of his machete. Coughing up a mushroom-soup gruel, the goblin turned to its side, issued a ear-aching shriek, and died.

Bryan crawled away from the thing, unarmed, and he raced on. Under attack, the ceiling was being ripped apart from the floor above them. Sinewy arms laced with pink gristle reached down and scooped up the fleeing victims surrounding him. They twisted off heads, squeezed torsos until guts and blood issued out both ends, or lifted them up into the ceiling, the sound of munching and crunching soon following.

Recovering a blood-covered 12-gauge from the floor, Bryan blasted at the ceiling. Two steps, *Ba-BOOM!* Four steps, *Ba-BOOM!* Six steps, *Ba-BOOM!*

Chunks of dried bones chinked and rattled down upon him, and one complete monster crashed down to his level. It was a creature with twelve arms and a body made completely of bones, like a fossilized dinosaur.

The way was safe for a few seconds, and he zipped ahead into a closing elevator. The five others already inside were gasping and out of breath. Their eyes were doubled in size, in constant awe, covered in various shades of green, brown, and red blood. Nobody said a word as the elevator closed and rose to the higher floors.

They talked amongst themselves after managing ten floors up, but Bryan blocked there voices out. His eyes roamed from the ceiling, to the floor, to his fellow human beings, and repeat, waiting for something to jump out at him like a psychopathic jack-in-the-box. During his watch, he caught a few words of what the group said.

"How many are left?"

"It's not like we can all survive..."

"You think they'll own up to their promise, and let one of us live?"

"...kill or be killed anyway..."

"This is the government's fucking fault..."

"Did you see President Yearling become a zombie on live TV? That shit was..."

"...no going back now..."

"...no, I can't...I can't keep fighting..."

"...she's right, we're dead..."

"...get a grip people. At least we have weapons!"

Even the fragments of conversation he heard were now ignored, as from the top of the elevator car, a bright green foamy substance slithered its way down the walls. It forked and shot up a man's nostrils, turned into a noose and strangled another, pried open a woman's mouth and shattered the victim's jaw as the green trail forced its way into her mouth and burst out of her belly.

Bryan shot at the green monster, but the bullets only served to tear up the walls. "Goddamn it!" he screamed.

He punched the button for the next floor up as webs and arterial branches of green were edging towards him, to squeeze him of life.

"Leave me alone!" Bryan demanded when the hot barrel touched a sliver of green, and it shrank back, its body smoking and curling up. "Take that, you bastards!"

Increasing the temperature of the barrel, he fired another round—each of his elevator mates jittering in nervous spasms as the green tore up their insides—and pressed the heated metal up against his enemy until the elevator doors opened. He fell out and was soon running for his life once more.

There was no row of offices or open space where he ended up; he'd entered what looked like the pink tissue of a human throat, though the walls were jagged with teeth. Any moment, the walls could close in on him and run him through. There was no end in sight, and he couldn't turn back to the elevator, so he used the last five shells in the 12-gauge to create a hole in the wall and force his way out through the strings and cables of broken meat.

He entered a large open foyer, where the walls were laced with the same pink throat meat. At each wall was a slit where mucous and blood slithered free, and then out came another horned creature, then a series of zombies, each rotten and fetid with black skin. Vampires with and without wings soon appeared, then balls of fur clawed their way free, what would soon turn into werewolves.

Then 'Hell's Abortions' were birthed: a head with two arms sticking out where the ears should be, another that was merely a spine snake creature, then a human who could shoot out visceral coils from its hands, the ends laced with lamprey suckers, then a woman whose hair was strands of flesh, the flesh itself wide enough to harbor mouths, teeth and a throat to swallow with.

The horrors kept coming, bursting forth onto the killing floor.

A man on a motorcycle kept burning out his tires, kicking up flesh and blood from the meaty floor, and stopping a moment, he opened fire on the room with an assortment of machine guns. Then a grenade exploded from another pocket of the room, though the person hadn't thrown it far enough, and he was struck by a burning hunk of metal, though he'd also destroyed the flying vampire stuck to the ceiling.

Bryan had nothing to defend himself with, and he was vulnerable, so he kept still, watching and waiting and expecting a fleshy enemy to snatch him up and end his existence, much like they had his wife.

Without anticipating it happening, a stick of dynamite detonated, and he was struck down by the shockwave, the sinewy floor cushioning his fall.

Bryan woke with a start, catching a wide berth opening on the wall a sprint's distance from his position. He got up, though he was weak with exhaustion. He'd been clubbed on the back of the head by a flying appendage, he gathered. The monsters were coming after him, and up he went again, storming ahead of them, to escape, to reach the top of the building, for a chance to win his survival.

He followed the dissipating fumes from the motorcycle; he heard the motor's churn, the bark of it, as he ran up stairway after stairway. He was running on the emergency stairs, he realized, as he stumbled up one tier after another. Guns blasted from near and afar. How many people were still alive?

Not many, he assumed, as he forded the next turn on the stairs, and the walls were suddenly encased in human tissue with hands, arms and heads biting and reaching and grasping for their victims. He easily avoided them, ducking, weaving and bounding out of their range, but a woman near him was snagged by a human hand, and held in place. A head seemed to swim down the flesh wall, the ripples giving the skin a waxy soft texture, and its teeth bore down on her. The last he saw of the poor woman was her lipless scream, before her throat was torn out!

He charged ahead, picking up speed, having to dodge strewn torsos on the stairway. Any moment the monsters would overtake him; they were playing games with him, enjoying the fear boiling and churning in his system.

Judging by the lack of gunfire, the motorcycle rider was the only other person alive. He wished the man no ill thoughts, nor did he want him to die. The monsters would kill them both, he believed.

The competition was drummed up for their enjoyment, the thrill of the kill. He'd hidden in abandoned apartment building and sewers in hopes of evading the creatures weeks ago, and they'd sit outside and wait him out, only to move on, after being pleased by the level of terror they'd put him through. He'd also discovered random items during his journey to New York. Backpacks stuffed with food and bottled water. Assortments of small firearms and First aid kits. Cars, trucks, and vans with the keys left inside and a full tank of gas.

Slaughtering humanity was their ultimate game, and they intended to extend the game for as long as they could.

Bryan was near the point of total exhaustion, and his injuries caused his pace to slow down to a weak jog. Nearing him, drawing closer, the monstrous shadows followed.

His end would be soon.

Slipping on blood, Bryan crawled on his hands and knees, both caked in red, shivering, and keeping on. He wondered how his body could still move after they'd stampeded through him. He managed back to his feet, though he was dizzy and disoriented and so confused. He marched in a straight line, traveling up yet another staircase, and when he arrived on the next floor, he saw double doors opened and the motorcycle on the stairs, mashed to pieces and dripping with blood.

He realized he was the last person to survive.

Entering the room the monsters were in, he heard the words being announced to a giant crowd of monsters; hundreds of them filled the room to capacity.

"It's a great disappointment—and no great surprise—that we've slaughtered them all once again! And in so short a time!"

Malicious laughter filled the denizen of beasts.

"Tomorrow, we find the next batch of humans. We'll have to plant more weapons. Select the stronger of the survivors."

The speaker was at the head of the ballroom, behind a podium; it was the vampire who'd led the group to the building and announced their fate to them earlier.

But he was alive! He'd outlasted everyone else.

How, he didn't know.

Bryan feared crying out and telling them the mistake they'd made because he couldn't trust their word. He'd wait them out, he decided. Let them go about their way, and he'd slip back into the city and return to hiding once more.

Then he was lifted up by the armpits by a great ogre who stank of shit and blood, and the deep-throated monster bellowed in a dumb voice, "This human! This human!" The ogre raised Bryan up high and shook him like a rag doll. "This human! This human!"

The entire room spun around and gawked at him, their object of attention.

Admiration.

He soon learned how he had lived this long.

The vampire speaker parted the crowd as he headed towards Bryan, and the moment the creature met up with him, it began removing the large set of jaw bones from one of

'Hell's Abortions' that had somehow landed on top of his head and stuck there.

Guts and bolts of tissue had piled up on top of Bryan's head, too, making him resemble one of the monsters. The change had happened in the pink room, where the monsters were being birthed left and right, and the explosion of dynamite had knocked him out. Whatever happened while he was unconscious, it had saved his life up to this moment.

They thought he was one of them...up till now.

Fearing their reprisal, Bryan cowered, but then another figure parted the crowd.

It was a female vampire. Naked from head to toe and proud of her form, she closed in on Bryan and held him close.

She whispered in his ear, "You're one of us now, my love." Her eyes lit up in a brilliant ruby red, and her slit mouth opened. She presented him with a wet kiss laden in blood and the stink of flesh—and he didn't care!

The vampire was his wife.

Karen raised her thumb up to his face and dragged a talon down the center of it, causing her to bleed. "Drink my blood, darling, and become one of us."

Sticking the bleeding digit into his mouth, Bryan sucked and lapped her deliciousness. She stroked his wet-with-death hair and cooed sweet words to him, bribing him with her love to drink more of her blood.

The group began to chant, filling the room with their continuous din. "*One of us...one of us...one of us...*"

And then he became one of them.

RASPBERRY

COLIN M. MAGUIRE

Lora managed to lift herself up on one arm. The effort made her head spin. In the doorway to the bathroom, silhouetted, was a large, shifting form in a silk kimono. A kimono? What was he doing in a kimono?

"Hey," she said. "Come let me see you."

The form revealed itself. She barely recognized him. "Wh...why'd you cut off your hair?"

"Part of the formality. I have to."

"Well, I don't even know you."

Steven gave her a disapproving glare, then vanished into the enormous closet and began ruffling around.

"Okay," he called out, "remember, I have to go today, like I told you. It's important."

Lora rubbed her eyes in confusion. "What?"

He came out and began setting various garments over a chair. "I'm leaving for two weeks. It's important that I look top drawer," he said, slipping into pressed black slacks. His undershirt revealed that his chest and back were waxed and polished. He preened himself, smoothing his short hairstyle.

Lora shook her head and slid her thin legs over the side of the mattress. She sat up as straight as she could, creasing her brow. "I want you here."

He laughed. "No. No. This is business. It's crucial. You'll have to be alone for two weeks straight."

She moved a lock of hair out of her eyes. "I don't know if I can do that."

"You can."

"Well, I don't want you to go. We just moved in here, didn't we? I'm just getting used to it."

"Yeah," he said as he stepped into his shiny black shoes, "that's just too bad. You'll like this place more once you have it all to yourself a bit. Besides, it'll be good for you to be without me for a little while."

"I liked our other apartment better."

He laughed and moved back into the bathroom. She lay back down, exhausted. She hated this damn place. All sterile and white—it was synthetic. Looked like something right out of a businessman magazine. Just cold as hell. How do you go from sterile to more sterile?

Each apartment had been colder and more clinical than the last, each neighborhood less eccentric and closer to the city. How many times had they moved now? She missed the place they'd rented a few moves previous! *That* place had been so cozy and warm—when he was first moving on up in the world. What a great apartment that had been! All the Bohemians surrounding them, the interesting shops and unique restaurants...

She tried to remember the time and area more clearly. Hazy images and feelings flitted before her, and she drifted off to a time long gone.

He had been so handsome back then. His hair still long and his body still skinny and wispy...he had been real cute and fuzzy and charming. He was just beginning to change, then. Now he was a sleek and polished machine.

Over time, the long hair had become a mullet, and then the back had gotten shorter and shorter, his hair becoming more perfect, to match with the job's economic progression. Not a line out of place. This latest haircut was like the plastic hair on a Charlie McCarthy doll.

She forced herself up onto one arm, observing him as he buttoned up his crisp white shirt.

"Is that a new suit?" she asked.

"They're all new suits, Lora," he said.

"It looks nice. Your hair is so short, though."

He laughed. "The shorter, the better."

"It doesn't even look like you."

He assessed her coolly. "Lora. It *isn't* me."

She sloughed back down into the sweat-smelling pillows and tried to keep her eyes open, to watch him before he left. "You look so pretty. I feel kind of nasty."

Adjusting his gold watch, Steven moved deeper into the bedroom and looked critically at her. He sat down on the mattress and brushed her hair away from her eyes. "Now remember, while I'm away on my trip, you need to eat your fruit. I've written on the calendar all of the days I'll be gone, and which day I'll be back. Do you remember how we talked about that?"

Lora nodded. "Yeah."

He patted her oily hair against her jutting bones, caressing her like a pet. "You honestly remember?"

She looked him in the eye. "Yes, yes. The days are marked on the calendar and highlighted, and all the money is in the briefcases under the sofa—in case I have an emergency."

Steven grabbed her firmly by the jaw. "In case you run into an emergency or?"

"I dunno!"

He squeezed her jaw harder. "In case you get hungry."

"I don't like to eat. I hate those soft bananas."

"You need to eat the fruit. It's essential. Now say it all back."

Lora reiterated. "You'll be gone for two weeks on business. It's important. I'm going to stay here and wait and not get into any trouble. The days you'll be gone are marked in highlighter on the calendar, and the day and time your plane gets home is clearly marked in red. In case of an emergency, I'm supposed to use our money in the briefcases, but *only* in emergency."

"Or?"

"Or if I need more fruit. And if I need more fruit, I should call the grocer's number on the fridge and not try to go out on my own because…because the cops will find me and put me away. And then there wouldn't be any more Raspberry and I would end up in jail or the loony bin."

Steven beamed, and patted her face hard with his palm. "Perfect, Lora, perfect. There's a good girl. Now, you shouldn't have to call the grocer, because I've already bought plenty of fresh fruit and put it in the fridge. You need to make sure you get up and eat some today."

Lora blinked at him in disbelief. Certainly he should be able to tell her condition. "Baby, I can barely make it to the fridge anymore."

He sighed heavily, as if disappointed. "I'll bring some fruit in here and leave it by the bedside, if you don't want to be a big girl. If I do that, will you be sure to eat it?"

"No, no. I'll get it. I'll be a big girl."

"You have to make sure you eat it."

"I don't want to, though."

"If you don't, then you get no Raspberry."

Lora stared at him with her half-open, weighty eyes. "Baby, you shouldn't say things like that."

"You need to eat your fruit."

"I want to go back to our old apartment."

"We live *here* now. And in a couple of months, we'll move up to a nice penthouse on Farnam Street. I need you to promise me to eat fruit while I'm gone. If you don't eat the fruit, you won't be able to get around by yourself—you know that."

"You mean if I don't eat fruit, the Raspberry won't be as good for you when you get back home."

He stared at her coldly, then snatched her by the hair and pulled it hard. His hand shook with anger and he pressed her into the pillow. She squealed in pain.

"Just eat the goddamn fruit, all right?"

"Ow! Ow! All right, all right! I'll eat the damn fruit. If it means that much to you— I'll eat it, I'll eat it!"

Steven let go of her. He slicked his oily hair back into its faultless position and smiled at her with satisfaction. "There's a good girl. There's Daddy's little girl."

She rubbed at her head where he'd hurt her. As Steven began to roll up the right sleeve of his shirt, she knew what she had to do, and obediently moved closer to him. When his sleeve was rolled high up to his armpit, he said his quick command, "Give."

Lora laid out her right arm as well, staring up at him. Her breathing had become rapid with expectation. Drool leaked down to the pillow from the crook of her mouth. Her inner elbow lay vulnerable, open and revealing.

Steven brought his arm to Lora's, so that the two appendages lay abreast of one another. At the very center of his inner elbow was a small grayish lesion. The lesion sported a tightly contracted hole in the middle, encircled with embossed ridges of puckered skin. Slowly, a thin, coiling pink proboscis emerged from within the cavernous sphincter. Unfurling and growing, the thin tendril felt its way around, reaching and seeking.

Lora's arm responded. Her own protrusion sprouted from her inner elbow. It was similar to his, yet was a completely different extension. Hers rose, lifting from her skin—fat and long, thickening as it became more erect. Swelling rhythmically with her excited pulse, the burgundy-hued orifice stretched out willingly, until it resembled an elongated raspberry. The bumpy texture throbbed, and the thickened nodule wriggled around.

The mouth-like maw at the tip of the protuberance smacked hungrily, anxiously searching for its counterpart. The thin strip of tendril crept along from the low, ribbed cavity which rested on Steven's arm. It poked around Lora's arm with blind familiarity until it touched upon her hardened Raspberry, and then excitedly wisped upward along its bumpy, pulsating surface until it found the top. Clamoring to Raspberry's mouth, the proboscis stiffened, then smoothly jammed itself into the gaping hole. Lora's Raspberry began swiftly nursing the cord like a hungry baby.

Both Steven and Lora gasped in unison—their eyes rolling back, their bodies becoming rigid. The pink proboscis became dark as the thin line of black, slimy liquid streamed from within her, willingly surrendering itself into Steven's sucking extension. They both became less stiffened, and their bodies loosened.

As the tendril fed from Lora, it began to expel a responsive secretion from its coating—entering the inner walls of her Raspberry and therefore saturating her with an intoxicating elixir. Lora's Raspberry absorbed the secretion greedily, the effects of which caused her to slacken completely. Her eyes fluttered and her mouth fell wide open as she became lost in the array of colors and sensuous feelings that soared through her mind.

Steven's protrusion, becoming full on the nectar it exuded from her elongated polyp, slickly removed itself and retracted fatly back into the small lesion in his arm. He wiped the small dab of black liquid from the hole and licked his finger. Rolling down his crisp shirt sleeve, one would never have known there was anything beneath the cloth but ordinary skin. Not even a drop remained.

He stood upright quickly, his strengthening mass bulging out with renewed vigor. His chest thrust out like a dominant primate. He took in the gush of power and energy as it coursed through his veins. He straightened his tie.

He looked down with disgust at Lora, whose protuberance had gone slack and withered, and was limply shrinking back into her arm. Her eyes rolled unseeingly and drool ran down her face, soaking the pillow.

"Now you eat that fruit like a big girl," he said, his voice trailing fainter into the next room. "Just eat the fruit and you'll be okay."

Then his voice disappeared completely, and all Lora could hear was the door clicking shut and the lock being secured.

She lay comatose for what could have been two days or so, maybe longer. The room began to come back into view and she came down harshly—left without the juice to keep her mind in the void of space and floating planets that she occupied from day to day. She remained on her side for hours and hours, until the effects of the Raspberry exchange had completely worn off and dispersed from her system.

"Dammit," she cursed, rolling over onto her back and staring up at the cold, foreign ceiling's cross-hatch. What was she going to do for two weeks? She scratched at her arm, and could feel the stickiness of her oily skin against her finger. After a few hours, she became clear enough to where the putrid rotting smells infesting the slimy bed became apparent to her, and her mind began to sharpen enough for her to realize she was disgusted.

Lora pulled herself up and then remained seated on the edge of the mattress. She stared at the floor ahead of her. The carpet was grotesque, seething with nastiness.

How could the apartment be so well-kept and pristine in every room except the one she occupied? Did Steven really value her so little as to just let her lay in her own filth and rot?

She felt her skin crawl, and her unpolluted mind began to send signals to her that she hadn't been clear-headed enough to hear in a long time. She decided she was going to clean herself up.

Lifting herself off the mattress was a grueling experience. She bent and picked up her bedpan, her entire body popping and snapping as she did so. She grunted; the weight of the pan shaking in her hand. She had to adjust and carry it with both palms, so it wouldn't spill onto Steven's precious carpet. By the time she shuffled her way into the white-tiled bathroom, both of her hands were quivering under the weight of the soup-filled pan.

She flushed the fecal mess down the toilet, then washed the bedpan out in the ivory ceramic sink. Setting it on the counter, she avoided looking in the mirror—it was something she didn't want to see, her reflection.

If she just kept her eyes away from her reflection, then she wouldn't be reminded of who she used to be, and who she used to be was becoming more and more lost to her with each passing...

Week?

Month?

Year?

No. It had been years, now.

Lora braced herself with her pale thin hand, and eased herself slowly onto the edge of the tub. Been a while. She wasn't sure if she could even turn the faucet on, but with some effort she managed to maneuver the knob and get a good flow of steamy hot water going.

Years, now.

She wasn't even sure how old she was anymore. Yes, it had been years...but how many? The ripples cascaded and cast a brief spell, while she tried to remember how long she'd been climbing the ladder with Steven. She thought they had met when they were nineteen...and she could remember a couple of the apartments they'd both occupied—quite a few at this point—but she couldn't exactly tell how long this whole experience had been bleeding and drifting into such a grimy smear of nothingness. She turned the water off, and stripped.

She peeled off her tank top, and it stuck to her oily skin. She was more than a little repulsed. Was this really her? How had she come to this? It was peeving her that she didn't even remember what age she was now—what year was this, anyhow? She rose on her rickety legs and attempted to pull her stained panties off, but as Lora had them down to her knees, she began to feel dizzy and had to settle back down on the tub and pull them off while sitting down.

She stared at her gross underwear and splotchy tank top on the white tile in disbelief. *Years, now.* Between the bed pan and the plastic covering beneath the sheets, she didn't know which was more humiliating. Usually she didn't take note of it, but usually she didn't have to get up to bathe. How long? How long had it been since she'd even bathed herself? Was this really real? Was this really what her life had become?

She grunted and it took both hands to lift her quivering little right leg and hike it into the steaming tub. She lifted the left, and put that foot in—then managed to submerge the rest of her tiny little body with greater ease. She could feel her skin absorbing the moisture, the heat.

Lora slid down until the water was up to her neck. She let out a long, drawn sigh. She felt her frail muscles relax and unwind. Immersing herself, she let her head go under, her thin black hair lilting around the features that peeked out. She smeared the hot water on her face, wiping away the thick oiliness from her forehead, eyelids, everything.

Looking up at the ceiling, she felt displaced by the unfamiliar spackle. She rubbed at her face some more, letting her fingers feel her unfamiliar contours, then she pulled herself up into a sitting position, leaning her head back along the rim of the tub. The bathroom echoed her minor splashes as she enjoyed her revitalization.

When Lora opened her eyes again, she gasped in shock. Her bony knees jutted out of the steaming bathwater—revealing not only skin that was discolored a dank brown, but also bathwater that was a putrid brownish-gray color. She looked in horror at the water that had become muddy just from her sitting in it for five minutes.

She held up her arms, and although cleaner, there was still a layer of filth to them. She gagged, drained the water out, pulled the vinyl curtain around the tub, and turned the shower on. She let the searing water pelt over her, until the thin stream racing down the drain no longer had any gray, then she turned the water off. The remaining rivulets of water disappeared down the drain, and then she started the bath again.

She observed her body closely as she splashed the hot water over her, wiping her face intensely. Her legs were so thin and frail. She could fit her entire hand around her calf. They were coated in long black hairs, and her knees were brown and patchy. She observed her thin little wrists and pathetic arms, and felt at her jutting, sickly ribs poking out. Lora could feel every detail of her skeleton, pressing at the surface.

She felt her breasts, although always small, she supposed…now they were mere nibs across her flattened chest. She felt up her bony neck, to her face. What did she look like now? She had to see her face. She dunked herself under again, then pulled the plug and watched the remaining grunge fade away. She wobbled as she pulled herself up. It was an awful strain. Her arm shook as she rose, then her legs quavered as she got her footing.

Lora managed to step over the lip of the tub with first one leg, and then the other—holding herself steady with her hands against the wall. Dripping on the sterile tile, she made her way up to the sink and supported herself there. She kept her eyes to the porcelain sink, afraid, her body shaking with the strain.

Dare she?

Dare she actually *see* what she had become?

She lifted her eyes slowly and wiped the steam from the cabinet mirror before her. She touched a face that was at once unfamiliar, and yet still very distinctly the person she remembered herself to be. Her thin fingers probed where her jaw had become incredibly prominent; there was no light double chin like she used to have. It was just skinny neck with a sharp cut of jaw set at the top. She had always liked that cute little double chin.

Her face was now hollowed at the cheeks, accenting sharply protruding cheekbones. Lora could vaguely recall that her nose had always been long, and at least that looked pretty much the same, which was somewhat reassuring, but her eyes were surrounded by dark—nearly black—skin.

She couldn't believe she was looking at herself!

Lora opened her mouth and examined her teeth, letting out a sigh of relief. Her mouth seemed impossibly intact, her gums healthy—her teeth enormously large and chisel-like. She took Steven's toothbrush and got some toothpaste from the mirrored cabinet. She brushed her jagged teeth until she could no longer feel any residue on them, then returned the toothpaste to the cabinet.

Feeling slightly stronger, she made her way out into the unrecognizable apartment. She didn't even know this place. They had been here a while, she supposed, though none of it looked familiar to her. Not the illustrious leather couch, nor the enormous television and sleek VCR. Not the paintings, not the bookshelves. Nothing. She wondered if she had ever even really ventured outside of the blackout-curtained room she occupied.

Lora ran her tongue along her squeaky teeth. Fruit. She needed to eat some fruit. She shuffled through to the polished kitchen and opened the refrigerator. There, on the shelves, was a dazzling array of exotic fruits for her to eat.

Lora felt the Raspberry throb with excitement, and her stomach gurgled as well. She was surprised by the nice selection he had left her. He usually didn't get her anything quite as unique as what she saw before her: a few papayas, some kiwi fruit, green grapes, pears and plums. Usually it was just softer fruits. She was so sick of them. *This* selection was quite a luxury for her today. Lora plucked a couple of grapes and popped them in her mouth.

Immediately she could tell that both her body and the Raspberry were pilfering all the nutrients. She snagged up a fat papaya, which she proceeded to tear into with her teeth; eating the skin and everything. Juice ran down her chin, and she could feel her senses awakening.

She grabbed a pear and ravaged that, core and all. She hadn't tasted interesting fruits in a while, and not only were her senses and the Raspberry keen on it, but her taste buds were all alight as well. She recalled that she had once loved food and flavor, and had kind of forgotten that she enjoyed distinctive tastes and textures.

She took a peach and bit into it. Her sharp gray teeth crushed the pit, shattering it to pieces. As she gobbled up the mushy fruit, she chomped the core into tiny fragments without so much as a second thought.

Lora returned to the fridge, obsessed. It had been ages since Steven had given her anything but old lady bananas and squishy oranges. She was lucky to even get a crisp apple, which she would always gnaw all the way through, devouring the seedy center with a heightened sense of kidlike glee. She loved chomping, and the apples were seldom dispersed for her to enjoy.

But today, yes, yes, the fridge was full of goodies, and had more peaches with tough cores for her to chomp through...but there, she saw, in the back of the fridge...

Coconuts.

She giggled to herself. She clapped her hands, and snagged up one of the hairy orbs—her long steely nails roaming greedily all over its round circumference. She felt all along the hard armor, digging in. Her stone-sharp fingernails broke into the tough shell, splitting it open. The brown husk cracked easily, and she chomped gaily away at the inner meat and outer shell with abandon.

Her stomach rumbled in approval and she could feel her entire system devouring the food. After she had munched the last of the coconut, licking her fingers, she decided to investigate the unknown landscape that surrounded her. She washed her hands and arms in the kitchen, amused that she had become so enraptured with devouring the fruits that she had remained naked the entire time.

She went into the bedroom and scooped up the silk kimono that Steven had draped over the chair. As she put it on, she noticed her exposed tummy. It lurched and rolled forward, not an unpleasant feeling, moving and bulging, shifting beneath her skin. Lora pressed her hand to it, feeling it move around as though a living creature were inside her. It had to be the coconut shells.

Tying the kimono and patting her pitching belly, Lora wandered out into the enormous living area. The ceilings were so high! She sat down in the leather couch and took in the whole apartment. Everything was so black and white!

The paintings on the walls were ridiculous pastel portraits of women with sunglasses—something from an album cover or two, she somewhat recalled. Why would Steven have a smattering of beautiful women gracing their walls, and yet keep his own girl hanging from the last strands of existence in the very next room?

And that's what she was, wasn't she? A woman being kept barely alive in a room.

Lora patted her tummy as it rose and fell. She turned the television on and flipped through channels and settled on some music videos. Everything had changed, now. The videos were more about hair and clothes than before. The two of them used to stay up all night on weekends to watch music videos on cable. Not *so* long ago, perhaps—but then again, it was very far away from the present moment.

Looking around the monochromatic apartment, she spied a familiar wooden jewelry box resting on one of the bookshelves. Her eyebrows raised and a grin spread along her lips. *Weed.* She hopped up and went over to the small wooden box. She scooped it up and stared at the three digit combination lock. She flipped the numbers automatically—still memorized, and opened it right up.

Wow. My old pipe.

She stared at the paraphernalia within the small case. Her head reeled a bit. Memories fluttered at the edges of her mind. A couple of friends' faces, a mall, a gift shop where she had once gotten the box to hold her goods. She recalled posters of art—unicorns and beautiful women, a Hobbit poster from an animated movie; earring holders, hair picks, leg warmers, cherry-flavored lip gloss. How old was she then? What were those girls' names? Where had they been? What town?

She sat down on the couch and placed the box on the coffee table. Inside there was a full baggie, a lighter, some pipe cleaners and screens—everything. The weed must be ancient, though. When was the last time she or Steven had smoked pot? Why had he kept this one item of hers of all things? Lora pushed the table forward and settled down on the floor. She emptied the baggie and began de-seeding it, smelling everything as she did so.

As she took her first tokes, she spaced out on the music videos that played in between the long stretches of hair product ads. The smells and feelings took her back. She felt herself become more condensed and focused. She dwelt for a time on the faces of girlfriends of her teens, but was unable to recollect their names, or the details of their features. She couldn't even remember her parents.

What she found that she could recall was…well, she knew that she and Steven had been together as a couple for a very long time. Since about the time she remembered buying this wooden box. She had just been getting into smoking weed back then…and could place the date maybe…maybe to the late '70's or early '80s. No—it definitely had to be the late '70's, because if they had been watching music videos on cable, that would have been in the early '80's, and that would have been their first apartment.

That was long before the narcotics, when they were just smoking weed and doing soft drugs. Lora rubbed her forehead, trying to concentrate. Two men in white suits on the music video station were shaking their asses at a crowd of cheering girls who were oblivious to the obviousness that the men weren't so into girls. She turned the station off and held her forehead in her hands.

She and Steven had been a couple since high school. She knew that. They had left their parents' homes and moved into an apartment together. She remembered that. She had been working some job—but couldn't recall what. They both smoked pot, read and listened to a lot of radio and albums, she remembered that. But...

But they had gotten into some bad drugs, hadn't they? She seemed to remember them getting into harder drugs after they had lived together a while, after they were long gone from their home town, away from their families.

The Raspberry on her arm began to throb, as if reacting to her memories. Lora could recall that in the beginning she and Steven had shared needles, back when they were both shooting up.

It began to blur, there. She remembered they had used some weird dirty needle and it had had some kind of green moss on it or something.

Did she really recollect that the Raspberry had been some kind of...

What?

Alien virus?

Something?

Images of some alleyway flitted before her teary eyes as she pressed her knuckles into them. Some toothless someone, maybe? Somebody passing that damn dirty moss-ridden needle onto them? No. Had they simply *found* it?

Yes.

Yes, that's what it was.

The two of them had picked up what they deemed an 'alien fungus' from a contaminated needle they had shared.

And then everything had altered.

Lora wiped her eyes. Her mind couldn't take any more. She got up and calmed herself by eating another coconut. She smoked a bowl or two more, then spaced out on the couch watching music videos for the rest of the evening until she fell asleep. She slept soundly through the day until the next evening.

When she awoke, the first thing she did was take a hot shower; washing her hair and shaving her legs with one of Steven's razors. The jerk didn't even have any razors for her to use. No tampax, nothing. There were no female items at all in the apartment. Outside of the pot and her stash box, there was nothing of hers left.

She dug through the dressers, and all she found of hers were a few pairs of panties, jeans, all torn to shreds, and some old concert t-shirts from back in her youth. She put on the cleanest underwear she could find from the very back of the bottom drawer, then slipped into some holey cut-offs, and a black and white concert jersey sporting great art design for the *Journey Escape* tour.

She went to the kitchen, then ate what remained of the fruit. Out already. She devoured it, washed her hands, then sat down and smoked-out a while. Where were their albums? She couldn't find anything but a couple of trinkets and knickknacks that remained from their previous life together. What had happened to all their stuff? How could Steven go through life without any of their music? Where was all their shit?

Lora went back into the kitchen and picked up the phone, dialing up the number he had left for the grocer. On top of more coconuts and peaches, she ordered a razor for herself and some other feminine supplies. Over the next few days she pampered herself and tried to regain her identity.

As she moved into her second week alone, she began to focus on figuring out a way to get away from the situation she was in. She was stronger now, and less dependent.

So what would she do? Would she take the money and vanish? She had become so upset with the fact she was merely being *kept* so that he could feed off of her Raspberry. Once or twice she found herself poking at the creature in her arm with a steak knife, but she was finding out that—like an ordinary infection—it was beginning to shrink and vanish on its own accord.

It seemed that without Steven and *his* Raspberry's injections into her, the Raspberry in her arm was beginning to heal. Or at least, it felt like it was healing. It had become a bit, oh, harder somehow, like it was scabbing over or something.

All she knew was that it had changed from a soft seeking nub into a hard little branch, staying erect fully, and becoming less agitated red and more of a darkish brown color. The mouth at the end of it stayed closed, and wasn't smacking hungrily any more. It was strange, but Lora could have sworn the creature growing from her was cleaning out its system as well.

She wanted to kill Steven. She had thought about asking the stoney looking delivery boy if he knew where to score any Horse, but she figured that would be pushing it. She toyed with the idea of taking a bus into the bad neighborhoods and finding some on her own, but knew she could get ripped off or raped or beaten up…any number of things.

And then what? Wait until Steven returned home and then go shoot up an overdose into her Raspberry before letting him nurse? No, no, it would never work. He wouldn't let her go off to the bathroom for five minutes before attaching to her. It wouldn't work. Her best option was to leave with the briefcases of money and never look back. She could find some small town in Iowa to settle down in—the rent shouldn't be too high.

But she had no identity. No last name, no ID or Social Security—nothing. How would she find work with no identification? She no longer had fingerprints, she realized. Her fingertips were slick and featureless. Like her fingernails and her teeth and the growth on her arm, she had become alien and strange.

She had no formal ID. There was nothing that connected her to her previous life. She had gone through the entire apartment by this time. Nothing but her stash box and some ceramic poodles remained. No yearbooks, no photos—nothing. She couldn't even find an old paperback with her name written on the cover. None of her poetry, none of her homework, no letters from her parents. It was as if she had never existed at all.

A few days later, she ran out of fruit again, and then questioned the delivery boy about the area she was in. There was a gas station and a Laundromat just within a couple of blocks, and a K-Mart about a mile away. Lora ate some coconuts and showered and put on a t-shirt with one of Steven's long-sleeved shirts to cover the creature on her arm. She then jaunted outside with a bag of what little clothes of her own she could find. There were four more days until Steven was due back home, and she wanted to make sure she had her stuff together before then.

She got some quarters and a Twilight Zone magazine at the gas station, and did her laundry while reading short stories. She returned to the apartment with no problems whatsoever. She may have lost her long term memory, but she was clear as a bell with everything else. She remembered street names with no problem whatsoever, and felt that her first foray into the public world went without a hitch. Nobody had so much as looked at her.

She readied her clothes and munched on fruit while watching music videos. She had a map of the States sprawled out on the coffee table, and she smoked the last of her weed and made notes as to where she wanted to go.

One way or another, she could survive. If she were unable to get a job, then she would find some sort of social worker to help her. Surely she could find help. After all, if Steven could manage to find jobs with no history and no finger prints, then she could do it, too.

She had it down. She was going to get new clothes and a big suitcase at the K-Mart tomorrow, and then wrap up her packing and leave the following day. She would take a bus to maybe Dubuque or Sioux City. For some reason the Siouxland area seemed to ring true to her, and Lora felt maybe she'd had some association with that part of Iowa before. Something about cruising a mall there? She didn't think she was *from* either of those places, but for some reason those towns kept popping up in her mind.

She circled Dubuque and Sioux City in red pen, then tucked the map into her magazine. She sat back and fantasized about her new life. All she needed was a little place, just a studio or a small house. The idea of getting a small little home appealed greatly to her. She could start all over again. She pictured herself mowing her own lawn, and kicking up on her front porch. She could pick out a new name for herself and everything. Anything was possible.

Lora fell asleep on the couch, and then awoke and ate a couple of coconuts. Chomping the husks, she felt her weird belly roll the hard shells as it digested them. She cleaned up in the kitchen and took a long hot shower.

She was intrigued by what had happened to the Raspberry. It was as if it had taken on the characteristics of the coconuts she was ingesting. It had become hardened. It still looked like an elongated raspberry, but it was so tough that it seemed as though she could just break it off or snap it in two.

But she left it alone. She was determined to let her healing take its natural course. She would leave this prison and let everything mend in its own time. Drying off before the mirror, she swore that the Raspberry was in a sort of remission. It was dying without the injections from Steven. It was *dying*. Lora would poke at it and try to get it to open its mouth, but it just stayed clamped shut and stiff as a board.

She put on the *Journey* concert jersey again, as it was her favorite, and covered it with a long-sleeved shirt. She then pulled a couple hundred dollars from one of the briefcases filled with cash.

The morning was crisp and bright and beautiful and she had a great jaunt. She went to the K-Mart and found a perfect suitcase; it had a combination lock like she wanted, and had wheels so you could pull it.

If she could get just enough clothes to get by for a while, she could stash the cash on one side of the suitcase, and her clothes on the other. She would have to be as direct with her course as possible, in order to avoid heartache. If she were to get into trouble or mugged, that would be the end of the cash for her.

She would get on a bus and head straight to Siouxland. A bus or a train.

A train would keep her private. That's what she would do. She'd go back to the apartment, finish packing her clothes and cash, get a cab to the train depot, and then head for Sioux City. From there, well, she could start from there. A motel for a couple of nights and then talk to a social worker and act like she had amnesia or something. She tried to imagine all of her alternatives.

First thing she needed to do was get a bank account, and in order to do that she'd need an identity. Perhaps she should start first by renting a locker. If she could keep her stash safe in a locker, then she wouldn't feel so rushed and could weigh out her options.

She grabbed some more t-shirts and some jeans and a nice top or two. She picked up a couple of work shirts to cover her arms and a pair of Converse All-Stars. She had the cashier put everything into the suitcase and then she pulled the suitcase along as she trotted her way back to the apartment. The sun tingled on her skin, and she could feel her body soaking it in for the first time in what she calculated to be five to six years.

She took the elevator up to their floor, her excitement growing inside her. She was going to do this, she was *really* going to do this. Lora planned on eating a couple more coconuts and then hopping right to it. She was ready to leave as soon as humanly possible.

She unlocked the door and pulled the suitcase inside, then locked the door behind her. Perhaps it was Dubuque she was thinking of, after all. Sioux City seemed familiar; she was sure she used to go visit a mall there, but Dubuque kept popping up in her mind, like she had once planned on going to college there or something. Either way, if Dubuque wasn't the place, then she could always buy a train ticke...

Steven walked out of the bedroom.

Lora froze, staring at him.

"Going somewhere?" he asked, his right eyebrow raised in amusement or curiosity.

Lora simply stared. She couldn't move. Her brain registered everything. She could tell instantly what condition he was in. His ruffled hair, the black circles under his eyes, his cheeks gaunt and his skin blotchy.

Where she had begun healing from the Raspberry, he very clearly had *not*. He was in complete withdrawal.

"You're early," she said.

"Yeah, no shit," he snorted. "And not a second too soon, from the looks of it."

"Yup," she said. The hairs rose on her neck. Everything was different now. She had seen through this scam, and this was going to be her last plight come hell or high water. "You look terrible."

"I couldn't stand it. I had to come back."

"You're not touching me."

"We'll see about that. I bet your Raspberry missed me. Why don't we plug in and then we can talk?"

Lora straightened up. He was nearing her, and she was well aware of his true intentions. She couldn't have it. Once that dope got into her system again she would be helpless.

"I'm not letting you keep me half dead on a bed anymore."

"It was your choice," he said, moving closer.

Lora backed up. "That was never my choice."

"I never heard you complaining."

Lora was against the door, now, she had nowhere to go but into the corner. "You asshole. We were *infected*. This isn't us. These things are parasites! Remember?"

Arms outstretched, menacing—he looked withered and sickly. The look in his eye wasn't anyone she had ever known, and she was coldly aware that whoever this person once was—the man she had gone to shows with and watched music videos with—he no longer existed. This person before her was what the creature had made him.

"Remember what?" he teased.

"We called it the 'alien fungus', remember? Raspberry came from a dirty needle we found in an alley."

She was in the corner. He stepped over the suitcase and crept closer to her. "The alley in Denver? Off of Colfax?"

Lora stammered. "Was it Denver? I don't remember. Steven— it's *a monster*! You have to..."

But he was on her. He punched her hard in the jaw and then grabbed her hair. She screamed. He pulled her away from the wall and threw her tumbling onto the suitcase. He kicked at her with his shiny expensive shoes.

"Where'd you think you were going, huh? You think you're worth anything out there? You're just a little skank! Who's gonna want you?"

He kicked at her again and then jumped on top of her, flipping her over. He punched her again, straddling her. Lora covered her face. Steven squeezed her with his thighs, holding her in place. She could feel the suitcase digging into her back. He ripped off his shirt, his hungry Raspberry poking its long, starving proboscis out—ready to feed from her.

"Give," he commanded.

"No!"

"Fine, then." He began to force her right arm away from her face. She held him off as long as she could, but he pounded her when she resisted. Finally, pulling her arm away from her face, he straightened it out and held his own arm strongly beside it.

He forced up the sleeve of her shirt to reveal the orifice, his long tendril aggressively searching along her arm. Her Raspberry was hard and stiff and covered in hard shell. Steven looked queerly at it, not understanding her change, nor noticing until now. His longing proboscis wrapped its way around her woody nub, moving right to the top, where the Raspberry's mouth remained clamped shut.

The proboscis stiffened, and Lora's Raspberry finally opened its maw. Steven's tendril shot straight into the hole, pushing itself in as deep as it could go. His eyes rolled back in pure pleasure, then widened in startled terror.

Lora's Raspberry clamped down on the invasive strand as it forced its way into her. Its form, hardened by the coconut shells and peach pits, had developed a cavern of sharp, venomous teeth.

She stared as she watched her stiff Raspberry defend her. It closed on Steven's tendril, and bit into it with layers of fangs. She looked up at him, with his mouth agape and slobber falling from his chin, then tugged her arm away swiftly, tearing the proboscis clean in half.

Steven wailed.

Black fluid spewed from out of the flailing tendril as it whipped about his arm. From Lora's arm, her hardened Raspberry suddenly split open and shot out at Steven like five miniature arrows. It had detached from Lora completely—stabbing pointedly into Steven's flesh. He fell back, screaming as the needle points burrowed into his skin, digging into him.

Lora's arm leaked a thick green goop which began to coagulate immediately, sealing the orifice in her arm. She scooted back and quickly got off the suitcase, and caught her breath. Steven flopped around in front of her, clutching at his broken skin. His entire body was shaking. He looked up at her, his eyes filled with hate and anger, and he bellowed, his mouth opening incredibly wide. The sound was unearthly.

Lora began to back up. Steven clutched at his skin as the woody reeds tore through him. He began to step toward her. His mouth opened wide again. The skin on his face was splitting as he screamed, his lips tearing and stretching as his face opened wider.

Lora hissed at him. The voice that came from inside her was alien and instinctive. Her long nails elongated from her finger tips. She held her readied stance before him.

Steven shuddered. Long tendrils began to rip from his sides and whip about. His eyes expanded and popped open. Green pus shot from the openings. Lora hissed defiantly again, warning him to back down.

He didn't listen.

He came at her, the tentacles from his sides slashing the air until they found her, and they proceeded to wrap around her arms, trying to pull her close. Lora grabbed a handful of the vines and tugged at them. Her long nails tore a batch into pieces, slicing straight through them. The strands fluttered wildly, shooting green and purple ooze all over the white walls of the apartment.

She curled her claws into fists and she socked Steven in the jaw, following him over the suitcase as he backed away. She hit him repeatedly, her bones as hard as steel. She roared at him, tightened the tentacles wrapped around the other arm, and hacked at those. Steven wailed as they fluttered and sprayed fluid. He desperately tried to back away, but she clenched a handful of the sputtering strands and flung him down.

He slammed onto the floor, his skin continuing to split open as the daggers from her Raspberry tore his insides apart. Lora took her steely claws and slashed hard at his face, causing his entire jaw to burst open. She backed away, repulsed at the creature that was exposed before her.

Beneath his skin, his true self was revealed. His maw stretched—like a suction cup–growing and smacking as it pushed forward. Lining the inner cavity of the veined-green protrusion were several sets of jagged little teeth. It tore his nose open and split his face.

His eyes beneath were fish-like, and red. His ravaged scalp slid over his pulsating visage, the once perfect hair now dripping in clumps of skull and skin.

The creature grabbed at her leg once more, and she felt the pressure clamp onto her painfully. Lora screeched at him, but Steven was still determined, even as he fell apart. She kicked at him, but his grip remained firm, digging into her leg.

She jumped forward and bit into him with her jagged teeth, tearing at his shoulder as he pounded his fist into her, then she took the arm squeezing her leg and bit fiercely into that

Green liquid spattered her face, and she tore his limb off in two bites. The sucking protrusion from Steven's face bellowed. Lora released herself from his grip and gashed into the sucker-mouth with her sharp nails. His face split and shot green blood.

She took his skull in her hands and bore into it with her mouth. Her teeth penetrated his face, and she clamped down, tearing off the smacking sucker-mouth. Bile shot over her cheeks as it was ripped from his screaming skull.

She held his head tight and then brought her jagged teeth down on his eyes. Her jaw extended wide, and she bit down forcefully, bursting one of his eyes with the sharp top jaw, and popping the other with her bottom jaw.

She clamped them closed, then tore away with everything she had. Green and yellow slime drenched her face, spilling from her mouth to splatter on the floor.

Steven's body shook and jerked spasmodically, and soon all movement began to cease. Lora watched as his corpse stilled, and then she leaned forward and tore out his throat, just to be sure.

The creature was limp beneath her, and the shards that had been her Raspberry dislodged themselves from his skin, withering into dust on the floor. She wiped her lips with the back of her hand.

Steven's body began to collapse and fall in on itself. He was liquefying into a horrendous, gelatinous mess along the carpet.

Lora watched him melt away, breathing heavily. She then rose and wavered into the bathroom. She took the hottest shower she could, letting the hot water drench her, sanitize her.

Refreshed, she dried off, brushed her teeth, then dressed in some of the clothes she had washed earlier. She combed her hair and then went to the kitchen and ate a couple of oranges.

When she was finished, she washed her hands and took a sponge from the sink and went about cleaning the suitcase in the bedroom.

She scrubbed it down and got it as shiny as she could. She opened up the case, enjoying the combination lock, and pulled out the pair of sneakers and slipped them on.

She packed away all the money from the briefcases and then took whatever cash Steven had had in his wallet. Covering the money in the suitcase with her clothes, she packed it perfectly and closed it, setting it aside on one of the clean parts of the floor.

She called a local cab company, and watched music videos until the cab arrived and took her to the train station.

She made her way across Iowa to Dubuque, where her wounds finally healed, and she eventually managed to begin her life anew.

Yet somehow, in all of her various incarnations, through all her future achievements, marriage and children, Lora was never quite able to recall where she came from, or ever recollect her last name again.

SANGUINE TEMPERAMENT

BRANDON CRACRAFT

Oct. 12, 1908

I stared at my naked form in the mirror, almost forgetting that I was a man nearing his ninetieth year. The blood of my master brought me from the point of death and burned youth into my flesh. Men mistook me for a college lad, patting me on the head whenever I gave opinions. Women wondered what kind of fright I must have suffered to turn my hair white.

I placed two decades and an ocean between my ordeal at the asylum, but it was impossible to free myself from Prince Dracula. His blood burned on my tongue and scratched its way through my heart each night. I worried about walking anywhere at night, certain the vampire would emerge from the shadows and destroy me for my betrayal.

His revenge was far more sinister, preventing my death with a single drop of his blood left on my lips. My hunger increased, and I found myself sneaking into graveyards and lapping at the coagulated ichors in the bodies. I swallowed live spiders, centipedes, and even scorpions, desperate for that taste of life mixed with death. My body brought me the attention of men and women, and I indulged the worst of their perversions. I wanted to feel less empty and more alive.

I knew that I would never stop craving my master's blood. The monster left me starving, but it was worse than I deserved.

When I heard the door handle to my rented room begin to shake, my body tensed. I stood to my full six and a half feet and cracked my knuckles, preparing to strike. I'd struck Prince Dracula before, and I didn't intend of dying without a fight.

The ginger boy of twenty who opened the door held a candle next to his face, illuminating his smile. "You must be Ronald Renfield," he said, his voice thick with London fog. "Do you mind if I call you Ronnie? I figured that we should be mates if we're going to be roomies." He extended an athletic hand with spidery fingers to be shook. I hastily threw on a nightshirt and engulfed his hand in a firm shake. "My name's Duncan Herriot, but I'm thinking about changing it to Peter Black," he said. "I think that sounds more mysterious and aristocratic. What do you think, Ronnie?

"I paid extra for a single room," I said when he gave me a moment to speak, pointing to the child's trundle that the landlady insisted was a full size bed.

Duncan pulled a crumpled up piece of paper from his Norfolk jacket and compared the number to the one on my door. "I don't think you made a mistake, Mr. Renfield. Mrs. Carmichael would rent out my drawers if she thought she could make an extra coin. Most of the other rooms are two to three to a bed." Duncan looked at his pocket watch and winced. "A quarter past midnight," he said with an intense sigh, fear and frustration in his green eyes. "I don't suppose you could let me stay here for the night?"

"It wouldn't be the first time I slept on the floor," I said without hesitation, remembering my cell in the asylum.

He flopped next to me on the straw mattress. "We could share the bed, Ronnie, it doesn't bother me." Duncan pulled off his shirt to reveal a small wiry frame, an athlete in miniature.

For a moment, I thought about giving into perversion and carnality. I shook my head. "I think I shall be much more comfortable on the floor." He blinked at me, so I added, "I'm a very large man that needs his space to stretch out."

"What kind of work do you, Ronnie?" he asked after a moment of uncomfortable silence. "I'm an actor. I toured for three years as John in *Peter Pan*. I loved the role and making children happy, but I hated those horrible pinched voices women make when they pretend to be boys. Both Peter and Michael were played by girls, and they were both absolutely awful. After that, I did a stint as Duncan's son in the Scottish play; no lines but I got to die nicely."

"What play are you performing now?" I asked.

Duncan's face began to glow. "It's not a play, Ronnie. It's an actual motion picture."

"Like a nickelodeon? We have them at the small theatre from time to time. I saw one at the men's club that made me a man all over again." I gave him a wink.

"This film shall be so much bigger than a little nickelodeon picture. Charles Norman Smith, the director, told me that he plans on it being five reels long. It's going to be like a chapter play but for adults. He plans on it being bawdy and violent. He's looking for someone to add color to a couple of the climactic scenes."

My eyes widened. "Color? I didn't know they could do that."

Duncan became more and more excited. "They've been doing it for years in Paris. He also wants to use animation for a couple of the scenes, they call it stop motion. It's supposed to be a long process. Everyone's pitching in on the sets and animation, even the women. You won't believe what they can do these days with motion pictures. Charles Norman Smith told me that motion pictures will have full sound by 1910, just two years away."

When he was done with his tirade, he bit his lower lip. "Forgive me, Ronnie. I started rambling and never gave you a chance to answer my question. What do you do for a living?"

I shrank into myself, making myself as small as my muscular bulk would allow. "I just lost my job," I admitted. "I used to be a gravedigger."

Duncan slipped down to the floor next to me. "How about I make a deal with you, Ronnie?" Before I could answer, he continued to plow through me with his words. "I don't need this room for very long, just a few days. The director found some castle that a crazy prospector built to convince his wife to move out west. He bought the castle, and he wants us all to live in during the filming. If you let me stay here a few days in this room, I can see about getting you a job with the film. There's got to be a lot of brute work that needs to get done, hauling props and such." He clapped me on the back as an idea struck him. "I bet I could even get you a role in front of the camera. A movie like this has to have hundreds of extras."

I thought a moment. As extroverted as Duncan was, I knew I could put up with him. I needed money badly. I was living off some gold pieces I managed to steal from Prince Dracula. I wondered if each piece I spent led the vampires closer and closer to me.

"What's this motion picture about?" I asked.

Duncan hopped back on the bed and leaned forward. "Have you ever heard of a novel by Mary Shelley called *Frankenstein?*"

* * *

Charles Norman Smith screamed everything he said and wore uncomfortably bright clothes, terrified someone might not notice him. I saw him burst into tears and hysterical laughter within the first ten minutes of meeting him.

"He's quite a genius," Duncan whispered. "I hear that all the great geniuses are completely insane."

"Who are you?" he asked, pointing a fungal fingernail at me. "I don't remember casting you!" He looked around frantically. "Where's Wilber? Where the bloody hell is Wilber? Where's my monster? I want my monster!" He jumped up and down like a child having a tantrum, tears in his eyes. He turned toward the producer, as stoic as the director was dramatic. "What happened to Wilber?"

For a brief moment, the producer's hollow eyes focused on me. The strength of his gaze made me bow my head. "I haven't heard anything from Wilber. I suggest that you be kinder to that gentleman."

Smith grabbed the taller man's ascot. "Why?" he whispered, so loud it could be heard outside. "Is he some kind of film critic? I talked to my friend in New York. He said he was going to send a film critic."

The producer's face remained flat. "They don't send film critics until after the project is completed. What would he critique?"

"My casting!" Smith yelled. "My choice of location! I told you that we should've gone to California. They say it's going to be a Mecca for filmmakers. What kind of idiot decides to film in Arizona?" Smith ran up to me, standing on tip toes so that I would look at him eye to eye. "This location is authentic as possible. I needed some place beautiful and tragic. Lady Canter moved here from England under the provision that her husband replicate her castle brick by brick. She arrived to marry him only to have him die of exhaustion shortly after saying 'I do.' Lady Canter entered the beautiful castle he built for her and inspected all of the rooms before hanging herself. Her ghost still haunts this place. I've heard the banshee howling in the night." He turned his attention towards everyone. "I hope that no one is afraid of ghosts."

The producer tapped his cane on the floor. "Could you listen for a moment, sir?" After a few moments, Smith stomped back toward the producer and folded his arms. I expected him to stick out his tongue. "I shall take a horse and scout for your monster," he said. "If he is unavailable, I suggest you be extra nice to..." He paused and his gaze settled on me again.

"Mr. Renfield," I said when prompted.

He nodded his thanks. "I suggest you be nice to Mr. Renfield, because he looks like he could fit the costume for Frankenstein's creation."

Smith shook his head. "He's too young and pretty."

"No one would be able to tell once I get him into make-up," a young black woman dressed like a gypsy said; nervousness muted her voice. "I would just need to make a clay mask of his face."

The producer nodded his approval. "Thank you, Miss Pross. I'm sure you shall do phenomenal work. I trust you completely." He motioned from the young woman to me. "Mr. Renfield, meet Miss Lottie Pross. She plays Justine Moritz and she acts as our make-up supervisor."

Duncan introduced me to each member of the cast in turn, and I turned on my charm. The thought of being in a motion picture excited me."

"He's not in the movie!" Smith pouted. "I want my monster! Someone find Wilber for me!"

The producer bowed. "I shall fetch him." Something under his voice reminded me of Prince Dracula and I shivered. "I hope he's not unwell. The lack of fortitude of some of these actors still surprises me. Poor Miss Waterford."

"Who's Miss Waterford?" I asked after we heard the producer's black horse gallop away.

"The broad who killed herself," a tiny woman with brassy hair and a Jersey accent said, stomping over in three inch high boots. "I'm Katie Culliver." She extended her hand to be kissed and I inhaled a toxic amount of cheap perfume. "I'm playing Little William Frankenstein."

Duncan blanched. "A girl is playing my little brother?"

She waved her hand dismissively. "No one can tell the difference. No one's going to know the difference once she drenches herself in powder and the light hits her." She turned on her heels, trying to give Duncan and I a better view of her backside. "Everyone tells me that I act just like a boy. I'm telling you. No one's going to know the difference and it has got to be better than working with a brat. I watched the production of *Peter Pan* in Trenton. The gawky little pest they had playing John was absolutely horrible. I wanted to boo him offstage."

I put my hand up to keep Duncan from reaching over and slapping her. "That was me," Duncan said between gritted teeth.

"I would like to know what happened to Miss Waterford," I said, hoping to prevent a fight. "Does anyone know?"

Lottie Pross played with the beads on her shawl and raised her hand like a school girl. "I was there when it happened, Mr. Renfield. Iris Waterford killed herself. She came over early for a make-up test. I went to get her wig, and she was staring at herself in the mirror. I came back and she had shattered the mirror. She used the pieces to slice off her face."

Duncan turned green, and I thought he was going to choke up bile. "She killed herself...right here?" He went over to the mirror and found the shattered one. He pulled back like he had been bitten.

"This is why I didn't want anyone to know!" Smith exclaimed. "I know someone would blow the whole thing out of proportion." He rolled his eyes and began his theatrics. "She was naked when she died! Anyone want to make a big deal about that?"

"Really?" the actor who played Henry said. "Was she completely naked?"

"Like you care," the actress who played Elizabeth said. "We all heard you and Duncan grunting away." Everyone in the cast burst out laughing except for Lottie. The memory of the young woman's death remained within her.

I walked over to her and told her gently. "I saw someone die. It was horrible, but you can get over it."

Lottie smiled nervously. "Thank you, Mr. Renfield." I turned away from Lottie's gentle gaze, repulsed by the abominable things I wanted to do to the young girl's body. She sighed and walked back to her powders and wigs, stealing glances at me whenever she could.

"Where is Wilber?" We all sighed as Smith renewed his rant. "I should've known he would ruin my picture. What am I supposed to do without a monster?"

"I would be interested in the role," I hazarded to say. "I'm quite a fan of the novel."

Duncan put his arm around me and said, "My mate would be perfect, boss." He gave me a playful swat. "Absolutely perfect."

"I thought this was a professional operation," Katie Culliver said. "Where is the stage manager? I need a whiskey." When no one responded to her, she sighed as loudly as she could. "I never should've left the theatre."

"I hope you didn't think that all the drama was going to be in front of the camera, Ronnie," Duncan whispered.

When the producer returned, Smith stomped up to him with his hands on his hips. "What took you so long? Where's Wilber?"

The producer waited for the questions to die down. "I have sad news for everyone," he began, tone as indifferent as ever. "Wilber was hospitalized this morning with an undiagnosed blood disorder. He appears to be getting worse and worse." I held my breath as the pulse of vampire blood sang in my ears. "Whatever is causing the reaction appears incurable. I suspect he shall die soon."

Smith refused to listen. "When is he getting here?"

"Mr. Renfield shall have to take on the role of the monster." The producer put a cold hand on my shoulder. "I suspect he shall be glorious." He turned his attention toward Lottie, and I was relieved when he removed his hand. "I expect you to perform his make-up test by tonight. We have had too many delays."

"Yes, sir." She shot me one last hopeful look before disappearing down the halls to find her molds.

"Thank you very much," I said. Duncan hugged me, and the other actors nodded in my direction. Katie Culliver rolled her eyes.

"Should we visit him in the hospital?" the actress playing Elizabeth asked.

The producer shook his head. "I think it would be best for the production if we simply moved on," the producer commanded.

Smith nodded. "Consider this a warning people! You miss a day's work and you'll be replaced." He walked over to me and gave me an artificial smile. "I would like to welcome you to our cast, Mr. Redfield."

"Renfield," I corrected.

Lottie's sudden scream made us all jump. I ran to the threshold and she buried her face into my chest. My arm crawled around her back, and I comforted her.

"I saw a ghost," she said finally.

Smith threw his arms in the air. "I told you all about the ghost of Lady Canter."

"It wasn't Lady Canter." She dried her tears on her sleeves and forced herself to regain composure. "I saw the ghost very clearly. I know it wasn't Lady Canter. It was Iris Waterford."

"I hope one day I get to spend eternity as a ghost in the theatre," Katie Culliver said. Her lip curled in disgust. "I would hate to be trapped in a place like this." She let out a laugh, and Duncan glared at her. "If she sees how much better I perform the part of William, she will die a second time from shame," he said.

"What was the ghost doing?" I asked, loud enough to let Katie Culliver know that I wanted her to shut up.

"Iris kept trying to tell me something," Lottie explained. "She couldn't actually talk, just move her lips. After a few moments, I realized what she was trying to say. She kept saying the word 'murder' over and over."

"That proves it wasn't Iris Waterford," Smith said triumphantly. "She killed herself. She wasn't murdered. You must have seen Lady Canter. Maybe she really didn't hang herself. Maybe she was killed."

"I'm telling you," Lottie said, gritting her teeth, "it was Iris Waterford."

Out of the corner of my eye, I saw Katie Culliver casually walk over to the prop table and stab herself in the mouth with a pitchfork. Blood erupted out of her skull and sprayed the actors behind her.

Everyone stared in silence as the second woman to attempt to play young William Frankenstein shoved the weapon further into her head until she managed to rip off most of her skull. Her body continued to convulse for several minutes, even after she was dead.

* * *

Hunger scratched against my stomach, nearly doubling me over in agony. I licked my chops like a starved hound whenever an insect scurried past. The vampire blood craved something sweeter, the blood of a suicide.

"Good news, Ronnie," Duncan said, running up to me. "I convinced the producer to let us stay roomies. I don't think I can even fall asleep anymore without the sound of your snoring in my ear." He put an arm around me, speaking low. "I don't want to be alone after what Katie Culliver did to herself. That was pretty gruesome."

"I've seen worse," I said before I could stop myself.

Duncan looked at me quizzically. "Were you in one of those Indian wars, Ronnie? I heard they take scalps."

Lottie wandered the hallways, waiting for us. She put a hand to her lips and stepped back like she was surprised. "Mr. Renfield," she said, "I wanted to apologize for my behavior earlier."

"That's quite all right, Miss Pross." I hoped my smile didn't look too predatory as I imagined removing her clothes. My hunger worsened as I contemplated what I could force Duncan to do to Lottie.

"Excuse me, please," I said, racing to solitude. I slammed and locked the door behind me. The darkness and silence taunted me as I crawled on the floor on my belly, desperate for prey. I found a colony of ants and began lapping them up off the dusty floor.

I surrendered to my hunger, savoring the screams of a rat as I tore into its spinal cord with my teeth. "I need to get to the graveyard," I admitted, wiping blood and fur off my mouth. "I need to taste Katie Culliver's blood."

Duncan never made a sound as he slept, occasionally even sleeping with his eyes open. I snuck out of the room in stocking feet and locked the door behind me. I hoped that my roommate was actually asleep at the time.

I dressed in all black, wrapping myself in a scarf. I kept a knife and syringe in my scabbard beneath my underpants where no policeman would ever dare to check.

The guard at the graveyard made a better scarecrow than sentinel. His milky eye and pronounced limp scared children and housewives. College students told legends about trespassers being chopped up and cooked in his stew.

The old fool never noticed anything right in front of him, though. I eluded him with ease. Using the key the mortician never realized I'd stolen, I unlocked the back door to the morgue and crept inside.

My time as a gravedigger familiarized me with the habits of the mortician, and not simply his annoying habit of playing the phonograph as he slept. The body of Katie Culliver would lay in a bath of preservative overnight before he even attempted to embalm her. Saliva dripped from my mouth as I imagined her ichors hardening in her body like candy.

My heart sank and my stomach groaned in protest when I saw the dismembered form of Katie Culliver. The young woman had mutilated her skull but had left the rest of her body pristine. A grave robber had chopped her up with the skill of a surgeon. The organs seemed lovingly removed, as if the carver was careful not to spill even a single drop of bile and blood. He used the cuts on her skull to remove her spine without disrupting the ribcage or pelvis.

I felt a hand brush against me. I jumped around, but there was no one there but a corpse on a table. The mortician had covered the body in black velvet, an object of shame rather than the masterworks of human flesh he believed he created.

Compulsion drove my feet forward, and I walked slowly toward the dead figure in velvet. The name on the table read Iris Waterford and even though there was no wind, waves rippled the velvet.

After taking a deep breath, I pulled the sheet off. The grave robber left nothing but a torso. He even pulled out Iris Waterford's teeth, leaving her mouth in an eternal scream.

"Just like Dr. Frankenstein," someone said from behind me.

I almost attacked Duncan out of fright. He peeked around my arms to get a better look at what was left of the two women.

"What are you doing here?" I demanded, thankful for the mortician's awful music. It covered my shocked voice.

Duncan continued to stare at the dead bodies, oblivious to my fury. "I followed you, Ronnie. I got worried when you snuck out. I would've been here sooner, but..." He paused for a moment and shook out some horror. "I found something. Or rather, I found some*one*." He took me by the hand and led me as silently as possible to the horse-drawn hearse. He stayed by the threshold, too scared to move any closer.

"He must've just picked up the corpse," I said. "He never leaves a body in the hearse." I turned toward the pale form of my roommate. Duncan urged me to take a look. "It isn't another member of the cast, is it?" I asked.

Duncan hugged himself. "Look for yourself, mate."

Even though I never saw him before, I knew the naked body lying in the coffin belonged to Wilber. I recognized the paleness of his skin, no blood to congeal, leaving his entire body stiff to the point of complete immobility.

His long brittle hair covered his neck. Strands broke off in my hand as I tried to move it. I looked around, expecting to be attacked at any moment. The blood of my master pulsed within me. Horror and pleasure replaced my hunger.

The breath left my body when I saw the telltale signs of a vampire attack on his neck.

I made Duncan swear not to tell anyone what we saw at the morgue. He looked confused for a second, then took out a knife from his boot and pressed the blade against his palm. I took it from him before he could break the skin.

"You sound very serious, Ronnie," he said. "I figured you would want a blood oath. Haven't you ever shared a bloke's blood, been his blood brother?"

"Your word is enough, Duncan," I said. "I trust you." His face lit up and he gave me a hearty hug, pulling back when he realized I was shaking.

Before he could ask the obvious question, I said, "I'm fine. Let's go home. It's almost dawn."

Duncan took one last look at the hearse. "We're both going to need at least a little sleep if we want to function tomorrow."

The closer I got to the castle, the more relaxed I became. I barely managed to remove my trousers and shoes before I collapsed on the bed with Duncan beside me. As I drifted to sleep, I realized how unnatural my tiredness felt. Such a shock should have kept us both wired, perhaps for days.

"Hypnotism," I whispered, barely conscious. "That's how he killed those two girls. I saw Dr. Seward do it all the time to get us patients to reveal things to him. There was a Mesmer artist in London. He made this woman dance like a gypsy and he commanded another man like a dog."

"You lived in London? I didn't know you were another Brit." Duncan gave me a drowsy look and fell asleep with his eyes staring wide ahead.

"It has to be hypnotism," I said, struggling against the pull of sleep. "Dracula used it on me when I tried to kill him." Dizziness made me prone. My last thought as sleep overpowered me was that a part of me wanted to see my master again.

Instead of the call of a rooster, the castle woke up to Charles Norman Smith screaming his head off. I fumbled for Duncan's pocket watch, certain I'd gotten only a few minutes sleep. I jumped up when I discovered it was half past noon. The late night soon stung me in the face as I looked around for the clothes I'd kicked off. My suit trousers were hung up and my shirt and underclothes placed in the dirty clothes bin. Even though I was positive I went to sleep half-dressed, both Duncan and I were wearing pajamas. Duncan was tangled up in his bedclothes, because he was actually wearing mine.

I shook Duncan.

"We overslept," I said. He fidgeted in his sleep and his eyes burst open. He pointed beyond me. It took me a few moments to realize he was still asleep.

When the afternoon sun hit the floor, I noticed something glinting. I looked closer and saw a wet footprint, far too small to belong to myself or Duncan. I ran to the mirror and inspected my body, expecting to see a bite mark somewhere near an artery, but my skin was unmarked.

"This doesn't seem like my master," I said softly, looking over to make certain Duncan didn't overhear. "Dracula normally prefers his thralls naked."

The screaming got louder and louder outside. I tried to wake Duncan up again, but he continued his silent sleep. I wondered if we were still under the influence of the spell. When I heard something crash against my wall, I threw on Duncan's robe and ran out to investigate.

"Mr. Renfield!" Charles Norman Smith pointed at me, his face twisted by malice. "What are you doing out here dressed like that?" He paced back and forth in front of me, his shirt hanging out of his trousers and the legs of his trousers bunched up on his calf. He tripped over his untied laces a couple times. "You never, never leave your room in your bedclothes, Mr. Renfield. There are ladies here." His lip curled into a sneer. "And a child, evidently."

The producer was dressed in a smart blue suit and long opera cape. His lifeless eyes stared at the director. "I wish you would stop embarrassing yourself, sir," the producer said. "I think this boy is our best option." He gestured to a small boy beside him with thin hair and covered in grime from head to toe.

"Best option for what?" I asked.

Smith tore at his hair. "Why are you still standing there. Mr. Renfield? I told you to get dressed. I'm the director. I know you're only an amateur, so I will explain it to you. You have to listen to me."

I turned to go back to my room, but the producer bid me to stay. I found myself frozen in place. "We need your opinion, Mr. Renfield." Even before I was asked, I knew I would agree with the producer. "I searched the city for a young woman to play Frankenstein's brother, but I found none that looked appropriate. I saw this lad begging for chocolate. He spun all kinds of yarns about sick parents, and I figured that he was a natural actor. When I found out that his name was William, I figured it was providence." His brow narrowed. "Don't you think it was fate that I found this boy, Mr. Renfield?"

"I think it's a great idea to have an actual kid play William." Duncan appeared behind me, completely dressed and groomed. I could feel the relief wash over him at acting with a boy instead of a diva.

Smith looked ready to attack me. "This is stupid. I wanted a girl. William is supposed to be beautiful. Boys are disgusting. Women are beautiful."

The producer ignored everyone but me. "Don't you think boys can be beautiful, Mr. Renfield?"

I looked over at Duncan and sighed. "I think it's a good idea to cast a kid as William."

"Who's going to look after him?" Smith asked. He repeated the sentence louder and louder until the actors emerged from their rooms. Thankfully, I was not the only one still wearing his bedclothes. My eyes settled on Lottie's white nightdress before returning my gaze to the producer.

"I can look after myself," the boy said. "Look, I need the money. This man promised me money and a dry place to sleep."

"I hope you don't expect Lottie to look after him," Smith said, directing his comments back to the producer. "She doesn't have time to look after him. She has to get the costumes ready."

"Have a heart," the boy said, trying to get Smith to actually acknowledge him. "You can't send a kid back on the street."

"It would be different if his parents were in the cast," Smith said. He turned toward the boy, turning his eyes into a weapon. "I bet he's a bastard. I bet you don't know who your father is? Your mom was probably some whore, and you never knew your father." He spat on the boy. "Filthy little bastard."

I stepped up, cracking my knuckles. Smith stepped back, and I kept myself as calm as possible. I wanted to deck him. The producer studied me, and I wondered if I was playing into some kind of plan.

"William, is that you?" I asked, trying my hand on acting. "Why aren't you with your grandparents?"

William winked at me and mouthed gratitude. "Sorry, Pop. I couldn't stand it there. I had to go looking for you."

Smith threw his hands in the air. "Am I supposed to believe that you didn't recognize your own son, Mr. Renfield?"

A life on the street taught William to tell big lies, and he began his story without hesitation. "The reason Pop didn't recognize me is that it's been years since he saw me. After Mom died of the fever, he sent me to live with my grandparents in Maine. He moved out west and was going to send for me when he got a farm going. I guess you decided to do this acting thing, though."

Duncan played along with the lie. "Ronnie used to talk about his kid all the time, wondered what happened to him. I guess we don't have to worry about hiring some bitch, Charlie. We got the perfect William Frankenstein."

I offered my fake son a hearty handshake and tried to look comfortable in the hug. He felt so fragile, I was afraid I was going to end up squishing him. "It's good to see you again, William."

He made a face. "Will. Everyone calls me Will, Pop." He laughed, playing up to the crowd. "Pop hasn't seen me since I was seven years old."

"You haven't seen your son since he was seven?" Smith asked, his emotions hard to read. "How old is your son now?"

Will mouthed me his age, but I couldn't tell what he was saying. "Nine years old," I guessed. "It has been two years since I saw him." From the offended look, I knew I guessed younger than he was.

"You don't look old enough to have a nine year old son," Smith said. "Were you nine years old when you became his father?"

The producer gave me a knowing look. "I'm certain that Mr. Renfield is older than he looks."

I held my breath and put a protective arm around the boy who claimed to be my son. I wondered if I was staring at the cold eyes of Dracula. I've seen him change his form and voice many times.

Smith looked calm, and I went to get dressed. Will peeked his head in. "Thanks for covering for me," he said, "but I'm almost thirteen years old." He looked at his tiny frame and gave a firm shake of the head. "All right, I'm eleven."

"I don't care what lies you tell that fool out there," I said, "but I expect you to be honest with me." Will thought a moment than reluctantly nodded. "Don't worry. I won't ask you about your past," I said.

"I guess I was the one stupid enough to give you permission to punish me if I get caught screwing up," he said with a sigh.

Something crashed against a wall and Will ran into the room. He hid in my chest then pulled back, trying to pretend like he was never scared. I read a lifetime of abuse in his eyes as he stared at me, crying as silently as possible.

"I won't let him hurt you," I whispered to him, surprised to hear the words leave my mouth. I never saw myself as the parental type.

"You're his father!" Smith screamed as we emerged from the room. "You need to get him cleaned up. He's filthy." I was about to follow orders when I heard a high-pitched, annoyed grunt from the director. He rushed up to us. "Are you sucking your thumb?"

Will flushed with embarrassment and shoved his hands into his pockets. "Sorry about that, sir. I know it's a bad habit. I haven't been able to break it."

I looked down at Will, remembering that a day ago I was feasting on vermin. "There are far worse habits," I said.

Smith ran to the prop table and picked up a kitchen knife, swinging it in the air. "The next time I see you sucking your thumb, I'm going to cut it off!"

The producer raised his hand to keep me in my place and approached Smith. "Stop this behavior at once, sir. You're embarrassing yourself."

He whirled on the producer, holding up the blade. "Don't tell me what to do! I'm in charge!"

The producer moved with the speed of a cobra, striking before most of us had a chance to blink. We all flinched when we heard the slap, followed by Smith's agonized yell. Pain sent Smith to his knees, tears leaking out of his eyes. Without losing his demeanor, the producer broke Smith's left thumb in three places.

Lottie gasped but the rest of us remained silent.

The producer circled his underling. "From now on, Smith, you shall eat with nothing but spoons. If I ever catch you touching a knife or fork, I shall break both of your hands one bone at a time." He walked away from the pleading form. "If you will excuse me, I'm not used to this bright daylight. I shall retire to my room until nightfall."

I gave Will one of my pajama tops and it fit him like a night-shirt. Duncan started to say something about the scars on the boy's back and chest, but I covered his mouth and shook my head. Even though Will complained he wasn't tired, he quickly fell asleep after I tucked him in.

"I never thought you would make such a great father, Ronnie," Duncan said. "No offense."

I shrugged. "Neither did I." I tried to speak as quietly as possible, not wanting to wake Will. "I think I'm starting to believe all this father business."

"How long have you been in the states?" Duncan asked. "What part of England are you from?"

"I really don't like talking about that sort of thing. I have bad memories." The image of the producer's eyes remained in my mind, my imagination superimposing Prince Dracula's stare over them.

"I thought I remembered something about you being in a mental institution." When he saw the shock on my face, his lip quivered nervously. "How about I pretend I never heard any of that?"

"Thank you."

Duncan made a frustrated noise, and put his pajamas back into his trunk. "I don't even know if I'm really tired. Maybe I'm just being hypnotized again. I know I wasn't wearing pajamas when I went to bed, especially not yours."

I grinned at him. "You're a lot smarter than you look."

Both of us started yawning. "I just hope I don't wake up wearing Lottie's nightgown. I look horrible in bows." He laughed a little while lying down. "It kind of hurts to keep my eyes open."

"I don't think it affects me as bad as you," I said. "I used to get hypnotized by someone else. I think I developed some kind of tolerance to it." I looked over at Duncan. He'd fallen asleep sitting up. Normally, I would have been possessed by thousands of untoward and unhygienic thoughts. All I did was help him into a comfortable position and covered him up.

"You can fight this," I whispered over and over to myself. "I've got to show Will that I'm not just playing house. I told him I would protect him." Even though my head ached and my hands and feet felt like they were being crushed, I refused to fall asleep. A soft voice in my head told me that all the pain would go away if I simply surrendered to sleep. I shook it off even as pain ripped through my body. I pushed all of the new pain aside and focused on the familiar scratch of the vampire blood against my veins.

The handle to my door began to shake, and I tried to make my way to my feet. I fell onto the floor, cursing under my breath. Lottie walked into the room slowly, dripping wet. She opened her mouth to speak but no words came forth.

I called her name, but she didn't respond. Duncan and Will remained unconscious and before I could call out for help, she spoke.

"Murder," she said in a banshee's whisper. She walked over and reached a dripping hand toward me. "Murder."

Taking a chance, I said, "Iris."

Her head turned to me slowly. "Help me," she whispered. "Save me before he kills me again."

"Dracula," I hazarded. The ghost behind the woman's eyes didn't recognize the name. "He's a vampire. A very powerful one," I said.

"I can't fight him," she said. I heard the sound of two women screaming. "I tried to wake her up. I tried to wake her up." The screaming grew more and more distant until the sleepwalking form of Lottie stood in front of me, the ghost of Iris Waterford was gone, hopefully to the next world.

Lottie walked out of the room, and I forced myself to crawl after her. With a supreme amount of effort, I made my way to my feet. "Lottie," I called out, "it's Renfield."

She picked up a silver comb with a long pommel in the shape of a dagger. She placed it against her eye, but I reached her and broke it before she could kill herself with it. She searched the prop table, trying to find an item to commit suicide with. I finally restrained her and took her back to her room.

Lottie's eyes fluttered. "Renfield," she said, her eyes still glazed over. "Is that you?"

I hugged her, our lips brushing for the slightest moment. "Iris tried to protect you. The same man who murdered her just tried to kill you."

"Iris killed herself," she protested. "I was there."

"She was hypnotized to kill herself," I explained. "By the same man who makes sure we go to bed like good children." She looked confused. "I wish I could tell you more but I swore a blood oath."

"I don't understand."

"You need to understand, Lottie. Someone is trying to kill you. I don't know why but he kills young women, makes them destroy their heads." I expected her to be in hysterics and accuse me of being a lunatic, but she simply listened carefully. "He needs their bodies. He chops up their bodies afterward."

"Do you think he's creating some kind of Frankenstein bride?" she asked. "Taking parts of each girl that he liked? It would make sense for him to let them destroy their heads and brains if he had already had the perfect face and mind."

I let out a nervous laugh. "I'm surprised you're taking this so well."

"I keep seeing a ghost, Mr. Renfield," she said. "I'm just glad I'm not going insane."

"Ronnie, please call me Ronnie."

She leaned close, begging me to kiss her. I ran my hands through her ebony hair, and I didn't have a single violent or perverse thought. I only wanted a kiss.

Before I could press my lips against hers, the sound of Will's scream returned me to reality. "It's my son," I said.

"Is he really your son, Mr. Ren... Ronnie?" she asked.

"He is," I said. It didn't feel like a lie. "I hope you don't mind that I have a child."

"I think it's wonderful," she admitted. "It was great to watch you with him."

Even though I didn't have more than a second, I kissed her quickly. Lottie smiled and blushed, blowing a kiss to me as I ran to Will's aid.

I regretted lingering with Lottie when I saw Will sprawled on the floor in a pool of blood, the nightshirt ripped to pieces. I tore off my shirt sleeve, and used it to bandage the wound on his neck.

"It hurts so much," he whimpered.

I held him in my arms, trying to will the blood back into him. The blood began to clot, and Will began to drift back into sleep, his thumb in his mouth. I placed him back into the bed.

"Leave him alone," I said. "I don't care what you do to me, but leave him alone. He's only a little boy. I betrayed you, Lord Dracula. The boy is innocent. If you want to hurt someone, attack me."

I waited for a moment until I heard the sound of footsteps approaching. I said a final prayer and waited for my fate. The producer stopped in front of my room and entered, looking from the boy to me. He walked over to the boy and checked his wound. "Far too messy for a vampire bite," he said.

"Are you Prince Dracula?" I asked him. "Did you do this to him?"

"I have no reason to harm him, Mr. Renfield. Someone else injured him. These marks were made with a knife. A vampire may have killed your predecessor, but they had nothing to do with the deaths of Katie Culliver and Iris Waterford. Dracula didn't attack your son, Mr. Renfield."

"Who did?"

The producer stared at me. "The only thing I shall say is that the man responsible for the death of Miss Culliver and Miss Waterford attacked William."

"He wanted to frame a vampire for the murder?" As soon as I said it aloud, I knew it made no sense. "He's trying to find a vampire. Lottie was right. He's trying to create Frankenstein's monster. Lightning can't bring her back to life, he needs something else." The idea struck me. "Vampire blood. It kept me young all these years. It brings people back from the dead."

"The question remains, Mr. Renfield, how are you going to find this modern day Frankenstein?"

"Lottie," I told him. "He tried to kill her. He needs her parts. She can lead me to him. I just have to figure out how." I started to leave but froze in place, taking Will's hand.

"You have my word, Mr. Renfield, that no one shall harm this boy as long as you are alive." He touched Will's neck, and the wounds began to close. "Should you die, I can guarantee no one's safety. I strongly suggest you find the killer tonight."

* * *

Lottie tied herself to the bed, making sure that anything toxic or sharp was far away from her. She looked at me drowsily, trying to fight the hypnotic call.

"I figured I won't be able to hurt myself this way," she explained. She slammed her fist against the bed, and I was surprised by the sudden burst of violence. "Why is this happening to me? I lived on my own since I was barely older than your son. I know how to take care of myself. One week in the frontier and I become a whimpering damsel from a pulp novel."

"If you weren't strong," I said, "you would have died the first night." She gave me an uncertain smile. "I saw a wet footprint in my bedroom. I think the hypnotist tried to kill you last night and failed. You escaped to my room, looking for someone to help you." I thought about waking up wearing pajamas. "Maybe Duncan and I tried to help you."

"What happened with William?" she asked.

I shook my head. "I don't know. I honestly thought I figured everything out, but I'm not certain. The producer is looking out for him while I try to puzzle this thing through."

"That man terrifies me. Are you sure you can trust him?"

My mind trailed back to my first encounter with Prince Dracula. He was charismatic, seductive, and aristocratic. He promised to sate my endless hunger for the life force I drained from smaller animals if I worshiped him, even above God. "I don't trust him, but I know he'll keep his word."

Lottie tried to position herself to lie down, but the bonds refused to let her get comfortable. I saw a shadowy figure move amongst the wall. I grabbed a crucifix from my pocket, expecting to turn the demon away. The shadow settled on the wall, and I made out the silhouette of a young woman.

"Iris?" I asked.

When I acknowledged the ghost, she vanished once more. Whispers of 'murder' and 'murderer' echoed around Lottie's room, so intense that I covered my ears to block her out. When the chorus of madness died down, I settled into a chair, my hand absently fiddling with something in my pocket.

I took out Duncan's pocket watch and waved it in front of my face. I wondered if I could actually do it. Dr. Seward performed it several times in front of me, trying to sate a woman's sexual desires or a stop a man from howling at the full moon. I never actually tried to hypnotize someone myself.

When I splashed water on Lottie to wake her up, I realized why she had roamed the halls drenched. Even in her deepest sleep, she tried desperately to wake herself up. The woman was much stronger than she realized.

"Did I do something horrible?" she asked. "I didn't try to hurt anyone, did I?" Lottie relaxed, happy that her bonds remained in place.

"I'm going to try something, but I need you to be very brave." Without hesitation, she nodded. "I need you to put your faith in me. Before you agree, I think you should know that I'm not a very trustworthy person. Everything you know about me is wrong." She began to protest so I asked her a question. "How old do you think I am?"

Lottie stared at my face, completely without lines and wrinkles. "Probably close to my age, twenty-seven." Her mouth dropped open. "You're not really twenty-seven, maybe sixteen or seventeen. The white hair makes you look older, but you're still a child, aren't you?" She continued, and I didn't stop her. "I figured you lied to Smith about William being your son, but I don't understand why you lied to me."

"I think William is my son," I said. "Just not by birth." I rubbed my hands together. "When I look into his face, I can see a miniature version of myself. We even have the same color eyes, violet. I never met anyone else with violet eyes before him. I think my master brought him to me as some sort of gift. The more I'm around the boy, the less monstrous I am."

"You could never be monstrous," she chided.

The look in my eyes shocked her. I didn't know if I looked pitiable or horrifying. "I'm almost ninety years old. I'm kept young and vibrant through the blood of the worst of the demons."

"Satan?" Lottie pulled at her bonds, terrified. She seemed to imagine me sacrificing her to a dark lord. When she met my eyes again, she quickly relaxed. "No, you're not a Satanist," she said. "I've met many evil men."

"I served something evil, but he wasn't a man. I'm the thrall of the Lord of the Vampires, Prince Dracula of Transylvania. Even though I haven't served my master for years, I still feel him." After a swallow, I said, "I think the producer is my master. I don't think he's the one who killed those women or attacked Will. Dracula would have bragged about it if he did."

I figured she would be going mad, chewing at her arm to get away from me. "What do you need me to do?" she asked.

I dangled the watch in front of her, swinging it back and forth. "Just follow the watch with your eyes. I plan on fighting hypnosis with hypnosis."

Lottie leaned forward and kissed me. "I know you'll save us."

Once she was under my spell, I casually removed her bonds. She walked to the mirror but stared at something beyond her reflection. She pointed to the glass. "He uses this," she said. "The mirror tells us to sleep."

"Who is he?" I asked. I repeated the question several times, wondering if I would have to start over.

"I will take you to my master," she said. Her steps remained even. Despite the fact she was fast asleep, Lottie avoided hazards until she took me to a bare wall. I thought she was going to try to walk through it, but she pushed a button next to a candelabra and a door was revealed.

Electricity sparked up the staircase leading to an underground lab. The air was bitter cold despite the desert night and reek of decay. My nose wrinkled at a familiar smell—old blood.

Charles Norman Smith seemed calm, dressed in a sedate lab coat and suit. His broken thumb was hidden under thick rubber gloves. He adjusted his tie and spoke in a normal voice. "Well, this is a surprise." He took out a scalpel. "I never thought you would deliver the vampire to me, my pet." He smiled, revealing perfectly ivory teeth. "You were horrible at keeping yourself hidden, Mr. Renfield. First you defied all my hypnotic calls and now this."

"I'm not a vampire," I said. "I just serve one. Why did you need a vampire? What are you doing down here?"

"Life imitates art, Mr. Renfield," he explained. "I read Mary Shelley's ghastly little novel, and I knew I could do better than that idiot Victor Frankenstein. The flesh of murder victims is far more malleable than corpses dug from the grave."

"You're insane," I said, casually pulling a knife from its hiding spot. "And unfortunately for you, so am I." I tried to sink the blade into his neck, but a giant beast leaped out of the shadows. I turned and slashed at it but when I pierced the monster's flesh, no blood spilled.

"I would like you to meet my son," Smith said happily. The lights grew brighter and I saw a patchwork beast sewn together from parts of various women. The face was that of a little boy, and it had the genitals of a grown man. "You'll excuse me for attacking your so-called son, Mr. Renfield. I got jealous, because I thought my William was much more beautiful."

Lottie woke up from her trance and screamed. She threw beakers at the creature, but it continued to focus on me.

"I only need one final ingredient to make my son truly alive—vampire blood. I can keep him awake for a few moments, maybe even half an hour. After that, he returns to being a pile of discarded body parts. I'll take the blood from your veins, Mr. Renfield, then I shall use Miss Pross to replace any parts damaged in the fight."

I hit the monster with all of my might, and it backed off for a moment. It quickly recovered, but the look on Smith's face told me that nothing had ever injured the beast before. I hoped my unnatural strength would hold it off.

"Very melodramatic, sir," the producer said, descending the stairs and carrying the unconscious form of my son. "I thought I would see how all of this played out." He looked toward me. "After all, I do have a personal stake in it."

"Master," I begged, "help me." The producer continued to watch the scene, indifferently. "I need your help," I said. "I know that I have been unfaithful but..."

"I'm not Dracula," the producer said. "I resent the fact that you keep mistaking me for a vampire."

"What's going on?" Duncan yelled, stumbling down the stairs. The producer sidestepped to avoid having my roommate fall on him. His left eye widened. "I was right. It really was like the novel."

"Get out of here, Duncan!" I yelled. "I'll hold this monster off." The creature grabbed me by the throat and pushed me against the wall.

Duncan looked terrified. "You'll never defeat it, Ronnie! The monster's too strong!" His voice smoothed out, and I heard the familiar sound of Transylvanian nobility. "You need my blood, Renfield."

Prince Dracula's disguise melted away like wax, leaving bits of Duncan on the floor. Smith screamed, partly out of joy.

"I knew you would never trust me if I appeared anything like the man you knew," Dracula said. He caught Smith in his gaze, and he went limp. "I shall make a deal with you, Mr. Smith. Let me feed my thrall a fresh supply of blood. If he doesn't defeat your monster, my blood belongs to you." He released the mad scientist. "Trust me, my blood is far sweeter than the typical vampire."

"As you wish," Smith said. He whistled and the monster returned to his side.

I expected Dracula to offer me his wrist, but he shook his head. He pulled down his trousers, and sliced himself on the inner thigh. "I want Miss Pross to know what kind of man you are, Renfield."

"I'm doing this to save them," I said. I licked at the wound and then started sucking openly. Pleasure ran through my body, but I was able to control my perversions. People relied on me. There were far more important people in the laboratory than myself.

The blood increased my speed and strength, and I attacked and pounded into the monster until I finally broke its flesh. I grabbed organ after organ, hoping that a missing piece meant its end. The creature continued to move and fight, even without a heart.

"I can't believe you let me down, Renfield," Dracula taunted. "I can't believe you are going to let all these people die."

The producer looked at the vampire. "I would be careful what you say, Vampire Lord. I might consider such a tone a threat." I saw Dracula wince in fear. I wondered if it was just leftover impulse from his Duncan disguise, but it seemed genuine.

Smith yelled and jeered, telling me that I should just roll over on my back and let his monster kill me quickly.

"Think!" Lottie yelled. "There has to be something that can stop it!"

I nodded. She was right. It didn't matter how much blood I drank from Dracula, I remained my own man. I could think for myself. The monster was completely controlled by Smith. I punched it in the head, shattering its skull. I then reached into its brain and crushed it in my grip. The monster went limp as its parts burst at the seams. Ichor oozed from the hundreds of wounds.

"Impossible," Smith said, looking at Dracula. He cowered when the vampire flashed him his fangs. "What are you going to do now? Kill me?"

Dracula scowled at him. "I loved Mina Harker and Ronald Renfield, and I never gave them the pity of death. So why would I kill you? I hated you from the moment I saw you."

"What are you going to do to me?"

Dracula contemplated, then smiled. "I think I shall feed you to my hounds. That should take a few hundred years. I know all kinds of ways to keep someone alive and suffering." He grabbed the mad scientist by the collar and Smith went limp. "Consider yourself lucky. You get to be a part of my experiment."

"Don't forget our bargain," the producer said.

"I know better than to challenge someone over a thousand years my senior, Ramses," Dracula said. "I shall leave America immediately. From now on, all of my American assets shall be controlled by my clerk, Ronald Renfield."

My mouth dropped open. "You're letting me go, Master?"

"No. I can never let you go, Renfield. I could not let Mina go, either. You two shall belong to me for eternity." He raised a clawed finger. "I know that humans crave a family. I figured your madness made you immune, so I asked Ramses to find you a potential child. When I saw the two of you together, I knew I couldn't stand in the way of human instinct."

"I told you," Ramses said.

"Just remember," Dracula said, kissing me on the cheek. "You shall always belong to me."

"I must depart as well," Ramses said. "I leave my estate in the hands of my last living descendent, Ladonna Pross." Lottie asked a hundred questions, but the pharaoh only gave one response. "Do not end my line. I expect the two of you to have many children." He handed me Will. "Raise this one right. He needs a good father."

The two of them turned to leave, but Dracula paused and said, "I hope you two don't disappoint us. I would hate to have to return." With a flash of lightning, they were both gone.

Lottie came to me and I wrapped my arm around her, Will between us.

I kissed her.

For once, my future looked bright.

TRANSYLMANIA

WAKEFIELD MAHON

"It'll be fun, Leah. People backpack across Eastern Europe all of the time. Don't be such an old stick in the mud."

Leah rolled her green eyes. "Old? Dana, I'm nineteen. You're the one who buys the alcohol, remember?" She glanced at Dana in the mirror and then returned to brushing her shoulder-length blonde hair.

"That's exactly my point. If an ancient crone like me calls you old, that's saying something. Come on, I'm a senior this fall, is it wrong for me to want to do one fun thing before I have to grow up and face the scary mean world?"

"Fine, whatever, grandma. But this better not be like the Colorado fiasco." Leah turned from the mirror to look at Dana. "Do you at least have a hostel booked?"

"You're never going to let me live that down, are you? Tommy said he would drive us. How was I supposed to know he only meant one way? Anyway, you wouldn't believe how cheap this one is."

Leah sighed. "You do realize that you get what you pay for, right?"

"Hey, we are supposed to be roughing it. Lighten up, roomie!" Dana smiled an elfish grin, her brown eyes glowing with glee, and Leah relented. There was no fighting with her when she had her mind made up.

* * *

A heavy mist blanketed the graveyard. A wolf howling in the distance yelped and then fell silent. Leah watched her steps as she made her way through the overgrown brush surrounding the graves. Her thin white nightgown did little to protect her from hungry thorns eager for flesh and feasting on her calves and thighs. She sensed the presence as a chill crawled up her spine.

"Who's there?" Leah's voice trembled.

"Know you not, child? On the morrow, it is All Hallows Eve and a blue moon at that. Wilt thou truly venture in the devil's land?"

Leah turned around and saw a beautiful young woman. Her hair was like strands of gold and even by night, Leah could tell her eyes were green. Fear crept over her as recognition set in. The woman's face was nearly the same as her own.

"Fear me not, child. I am your grandmother seven times over. I am not here to harm you, only to warn you. Do not go on this trip or you will likely be joining me soon."

* * *

Whether or not it was a dream, the memory of the woman who claimed to be her ancestor rattled Leah. Her hands shook when she tried to do her make-up in the mirror, and she half expected her reflection to look back at her disapprovingly. It was too late now. Dana had already purchased the tickets and the flight left in a few hours.

"You're as beautiful as you're going to get," Dana said. "You are already better looking than me anyway. Would you mind letting us lesser mortals get ready, too?" Dana's playful mood was lost on her.

Leah apologized and moved out of the bathroom so Dana could get in.

While Dana showered, Leah packed as much as possible in her carry-on backpack. She checked around the room to make sure she hadn't forgotten anything she might regret later. She saw the old, oversized silver cross her mother gave her as a high school graduation present and decided to wear it for luck.

Once she was ready, Leah actually relaxed, that is until they boarded the plane two hours later and it began to taxi down the runway. She never enjoyed flying to begin with and her nerves rebelled against her.

Dana took her hand. "It's all right, girlie. We're going to have a blast! As soon as we get airborne, we'll get a couple drinks in you and you'll be good to go."

As it turned out, Dana was right. After a few drinks, Leah relaxed again. The flight from Boston to Heathrow was the longest plane ride either of them had ever been on, but they made the most of it. The airline showed a Bella Lugosi marathon and the girls laughed at the cheesy special effects, even though they still found themselves a little scared.

The flight from London to the continent was easier.

They boarded a bus at the airport.

"You never did tell me exactly where we're staying," Leah said.

"Oh you'll see. It's a surprise and the best part of the trip." Dana winked and flashed her famous grin.

Leah got off the bus and looked around. "You're kidding me right?"

"What, you don't like it?" Dana pouted.

Stepping off the bus was like stepping into the past. But that wasn't what was bothering her. "Transylvania is a real place?"

"Duh, it's like half of Romania, didn't you take geography in high school?"

"It's just so..."

"Quaint, rural, picturesque," Dana offered.

"I was going to say creepy."

"Well yeah, that's why we're going to the haunted castle tonight for Halloween, if the tour isn't over-booked already, that is. Maybe we'll meet Dracula."

"Now you're just being silly."

"Of course I am. Relax we're going to have a great time. Stroll through the castle. Check out the graveyard. Who knows what adventures we'll find?"

"Hooray for adventure." Leah swirled her finger in the air.

Dana swung her arm around Leah and laughed. "Obviously we still haven't gotten enough alcohol in you."

They checked into the hostel and an elderly woman in a tattered old dress greeted them. A strangely colored bandana covered her head.

"Where is our room, ma'am?" Leah asked.

"Baba Yaga."

"Excuse me?"

"You can call me Baba Yaga," the woman said.

"Oh of course," Dana said. "You know, from the old fables? It's all part of the ambiance."

"Oh, uhm okay, so do these fables have any food in them, preferably not little children in gingerbread houses?"

The old woman chuckled and hobbled over to a giant black cauldron. "Stone soup, don't worry, the stone is only decoration, it's perfectly sanitary." She started to sing and hum "Stir, stir the witches brew…"

"Yes, yes of course, double, double toil and trouble…" Leah said.

"STOP!" the old woman hissed.

"What's wrong with you, lady? First you people want me to get into the spirit and then you yell at me?"

The old crone leaned in conspiratorially. "It only takes three of us for a big spell and you never know when a body is lurking about."

"Dana, this lady is crazy. Let's go somewhere else."

"Suit yourself. The restaurant is half a mile east of here," the old woman said.

Minutes later, Leah and Dana dropped their bags in their room and headed down the street.

"I can't believe I let you talk me into this, Dana."

"I'm sorry. Look, I know the old woman was a little weird but I promise we'll have fun tonight. Besides, look at this place, it is like stepping into the past."

As they walked around the corner and saw the golden arches in front of the ultra-modern building, they both laughed.

"Now that is my favorite kind of architecture, Dana."

"A burger, fries and a beer, you can't top that."

With some food in her stomach, Leah felt better. As they walked out of the restaurant, they ran into an elderly man who identified himself as Sasha.

"You girls must be here for the Haunted Castle. That should be delightful. Are you staying at the Grand Hotel?"

"No, we're staying in the hamlet at the hostel."

"Oh you are the adventurous types, I see. Have a brochure map. This should help you find your way around our little village. You might even find some treasure that the regular tourists missed."

The girls thanked him and he headed off.

"My grandfather wears that cologne," Dana whispered.

"So does mine!" Leah giggled.

They returned to the hostel to prepare for the evening.

A line snaking around the corner greeted them at the castle.

"This is more crowded than I thought it would be," Dana said. "Don't worry though, it'll be fun."

Leah held up the area map. "Why don't we try this one?"

"That's just an old ruin. It's not even listed on the regular map."

"You said you wanted adventure. This line isn't adventure. We're going to be here all night just waiting."

Dana smiled. "That's the spirit Leah, let's go!"

It was nearly time for sunset. The air cooled rapidly and a heavy fog rolled in. They followed the street lanterns to the place on the map that indicated the path to the ruins. A wolf howled in the distance.

Dana took Leah's hand when she hesitated. "Come on, this was your idea, remember?"

"Give me a second, Dana. I just have a bad feeling."

"Oh no you don't, you're not chickening out now. We already lost our place in line at the haunted castle."

"I know, I'm sorry, just hang on."

They came to the end of the cobblestone street. Torches lit the path from the street down to the ruins. Silence hung in the air as heavily as the fog.

"Come on, let's go," Dana said and started down the path alone.

"Wait for me, I'm coming."

The full moon shone brightly above, illuminating the mist. Ivy vines swallowed up much of the walls of the ruined castle. A musky smell pervaded the chilly night air.

Leah was the first to hear the growl.

"Dana, listen!"

"What is it?"

"It's probably that wolf we heard howling. I can't tell which direction it's coming from."

"Behind you!"

"Are you sure?" Leah turned around just before the massive wolf pounced on her.

Dana screamed and grabbed a stick off the ground to hit the wolf.

The wolf snapped at Leah's neck but missed, having difficulty managing both of the women at the same time. Leah scrambled to get out from under the beast, but no matter which way she moved, the wolf shifted with her. She screamed and beat on the beast with her fist.

The wolf snapped again. This time the teeth grazed her clavicle, but the wolf got a bite of the large silver cross she was wearing. Its head jerked back and Leah smelled the disgusting smell of burning flesh mixed together with her grandfather's favorite cologne. She took advantage of the moment, rolled away from the wolf, and got to her feet.

The beast was blocking the path back to town, so she grabbed Dana's hand and ran down the other path, deeper into the wilderness. Thorns and bramble covered the path, but they didn't dare slow down. The thorns ripped at her skirt and her bare legs. Leah was grateful they had at least worn sensible shoes.

The howl of the wolf let them know he was closing in. He couldn't be that far behind them. Then they heard the yelp. A thrill of hope coursed through Leah's veins. When they saw the graveyard ahead of them, her heart sank. Hope had devolved to fear. She'd seen this place before; this story wasn't going to end well.

"Hey, Leah?"

"What's up, Dana?" Leah's eyes darted around the graveyard. Death was nearby. She just didn't know what shape it would take.

"Was it just me or did that wolf smell like it was wearing cologne?"

"You just had to go to the devil's land on a blue moon Halloween didn't you, Dana?"

"What are you talking about? Vampires and werewolves are all fables. I just thought it would be a fun vacation," Dana said.

"Are you having fun now?"

Dana was silent for a moment. "Oh no, maybe that wolf attacked poor Mr. Sasha."

Leah's eyes danced in the moonlight. "Or maybe that wolf *was* Mr. Sasha."

"Stop, Leah, you're freaking me out."

"Transyl-freaking-vania, with a full moon on Halloween," Leah chuckled.

"It's just superstitions. Your mom has a black cat and you never met your father, that doesn't make her a witch, does it?"

A grin grew across Leah's face and maniacal laughter shook her entire frame.

"Note to self, check Leah into the hospital as soon as we get back to the States," Dana said.

"We're not going back to the states. She warned me, but I just didn't listen."

"Listen..." Dana said.

"Yeah, it's too late for that now."

"No, I mean listen to that sound. What is it?"

Leah inclined her head slightly. "It sounds like a cat scratching at the door."

"If that's a cat scratching, that loud, I don't think I want to see it."

"Aw, come on, maybe it's Mr. Sasha's playmate. Hey, maybe it's Mrs. Sasha."

"Look, Leah, I can understand why you would have a nervous breakdown because I'm kind of freaking out, too, but do you think you could maybe wait to go crazy until we get out of here?"

"Hush, there's movement in the ground. I can feel it."

"What, like an earthquake? I don't feel anything. You're imagining things. Come on, let's go."

"No, I mean I sense the hallowed earth being disturbed by evil. I told you we weren't leaving here, Dana."

Then they heard the earth breaking. Twenty feet in front of them, gnarled, rotted fingers, with meat hanging off the bone broke through and reached out of the ground. An arm soon followed and brought an entire rotting body along with it.

"This ground is tainted. It wasn't properly hallowed for burial," Leah told Dana.

To their left and right and behind them creatures broke out of their graves.

"What does that mean, exactly?"

"It means that the presence of a great evil can call zombies from the grave," Leah said.

"What great evil?"

"I don't know. We might find out, if the zombies don't eat us first, that is."

"Brains!" the first zombie called out, its voice garbled from a rotting tongue.

"Maybe we can run between them, they don't look like they move that fast." Dana started running between two of the zombies, but Leah grabbed her shoulder and stopped her, then pulled her close.

"What's wrong with you?" Dana screamed. Just then, another hand reached out of the ground, just where Dana was standing.

"How did you know?"

"I told you, I can feel them somehow and they're surrounding us."

"So what are we supposed to do?" Dana asked.

"I don't know. If we had some strong guys with hatchets and swords, we could cut their heads off, I guess."

"Well, it's just us here and I left my battleaxe in my other purse. Do you have any *other* ideas?"

"Hang on, don't rush me."

"I'm so sorry, I realize you're busy, but I don't want one of those things eating my..."

"Brains!" another zombie called out in a moan.

"Leah!"

"Stop already! God I just wish I had a torch or something." Just at that moment, a ball of flame appeared in Leah's hand. All of the zombies stopped. Leah panicked and threw the fire, which hit one of the zombies, instantly burning the corpse to a pile of ash.

For a few moments, there was silence. Leah and Dana stared at the pile of ash where the zombie had been, the night echoing with the panting sounds of their frightened breath while the remaining zombies stood still.

"Brains!" another zombie cried and they all moved forward again.

"Leah, do that torchy thing again, hurry!"

"I don't even know how I did it."

"Well, figure it out!"

"All I said was I wish I had a torch." Instantly another flame appeared in her hand. This time she aimed with purpose and another zombie burst into flames.

"Hurry, hurry!" Dana yelled.

"I'm trying, it's not exactly like I know what I'm doing here. I wish I had a torch." A flame appeared and she chucked it towards a zombie but missed. The remaining zombies were closing in slowly but surely.

"I don't know if this whole one torch at a time thing is working. Can't you call up more than one?"

"If you think this is so easy, then why don't you try it?"

"Look, all I'm saying is they're almost on top of us and at this rate we'll run out of time before we run out of zombies."

"Thank you so much for the play-by-play, Howard Cosell."

"Who?"

"Never mind, just shut up a minute so I can think. Wait a minute, that's it! My father's other favorite voice."

"What about your father's favorite voice?"

"Mr. Johnny Cash, Dana. I wish I had a burning ring of fire!" Leah called out.

There was absolute silence in the cemetery. The mindless creatures surrounding them paused, but nothing happened.

"Why isn't anything happening?" Dana asked.

"How the hell should I know? I did the same thing I did before when I made a wish. It's not like I ... oh." Leah doubled over, the air knocked out of her.

"Leah!" Dana knelt down to help her friend, oblivious to the zombies who had started moving again.

"Brains!" one zombie cried. "Br..." then the voice of the zombie was covered up by the howling sound of wind sweeping through the woods and the whoosh as suddenly the girls were surrounded by a protective wreath of flame that burned each of the zombies and turned them all to ash.

Leah gasped for breath.

"Good evening," a dapper gentleman spoke in a thick local accent. His clothing reminded Leah of a bygone era of aristocracy. "It is difficult work calling on magic, is it not?"

Dana started laughing hysterically, tears of relief flowing from her eyes.

"Dana, stop," Leah said while still trying to catch her breath.

"What? It's one of the actors. We're safe now. Oh man, you had me going, Leah."

"Yes, ladies, you are perfectly safe, my name is Vladimir. Come with me."

Something felt very wrong. Leah reached into her blouse and pulled out her cross. "Hey, Vlad, how do you like my jewelry?"

Vladimir hissed and his face twisted and contorted, revealing his demonic nature. His fangs extended and his eyes, by the light of the full moon, appeared to turn completely black.

"Still think he's an actor, Dana? Run. Get out of here!"

"I'm not going anywhere without you," Dana said.

"Oh, how sweet," the vampire hissed. "I guess that means two meals for the price of one."

Suddenly, Dana yanked the cross from Leah's grip, tearing the chain from her neck, and throwing it into the brush. Vladimir's countenance returned to a handsome young man's face.

"What the hell, Dana?" There was no emotion at all in Dana's face, she looked hypnotized.

"Oh, no, Dana, wake up. Snap out of it, please."

"Well, at least one of you is pliant. I suppose that means you can watch while I make a snack of your friend."

Leah tried to figure out where Dana had thrown the cross, but she was afraid to take her eyes off the vampire.

"Time is ticking away, my little dessert, what will you do?"

Dana was walking slowly towards the vampire. Vladimir, however, had his eye on Leah. His smug and toothy smile dared her to make a move. Leah felt paralyzed. She couldn't run and leave Dana, but she didn't want to watch Dana be killed either.

"Such a pretty friend you have, witch." Vladimir stroked Dana's hair as she stood before him and offered herself to his will. He placed his fangs on her neck, all the while watching Leah with a grin in his eyes.

Leah's stomach started to give way. Her head was pounding. His fangs found purchase. The first drops of blood began to run down Dana's neck.

"You won't be snacking on any of my boarders," the voice of the old woman from the hostel shattered the silence.

Vladimir's eyes went wide as he felt the power compel him to retreat from his meal.

"You may be powerful, old woman, but you can't hold me forever. It would take three witches to destroy me and this one hardly knows her strength. She could not lift a finger against me." Even though he was bound by the old woman's spell, the smugness returned to his smile.

"Then perhaps you should not have chosen here and now to corner these girls."

"I'm not afraid of dead bodies. None of these was a witch. Besides, the bones of witches have no power"

"That is right, abomination, magic lives in the spirit!" a new voice spoke. "Dead things should stay dead, but you would run about stealing the souls of others."

"Great grandmother!" Leah snapped out of her fear. She felt a surge of power flow through her.

"A few more greats than that but I'll take the compliment, dear," the ghostly woman smiled. "Let the body be at rest, let the souls be free."

The vampire once again took on its demonic countenance and snarled. The old woman who called herself Baba Yaga opened her hands to the night sky. "Let the body be at rest, let the souls be free."

Vladimir began thrashing about, struggling with each step he took towards Leah. Her vocal cords froze. This couldn't be happening. She didn't have the power, like the others thought.

"Leah?" Dana started to rouse from her trance.

Vladimir's demonic face filled with an evil grin.

Leah yelled out, "Let the body be at rest!" The vampire lunged at her. "Let the souls be free!" An explosion of ghostly faces, contorted in fear and pain, burst out of the vampire's body, leaving only a pile of ash behind.

"Leah?" Dana asked again.

"Yeah, Dana."

"I think I want to go home now."

MONSTER DETECTIVES 2: THE NEXT CASE

REBECCA BESSER

Hello, I'm Vincent Ortega, but I'm more commonly known as Vinnie, the vampire third of the Monster Detectives. The other two 'parts' of the team are Frank N. Stein, but we call him Frankie. He's a huge, green mammoth of a creature with bolts sticking out of his neck—quite clumsy, but he gets the job done. Then there's Zack...

He's a zombie—nothing more than a walking, decaying, eating piece of undead flesh. But, hey, we all have our purpose.

I suppose you're wondering what we do. Together we investigate occurrences involving anything of a supernatural or mythical origin. Monsters investigating the wrong doing by other monsters, you might say. The last case we were on involved werewolves. It was a mess! Frankie thought it was just one werewolf, but it had turned out to be five! Maybe next time we'll look before we leap. Hell, we didn't even get paid for that little fiasco, because we went charging in before we had a client. But, Frankie says in doing so we protected ourselves. Maybe him and Zack, but as for me, I've been around thousands of years and have remained invisible.

My coffin shook as someone banged on the lid.

"Vinnie, are you awake?"

With a heavy sigh, I unlatched the lid of my coffin and peeked out, just to make sure the sun wasn't still shining in. Sometimes Zack would forget about my aversion to sunlight and wake me up too soon. I don't know how many times I've lost fingers and suffered burns because of his carelessness when I wasn't wearing sunscreen.

It was Frankie, standing there looking anxious.

"What?" I asked.

"Turn on the news and you'll see," he said urgently.

Pushing the coffin lid all the way open, I turned on my built-in TV.

"What station?" I asked.

"Doesn't matter. It's on all of them."

I was about to ask 'what is' when I heard it from the TV anchor.

"...Burnt human remains have been found in the woods close to Overlook Point at the sight of a wildfire. Among the remains are said to be Senator Gregory Hastel and his secretary Joyce Willis. Speculation is that they were involved in some kind of ritualistic slaughter and burned. There were three other DNA samples found at the scene, but they have yet to be identified..."

"Damn," I said, glancing at Frankie.

"No shit!" he barked, gripping the side of my coffin so tightly I could hear the wood cracking.

"Easy, you're breaking my bed," I said, turning my attention back to the TV.

"Sorry," he muttered, loosening his grip.

"...In national news, thirty-nine bodies, with more expected, have been found in Appalachia, more specifically West Virginia. No one knows the cause of the deaths at this time. Our sources tell us the bodies are dried-out shells. No blood, no wounds, just dry husks. We'll keep you updated as information comes in..."

They cut to a quick video someone had managed to get of Federal agents carrying bodies out and laying them in a line to be taken to the morgue. It showed what the anchor had said. Human raisins, all dried up and wrinkly—merely shells of what they had once been.

"Shit," I sighed, sat up, and dragged my claw-tipped fingers through my hair.

"Yeah, who would have thought those werewolves were prominent citizens?" Frankie said. "What are the chances?"

I closed my eyes for a moment and willed some patience. Frankie's mind was still on the last case and I was already on the next. Typical. It was hard to work with the guy sometimes when I've had years and years of experience he didn't. Not only was my body faster, but my brain was faster as well.

"I don't know," I said, jumping sleekly out of my coffin to stand next to Frankie. "But that's the least of our worries right now."

Frankie turned his head with a barely audible creak. No one except for me could hear all the creaks and moans when he moved. No one else had my acute hearing, at least not anyone close by. My eyes flicked briefly to the TV screen. The news was over and they were moving on to something else.

"What's wrong now?" Frankie asked. "What could be more important than us killing a Senator and who knows who else! This is serious. It could attract more attention than we need. This could end us!"

In his frustration and fury, Frankie slammed his fist down, shattering the side of my coffin in an explosion of splintering wood.

He looked down at what he'd done, his eyes growing wide. "I'm sorry, Vinnie. I'll have someone in here to fix that right away. It'll be good as new by morning."

I just glared at him—this, after breaking three of my ribs last week. Taking a deep breath, even though I didn't need air, I counted to ten as I let it out slowly. I still found some human rituals could serve a purpose in my life. This was one of them.

"Where's Zack?" I asked and started walking toward the door.

"I really am sorry, Vinnie," Frankie said, thumping after me. Each step he took shook the floor.

"I know you're sorry," I hissed, spinning back toward him. "We have other stuff to worry about right now. *Where's Zack?*"

Frankie pulled up short, in mid-step, and just stared at me. It's no wonder. He'd never seen me like this before. Hell, I hadn't been this way in more than four centuries, but he didn't know that, because he hadn't known me then.

"I think he's in his office," Frankie said, frowning.

I turned back to the doorway and marched out into the hall. Zack's office was three doors down, to the left. I followed the passage, knocked briefly, and then steeled myself to enter. I hated going into Zack's office. Not only was I fast and had acute hearing, my sense of smell was stronger. Being around Zack in an enclosed space filled me with revulsion. I know he did his best to keep his rotting stench under control with Lysol, but all it did was burn my nasal passages even more. I tried not to fall back into my past 'human' actions when I was around him. I didn't need to breathe, but it was hard not doing it sometimes.

Don't breathe! Don't breathe! I chanted in my head before twisting the doorknob and stepping inside.

Zack was sitting behind his desk chewing on a human calf like most people would chew on a fried chicken leg. Blood was shooting from the flesh with each chomp of his jaw. It sprayed the ceiling and the walls, with a few drops landing on my face. I hissed and wiped it away.

"Sorry," Zack said around a mouthful of raw meat.

I nodded and walked in.

Frankie followed almost two full minutes later. "What's the rush?" he asked, still frowning.

"Sorry," I said. "I didn't know I was moving so fast."

"You were in here so fast," Zack said, taking another bite, "that I'd just opened my mouth to take a bite and you walked in before I could close it! Which explains why you got sprayed."

Instead of sitting down, I paced back and forth so quickly that Frankie and Zack didn't even know I was moving. I suppose to them I just looked like I was going blurry.

"What's going on, Vinnie?" Frankie barked, getting tense now. "Just spit it out! You're making us all nervous."

"It was the news," I said, coming to a halt. "The bodies, the ones in West Virginia, I know what, or I should say *who* is responsible for them."

"Really?" Zack asked, swallowing what was in his mouth. "Who? Is this going to be our next case?"

"I have a feeling it is," Frankie said, still looking at me. "Are you going to tell us what's going on? Or do we have to beg for information?"

I took a deep breath to calm myself and regretted it instantly. The smell of Zack and his meal burned my throat and lungs.

"It's hard," I said. "I'm not supposed to tell anyone. I'll get in serious trouble if I do."

"What do you mean?" Frankie asked. "Why can't you tell us? We're your partners for crying out loud, not to mention your friends!"

I thought about it for a moment. Trying to figure out how to break this to them without sounding like I didn't trust them. I did trust them. I just wasn't *allowed* to tell. They would hunt me down—they would kill me.

Sitting heavily on the dirty couch against the wall, I tried to ignore the squishing noise it made.

"Great!" Zack yelled, wiggling and wobbling to get out of his chair. "You found it."

I was scared to ask what I'd found, but didn't have to as he pulled up the edge of the cushion I was sitting on and extracted a quarter of a brain from beneath it.

"I've been looking for this for almost a week," Zack said, taking a delicate bite and chewing slowly, like he was savoring the flavor.

This time, I remembered not to breathe.

"I'll tell you what I can," I said, staring Frankie in the eye. "But the less you know the safer you'll be. You're going to have to trust me about the rest."

Frankie folded his arms and nodded, never dropping eye contact.

"The deaths...they're vampire related," I said slowly. "And I know which vampire is responsible. But I can't tell you."

Frankie raised his right eyebrow and I inwardly cringed at the high-pitched squeal that little movement made. I wanted to cover my ears and scream for him to be quiet.

"It's a long story," I said, holding my hands up. "Again, one I can't share. All I can tell you is we're dealing with a vampire older than me, and that she's very strong and dangerous. And *if* she's made others like herself, well. then they could be..." I sighed. "I can't even imagine how bad this might end up."

"She?" Frankie asked. "A *female* vampire?"

I almost laughed. "Yes, Frankie, there are female vampires."

Zack sucked the last bit of brain into his mouth noisily. "You know, for some strange reason, I always thought you were the only one. You know, like Frankie is the only one of him, and I'm the only one of me that we know of."

I did laugh at that. "There are many vampires. We're an ancient race, going almost all the way back to the origins of humanity."

"Why do I have a feeling there's way more to this than you're letting on?" Frankie asked.

"Because there is," I said.

"What are we supposed to do? Just jump in blind and trust that what you aren't telling us won't get us killed?" Frankie asked.

I sat silently for a moment, thinking. "Either that or let me go and handle this on my own."

"Not a chance," Frankie and Zack said at the same time.

While I feared for their lives, knowing they didn't understand what they were up against, it also made me feel good to know I wasn't alone.

"Thanks," I said. "I guess we should head out to West Virginia and see *if* it is her who's doing this, or if I'm letting my nightmares run away with me. I'll have to see one of the bodies or catch her scent at the crime scene to be sure."

"I don't like how that sounds," Frankie said softly, as he and Zack followed me out.

*　*　*

After getting the supplies I knew we would need, Frankie, Zack, and I climbed aboard our helicopter. It was a good thing I'd taken lessons years ago or we might have been hard pressed to find a pilot who only flew at night and didn't ask a lot of questions. We'd used it as our mobile camp for three years. It has a spare coffin for me, a cooler for Zack, and some kind of portable office looking thing for Frankie. He seemed happiest when he was working, and I have to admit, the nights he'd spent surfing the internet doing research has saved our asses more than a few times.

"We should be there in an hour," I said into the microphone attached to my headphones.

Frankie nodded and tried not to look nervous as we flew high above solid ground—his favorite place to be. Zack didn't seem to care. If I turned my head, I could see him sucking marrow out of bone fragments he'd brought along for a snack. I didn't want to think about what was in the cooler in the back.

My mind kept going back to the glimpse of the bodies I'd seen on the news. With the image came memories of a past that haunted

105

me. I'd thought I'd buried it deep and would never have to face it again. But I'd been wrong. Here it was, staring me in the face.

I kept hoping we'd get there and her scent wouldn't be on the bodies, that I wouldn't find the little mark I knew to be hers. If it was there, then the humans hadn't found yet—and may not ever find it. Unfortunately when I arrived at the scene shortly after landing, her scent was everywhere—taunting me, teasing me, making me remember.

I stood beside the old wooden church tucked into the side of the mountain. Towering trees stood around it, as if they were sentinels of protection, with a cross visible over their green tops.

Frankie and Zack had stayed behind to set up internet and communication links. There hadn't been anywhere close by where I could land the chopper, so it was faster and easier for me to scout alone. They couldn't help with the trail anyhow. Their sense of smell wasn't good enough to detect what I was after.

There was no scent of blood. I hadn't expected there to be. She'd always been meticulous about that. Her sweet voice echoed to me through the glade, but I knew it was only in my mind.

A drop fallen is a drop wasted.

Slowly, I walked around the church, looking for any signs of entry. I sniffed at all the windows and doors before going inside and sniffing the floorboards. She hadn't been alone. I could smell at least two more, and they were both like her. She'd made herself a few children—a family.

When I knew I'd uncovered all there was to be found, I leapt to the tree tops and made my way back to the chopper. The cool air helped clear my head. I had to be able to think clearly if I was going to make it out alive, if *we* were going to make it out alive.

I landed in the small clearing and noted the satellite dishes were in place and Frankie's face was illuminated by the artificial glow of his laptop screen. Zack was off to the side, sorting and tying up some wires, popping eyeballs into his mouth like they were cherries. He didn't seem to notice that the juices were dripping from his chin, coating all of the wires he was handling.

Zack was a conundrum. In life he had been a computer genius, and though now a zombie, he had carried most of his skill with him in *undeath.* I found it so ironic how he would act so much like a zombie in the movies, feeding and slobbering like a mindless ghoul, and then do something brilliant with computers.

I went straight to my coffin and opened a small compartment at the foot, extracting a chilled pouch of blood. Without warming it like I normally do, I bit into the bag and sucked it dry. My nerves were stirring the need to feed. Usually I could go a week or more without a meal, but right now I was going through two gallons of blood a day.

Frankie glanced at me. "How'd it go? Did you find what you were looking for?"

"It was her," I said, tossing the empty plastic bag into the trash bin, "and a couple of others."

"So, it's worst case scenario?"

I nodded. "Yes, I would say so."

"I found where the bodies are being kept," Frankie said, pointing to the screen. "The county morgue. This little burg doesn't have much to offer, which makes it easy for us."

"I don't need to see them," I said quietly, hopping up and laying on top of my coffin. "I know it's her."

"Are you ever going to tell us *her* name?" Frankie asked, sounding agitated.

"I can't," I said, looking in his direction. "If I do, she'll hear me."

Frankie turned his head slowly to look at me. The groan of it filled the interior of the chopper. Glancing at Zack, I thought it must be blissful not to hear it.

"Aren't you being a little paranoid?" Frankie asked.

I shook my head no. "She's in a cave close by. I found it on my way back. She won't pay attention to us unless we get in her way or she accidentally comes across us; we aren't food. But if I say her name, she'll know we know she's here and come and find us. We don't want that to happen. We want to surprise her, not the other way around."

"I wish you weren't so cryptic," Frankie muttered and turned back to his laptop, slamming his fingers on the keys. The little plastic pieces broke apart, ruining the computer as they shot down in and blew pieces off the motherboard. He screamed, picked it up, and threw it out the door. The wires detached mid-air, like Zack had designed them to.

Opening a drawer, Frankie pulled out another laptop and yanked the wires back over to where he could reach them, pulling Zack with them. Zack fell hard against the ramp they'd set up to get in and out of base. I heard a sickening crunch and some grinding of bone as his shoulder dislocated and his torso gave way, almost twisting the middle of his body all the way around.

"Damn it!" Zack yelled as his bowl of eyes dumped onto the floor of the chopper. "Be careful, you big oaf!"

"Sorry," Frankie muttered. He stood and stomped outside. He stormed all the way to the treeline before he stopped and just stood, watching the forest.

With a deep sigh, I got up, helped Zack semi-right himself so he could pick up his eyeballs, and went after Frankie.

"What's wrong?" I asked, as if I didn't know.

"I feel helpless on this one," Frankie said. "I'm supposed to be the leader, and right now I'm feeling like a newbie going out for the first time. I don't know how to proceed. You won't tell me! Don't you understand that! You two are my responsibility. If something goes wrong, if something bad happens, it's my fault."

"No, it would be *my* fault," I said. "I shouldn't have let you guys come with me."

He turned toward me and I noticed his movements were quieter out in the open.

"We wouldn't let you come alone," Frankie said with a half-grin. "Even if you hadn't let us come, we would have found a way and would be here anyway."

I nodded. "I was thinking maybe we should make this quick—get it over with tonight. It would be faster and easier. I don't like taking the chance they'll find us. Would that take a load off your mind? Just getting it done and over with and going home?"

Frankie frowned. "Yeah, but we only have a couple hours of darkness left. You'll have to get in your coffin or load up on the sunscreen."

"I've been working on something for just this type of occasion." I grinned. "I don't know if it'll work, but it's one of those now or never times."

"I take it you have a plan. What did you have in mind?"

I laughed, and together we walked over to Zack, who'd finished picking up his eyeballs and was eating again, so we could all discuss it together.

*　*　*

Moving through the forest at such a high rate of speed I knew no one and nothing could see me, I headed for the cave that I'd tracked the vampires to on my way back to the chopper earlier. It hadn't been hard. I was guessing that one of the 'children' was still relatively young, because their scent was easy to follow. But then again, they probably didn't figure on anyone coming after them. Knowing her like I do, I could bet she didn't feel threatened by anyone, thinking she would always be safe.

When I was in position, I gave the signal, which was nothing more than me pushing a button on a one-way remote. It would signal Frankie and Zack, but I couldn't receive anything back from them. I didn't want them giving away my position. That could get us all killed.

Darting swiftly to the mouth of the cave, I paused to listen. At first I couldn't hear anything, but after waiting a full minute, I heard what sounded like voices within the deep, dark depths. Checking swiftly over the concealing, black body suit I was wearing, I made sure everything was ready.

Slinking through the darkness, which I could see fine in, I traversed toward the innermost depths of the damp cave. Sounds would carry easily, so I had to be incredibly careful not to make any noise. It took me longer than I thought it would to reach the den of the coven.

Her scent overwhelmed me as I circled around them. There were five of them altogether—more than I'd counted on, but still manageable. They were all lying down in a square, head to head, foot to foot, with her in the center by herself.

I knew they were still awake; the sun wasn't up and the feeling of lethargy hadn't set in. It was as if all vampires had an internal clock, telling them when it was time to sleep by making them extremely tired.

There was one tense moment when my foot scraped against some loose stones along the edge of the chamber. A young female sat up and looked in my direction.

I froze.

When she didn't see anything, she laid back down, and I knew my suit was working.

Once I was in position behind the vampires, knowing they could easily get out of the cave, I waited until I started feeling tired—it wasn't very long. I hit the signal again, letting Frankie and Zack know I was ready.

Suddenly, she shot up from her position on the floor, flew across the small space, and slammed into me full force, knocking me off my feet. She hissed in my ear as I tried to push her off me, but she was too strong. Her clawed hands clamped down on either side of my head, and she was about to rip it off my shoulders, when she stopped.

By this time all of her children were alerted to my presence and they circled around us. She bent forward, pressing her face into my neck, breathing deeply.

"Vincent?" she whispered in shock, her body going limp.

Quickly, I pushed her off and stood. The others hissed and growled at me, still having a hard time seeing me.

"Vincent? Is that really you?"

"You know it is," I said roughly. "It's been a long time, Penchant."

"Yes, it has," she laughed.

Her children hushed, listening to their maker talk to me with interest.

Thinking fast, I jumped to the ceiling and then to the wall, positioning myself behind the group once more. Swiftly, I lit the UV lights I'd attached to my suit. The vampires around me hissed in pain and tried to hide. I knew the strength of the lights wouldn't kill them, but it would burn like hell.

"Why are you doing this, Vincent?" Penchant cried, backing away. "Why?"

"Need you ask?" I asked bitterly. "I'd think you'd have a better memory."

I walked forward, forcing them to move back toward the mouth of the cave. They withered and whined, crawling along the ground in agony. One of the young ones was brave. He jumped up, bounced off the wall, and hurtled himself at me. I didn't expect such a show of heroics. He caught me in the chest, knocking me down and breaking three of the six lights. His face sizzled inches from mine as he hissed, clawing at my throat.

I was older and stronger, easily holding him back. The others were turning back, ready to help their brother.

I heard Penchant laughing softly.

"I remember quite well, Vincent," she purred as she watched me fight off her children. "You always were foolhardy. It was one of the things that caused me to fall in love with you."

I clawed, bit and fought against the group of young vampires. Decapitating one with a twist and a yank, blood went spraying through the air. I could tell they'd recently fed by how much they bled. Quickly spinning and kicking, I knocked another off me and dragged the other two with me as I got to my feet. The young female who'd almost spotted me earlier tried to rip off my arm. Luckily, it was the one with the broken lights. Thinking fast, I lifted my other arm and held the light to shine across her eyes, burning her eyeballs to a crisp in her sockets. Her howls and wails as she fell away were almost deafening.

The one I'd knocked off started to get up and I knew I had to get out fast. If they managed to rip my suit, I wouldn't be able to leave the cave.

Penchant heard my panicked heart beat faster. "What's wrong, Vincent? Are you rusty? You used to spar with me and it didn't bother you near this much."

Angrily, I ripped the young male off my back and threw him into the one who'd just regained his footing. They fell in a mass of limbs onto a stalagmite. It penetrated one through the torso and the other through the neck. They withered in pain, crying out as they tried to free themselves but couldn't.

I roared, shaking the cave with the loudness of my fury. I could hear Penchant laughing over the screams of the fallen, but I couldn't see her anywhere. I knew my time was up and it angered me. Everything had almost gone according to plan. Turning, I ran quickly to the mouth of the cave and swallowed hard as I stepped out into the sunlight. Thankfully, Zack and Frankie were there with my coffin because there were multiple slashes in my suit and the sun was burning me.

*   *   *

When I woke up, it was night once more and I was in the chopper. I opened my coffin and peeked out. No one could be seen. It was just as we'd arranged. I climbed out and shed the skintight black suit I'd worn in the cave and threw it into the trash bin with the rest of the garbage. Retrieving a bag of blood, I sucked it down quickly.

"You know, years ago, the sight of you standing naked and sucking on blood got me excited," Penchant purred from the darkness beyond the helicopter. "And I have to admit, I still feel some of that excitement when I look at you now."

I turned to see Penchant standing at the top of the ramp. Her long, brunette hair hung free around her shoulders, being tousled by the night's breeze. Her soft red lips were slightly parted and she was panting eagerly, like she was thinking of pinning my down and mounting me like she'd done many times in the past. Her bright red pupils betrayed her though. They weren't filled with lust like they used to be, they were filled with anger and hate.

"And once, I liked that," I said, "but not anymore. You tried to kill me. Hell, you betrayed the entire coven. That's why you were exiled, and why I left. After standing up for you—when you *lied* to me—I couldn't stay any longer. Now you're breaking the laws again, and this time I'm not going to protect you."

She laughed, her head falling back in amusement. "You're so cute. Do you honestly think you can defeat me?"

I grinned and winked at her, lifting my foot off the trigger that Zack had set in the floor. Ropes soaked in holy water whipped around Penchant. She tried to leap back, but they still managed to tangle around her lower half.

I jumped out of the chopper, pounced on her, and shoved a clove of raw garlic into her mouth while she was screaming in fury. It wasn't enough to seriously hurt her, but it would knock her out for a while and make her sick when she woke up. After her eyes drifted shut, I put on heavy work gloves and untied her before the ropes burned completely through her body. After that was done, I dressed and made a couple of calls. One to let Frankie and Zack know our plan had worked, and one to the 'authorities,' to come and take care of Penchant. This time she wouldn't be exiled. This time she would be terminated.

Thanks to Frankie and Zack, the equivalent of the vampire police showed up and took Penchant, saying they would also take care of her children. While I had peace knowing I had done everything I could, I still felt a deep sadness. She was my first love after all, and who wanted to be part of their first love's death?

"Where is she?" Frankie asked, lumbering up the ramp. "Did she get away?"

"No," I said with a secret smile. "They came and took her. Our work is done."

Zack followed Frankie, eating a heart like it was an apple. "What? We don't even get to see her? What a crock!"

"Sorry, guys," I said. "But that's how it has to be."

Frankie frowned, and then grinned. "You know, I think this case has been '*Vin-dic-ated*'! Thanks to Vinnie, the best vampire Dic around!"

We all laughed. Everything was back to normal. Things were taken care of, and we'd done it as a team, even if I was the only one put in the path of danger.

FLATWOODS

TERRY ALEXANDER

Rodney Harper lay in the uncomfortable hospital bed, staring up at the ceiling tiles. The steady hiss of the oxygen machine annoyed him; the twin nubs sticking in his nostrils rubbed the tender flesh raw.

He glanced over to the medical drip and the IV stuck in his arm.

What a way to go out, he thought and shook his head sadly.

He gazed at the open doorway, expecting a special visitor today, one he desperately wanted to see. Paula, his granddaughter, had just finished her junior year of college. The girl had a good head on her shoulders with an excellent chance to really make something of her life.

Months ago, she asked him a question, one he refused to answer, but now it was time to come clean. Someone had to hear the story. Someone had to know the truth, so it didn't die with him.

Rodney closed his eyes, dozing lightly. He felt his bed shift as if someone had sat down, and he opened his eyes, blinked several times, to see a figure sitting at his bedside. As the figure slowly came into focus he saw it was...

"Paula, I'm glad you're here." The old man's smile looked more like a grimace.

The young woman in her mid-twenties smiled, showing even white teeth. "Grandpa," she said. "It's good to see you. I always enjoy visiting with you." Her smile grew wider, and she absently brushed her unruly red hair from her eyes. A line of freckles crossed her cheeks and nose. She reached over to him, holding his liver spotted hand in her porcelain one.

Rodney's faded blue eyes sparkled with renewed life. He winked at his granddaughter. "We need to talk, dear."

"What about, Grandpa?" she asked.

"You need to know about your family, it's time we talked about West Virginia." He squeezed her hand slightly.

A puzzled look crossed her face. "You've never wanted to talk about Flatwoods before. Every time I asked you've always changed the subject."

Rodney nodded his head weakly. "I know, but my time is waning, someone should know the story and you're all I have left."

"I'll need a tape recorder or a notebook," she said while rummaging through her purse. "I need something to keep a record."

"We ain't got time for all that, honey. You're going to have to rely on your memory." A shaky hand reached for the plastic water glass on the tray before him. He sipped through a straw, a stray drop clinging to his thin lips.

"It was September 1952 in Flatwoods, West Virginia, in Braxton County. I was a strapping young lad, just getting ready to graduate high school. My mom's brother Leon was visiting. Now Leon was an odd duck." He paused for a moment, letting the memories flood back. "At the time I didn't know how odd."

*　*　*

Leon Drummond sat at the kitchen table, sipping a glass of lemonade. His complexion was haggard and gaunt; red rimmed eyes were set deep in his head, his hard life etched in his face.

"Helen, that was a fine supper. Too bad Ralph had to miss out." He dabbed his lips with a napkin, as he glanced across the table at Rodney.

"He's working the night shift for the next three months, and then he goes back to days. I hate these swing shifts." Helen wiped her neck with a dish towel. "I don't know what I'd do if Rodney wasn't around to help me with all the chores that need to be done around here."

Leon's face wrinkled in pain, and his hands clutched his stomach. He avoided Helen's gaze, but not Rodney's watchful eyes.

"Are you all right, Uncle Leon?" Rodney asked.

"Yeah, I'm okay." He tried to hide the pain, but his face told the story. "Hey, sis, do you know of any good fishing spots nearby? I think I'd like to try my luck tonight." He rose from the chair slowly, still clutching his stomach.

Helen's lips puckered. They always did when she was thinking. "I'm not sure."

"Bailey Fisher has some good fishing spots on his farm," Rodney said, eager to wet a hook and discover what was wrong with his uncle.

"Where are they exactly? I want a place away from people so I can fish in peace," Leon said. "Maybe I could take a few sandwiches for later."

"I'll fix up three or four." Helen pulled a bundle wrapped in white butcher paper from the refrigerator. "It won't take me but a minute."

"I can show you where the best fishing hole is, Uncle Leon." Rodney offered.

Leon drained his glass. "No need, just point me in the right direction, I'll find it." He made it clear he didn't want company.

Helen handed him a brown paper bag folded over at the top. "That should make a good midnight snack." She stood on her tiptoes to give him a hug. "Remember, we're going into town tomorrow for a fancy sit down dinner."

"You bet, I'm looking forward to it." Leon turned to Rodney. "Whereabouts is that fishing hole?"

"You go down to the first intersection and take a right, go two miles and you'll see a big metal gate on your left, that's the spot." Rodney glanced down to the floor. "Mind if I tag along, Uncle?" he asked.

"Not tonight, kid, I've got some thinking to do," Leon said, holding the bag close to his stomach. He turned and walked slowly out the back door.

"Mom, what's wrong with Uncle Leon?" Rodney asked. "He's not acting right."

He hasn't been the same since he came back from Germany."

"Leon was at Omaha Beach during the invasion, but he won't talk about it. The memories are too painful to dwell on." She gave Rodney's shoulder a light squeeze. "War changes people, son."

"Still, I wish he would let me go with him." Rodney shook his head, glancing out the window. A look of puzzlement crossed his face. "Mom, where are the fishing poles?"

"Out in the tool shed where we always keep them, why?" She wiped the perspiration from her forehead. "This kitchen gets so hot."

"I'll be back later, Mom, I'm going out for a ride." He kissed her cheek. "Don't wait up."

"Where are you going, young man?" she demanded.

"I'm taking the motorbike for a ride," he said. "I thought I'd drop by Jimmy's for a little while. His mom and dad have one of those new televisions." The door slammed behind him

"Well, be careful," she called, shaking her head. "Televisions, those things will never catch on."

Rodney straddled his American Indian Scout motorcycle. He toed the starter peg down and stomped the kick-pedal. The engine caught on the third attempt.

He should be at the corner by now; maybe I can catch him before he gets to the Fisher place, he thought.

He squeezed the hand clutch and stepped on the foot shift.

He pulled into the rutted dirt road, twisting the throttle. Dust still swirled in the air from his uncle's departure, and Rodney knew the road well and kept the bike at a safe speed. He made the corner and caught a blink of taillights in the distance. Practiced fingers switched on his single headlight against the approaching darkness, as he eyed the dying sun in the red western sky.

Ten minutes later, Rodney spotted the '47 Packard parked under a row of trees, on the opposite side of the Fisher's iron gate. He stopped the motorcycle behind the huge V-eight.

Well, he found the gate anyway, he thought.

"What are you doing here, kid?" Leon said as he stepped silently from the trees.

Rodney spun around, surprised by his uncle's quiet approach. "How did you sneak up on me like that?"

"It's a knack I have. Now, why did you follow me?" Leon leaned against the rear quarter panel of the vehicle.

"You ain't going fishing, you don't have a pole or anything." Rodney stared up at Leon's slicked black hair.

"Smart-alec kid. Yeah, you're right." A spasm of pain twisted his face. "I'm not feeling good. I just needed to get out of the house and get some fresh air." Sweat beaded on his forehead.

A large, saucer-like shape flew by overhead, then seemed to hover just beyond the trees. It glowed with the same pale light of a full moon.

"What's wrong with you, Uncle?" Rodney rushed to Leon's side.

Leon doubled over in pain, hugging his stomach. "This can't be happening, not now. The full moon was day's ago," he said through clenched teeth.

"Uncle Leon, what's happening to you?" Rodney's eyes bulged in his head.

"Go away, kid. Get out of here. Go home." Thick hair began to sprout on Leon's face. He kicked the shoes from his feet, clumsily working the buttons loose on his shirt and dropping it to the ground. He loosened his jeans, letting them fall around his ankles, standing only in his blue boxer shorts with white heart designs. Rodney had purchased them at Christmas time as a gag gift for his uncle. "Get out of here." Leon's voice turned deep and coarse. He fell to his knees. His face bubbled and stretched. Bones snapped and popped, grinding together, muscles rippled and reshaped under the skin. Coarse black hair erupted, covering his entire body within seconds, growing longer and thicker. The bones of his face reformed, the nose and mouth growing to a pointed snout, the ears lengthened and tapered to points. The teeth grew to sharp lethal canines.

The beast jumped to its feet. Its feral yellow eyes fastened on Rodney. The teenager stared in bug-eyed fear at the thing that had once been his uncle. The beast stepped closer. Rodney desperately wanted to run, but his numb legs refused to carry him.

The monster crouched before him, saliva dangling from its open mouth. It hesitated, a glimmer of recognition flashing through the creature's eyes. The huge nose distended, inhaling Rodney's scent, the long lolling tongue licking his cheek. The feral eyes narrowed. It turned slowly, and after giving Rodney a final glance, it sprinted into the darkened forest.

Rodney stood statue still, allowing his racing heartbeat to slow. He drew in a deep breath. *My God, what was that? Was that a werewolf? That only happens in the movies? Uncle Leon can't be a werewolf, it's impossible.*

He caught a glimpse of ghostly white dots racing through the woods, chasing the disc of light crossing above the tree tops. "That must be it, that light, that must be why Leon changed." Rodney ran after his uncle, keeping the flying saucer in sight. After several minutes, the plate-shaped craft stopped. It hovered in mid-air, slowly settling to the ground.

The glowing saucer landed on the east side of a small hill. Rodney paused on the edge of the forest, filling his burning lungs with air as he leaned over, hands on knees, and closed his eyes. His sweaty clothes clung to his body like a second skin. He watched in fascination as a portion of the hull slid upward to reveal an opening.

They're real, they really exist. Spacemen! First a werewolf and now little green men from Mars. What's next unicorns?

A single figure moved from the doorway, encased in a green armored shell. The platform it rode floated above the ground supported by a cushion of air from its base. A metal-like cowl protected the back of its glowing red head. The creature lacked shoulders; its short stubby arms jutted straight from the thick chest. The tips of its three-fingered hands ended in sharp curved talons. The platform, which covered its legs, floated for a few feet and then settled to the ground.

Its face appeared scaly, lizard-like.

Make that big red men from Mars.

Rodney glanced away from the creature, scanning the forest using the glow from the flying saucer to see by. A movement at the crest of the rise caught his eye; four shadowy figures stood on the hilltop.

Who are they? What are they doing here? Who are those people?

A flashlight beam settled on the lizard creature. A loud hiss reached Rodney's ears. *What are they doing, trying to get killed?* He took a reluctant step forward, and at that moment he saw his uncle, still in wolf form, wearing the outlandish underwear, moving through the tree-cover.

"Run!" Rodney shouted. "Get out of here! Run!"

A blast of air lifted the creature into the air. The platform glided toward the group on the hill. Rodney's eyes began to fill with tears, his nose burned from the foul pungent odor coming from the vehicle's air drive. He wiped his eyes with the tail of his t-shirt, pulling the collar over his nose to act as a filter. A scattered mix of voices drifted down the hillside, sounding like the drone of bees. The group scattered, the glow of the flashlight traced weird patterns in the trees as they ran for home.

The lizard creature turned from the intruders, returning to the spaceship. Rodney watched helplessly, a knot of fear growing in his belly as the creature turned in his direction.

Leon rushed from the trees, the heart-dotted underwear flashing in the light of the ship. He stopped between Rodney and the strange floating monstrosity. The two creatures circled each other in a bizarre combative ritual, each sizing up their opponent. The werewolf's thick leg muscles bunched together, and it leaped at the hovering figure. Its claws hooked into the platform, and with a mighty heave, the beast pulled itself aboard, sharp claws slashing at the armor. The werewolf found a seam along the cowl and ripped it from the reptilian head.

It provided Rodney with a better view of the creature's elongated skull and blood-red skin. Its sharp talons raked and slashed at the werewolf's chest; the misshapen arms were far stronger than they first appeared. Blood flowed from the triple slashes across Leon's hairy chest. The werewolf threw back its head, and an unearthly howl of agony burst from its toothy jaws.

Twin rows of sharp canines glinted in the spacecraft's glow as the werewolf bit down on the scarlet neck. The alien's lips parted, showing a double set of fangs in the upper jaw. The short arms pushed at the powerful jaws, forcing Leon's deadly teeth from its flesh.

The talons sank into the corded flesh of the werewolf's thick hairy shoulder. The triple daggers scraped along the bone, the pressure from the beast's jaws relenting. The three-digit hand worked under the jaw and closed on the fur-covered throat, squeezing the windpipe.

Thick blood dripped from the ravaged, scaly neck to the armored chest plate. Slowly, it pushed the snarling beast away. Leon balanced precariously on the outer rim of the platform, and then a backhanded slap knocked him to the ground.

"Oh God, Uncle Leon!" Rodney took a second step forward, intent on helping his uncle, not knowing how he was going to accomplish this feat. He froze as the werewolf jumped up, then leapt for the platform above its head again.

A concentrated beam of red light blazed from the turret, the ray burning deep furrows in the rocky earth. The werewolf fell to the ground, as the scent of singed hair drifted on the light wind. Leon avoided the continuous blasts, running in a zig-zag manner while the ground vaporized around him.

"Leon, Uncle Leo! Get out of there! Leave that thing alone!" Rodney burst from the tree cover while waving his arms.

The platform spun on the cushion of air. The red-faced invader hissed, displaying curved fangs along its upper jaw. A forked tongue flickered in the air, seeking the source of the disturbance. Its beady eyes centered on Rodney.

The boy froze in a half-step, slowly letting his left foot touch the ground. He stared in slack-jawed amazement at the lizard man, his eyes showing white. He drew in a deep breath, sure in his mind that he'd met his end.

Flying bits of debris and twigs slapped his face, collecting in his hair as it was carried on a blast of compressed air.

It's gonna kill me! He gazed in silent fear, rooted to the spot as the lizard-creature closed on him.

The werewolf leaped to the platform, the fur from its shoulder and chest was burned away, the charred flesh covered by a cluster of bubbly, weeping blisters. Leon's claw-tipped hands closed on the metal breast plate, the metal shrieking as he tore it free and hurled it to the ground. The chunk of metal clattered at Rodney's feet. Hesitantly, he reached out his hands to touch it. Strangely, it felt cool to his touch. His fingers traced the etched patterns in the metal as he clutched it to his chest.

Rodney glanced up at his uncle. The beast's slavering jaws closed on the creature's forearm, the bone snapping with a sharp *crack*. Eagle-like talons slashed at the werewolf's injured chest, cutting through the mass of blisters to the burned flesh beneath. Bright crimson flowed from the open wound and down the werewolf's side, staining the tattered heart underwear.

A beastly howl shattered the night, as the werewolf's claws reached out, digging into the scarlet lizard-face, catching it on the lower jaw. In a tremendous burst of energy, it ripped one side away. The mandible bounced against the creature's stubby neck as it fell away. Leon's canines sank into the bloodied flesh, biting away great chunks of meat.

The creature pushed at the werewolf's injured chest to no avail; it lacked the strength and leverage to dislodge its attacker. The creature slowly grew limp, its arms hanging lifeless.

You're doing it, Uncle Leon, you're gonna kill it! Rodney ran into the clearing, as thoughts of fame and fortune filled his mind. He failed to see the second lizard man exit the craft until it was too late.

"Uncle Leon, look out!" Rodney shouted.

A blast of intense light struck Leon's back, and the werewolf crumpled heavily to the ground. The newcomer floated to his companion's side, and a series of clicks issued from its mouth. It hovered, awaiting a response, and when none came, a yellow beam of light enveloped the crippled platform and dragged it into the dark interior of the flying saucer. The sliding door closed silently after they passed inside, and within moments the craft lifted from the ground. It hovered for a moment and then shot off into the sky and the stars above.

Rodney ran to his uncle's side, cradling Leon's head in his lap. The wolfish features began to recede, returning to normal. "Leon, Uncle Leon. You'll be all right; you've got to be all right." Tears filled his eyes, threading down his cheeks.

"Afraid not, kid," Leon whispered. "I'm cashing in."

"Come on, Uncle Leon, we'll get back to your car and get to town, then we'll find a doctor," Rodney said.

"Not enough time. What was that thing anyway?" Leon's bloody lips barely moved.

"An alien. It came down in a flying saucer." Rodney wiped the blood from his uncle's face. "Just like in New Mexico."

"They're tough, I'll give them that," Leon nodded. "Hope we never have to fight them."

"What happened to you? What made you change into a werewolf? How did it happen?" Rodney asked.

"It happened in the war. My outfit pushed Hitler's boys back across the Rhine. I pulled guard duty one night, and something attacked me." Leon paused to draw in a deep breath. "I've been fighting this curse ever since. I hope it dies with me." Leon closed his eyes, his breath rattling in his chest as his body slowly went limp.

*　*　*

Rodney glanced at Paula, as a smile creased his face. "You should have seen it, a werewolf wearing blue boxers with white hearts." His face turned solemn. "Mom and Dad died a year later in a car wreck, that's when I left West Virginia and joined the army. I completed my basic training at Camp Chaffee in Arkansas. I met your grandma when I was on leave with some of my buddies."

"Grandpa, that story can't be true." Paula held the old man's hand. "It's too fantastic to be true."

"Look it up for yourself. They call that thing the Flatwoods' Monster now." Rodney coughed weakly. "I'm the only one that saw everything, and I'm telling you exactly what I saw that night."

"Okay, Grandpa," Paula nodded. "But it's just so hard to accept."

"My times nearly gone, dear," he wheezed. "There are two things I want you to do for me after I pass on."

"Just tell me what you want," Paula said, fighting back tears.

"There's a set of keys in that night stand, they go to the big locker in the old garage at my home. You'll find the breast plate inside."

Paula dug through the drawer, rattling the keys when she found them.

Rodney nodded. "After I'm gone, I want you to go to Flatwoods and find my mom and dad's grave. Leon's is right next to them. Put some fresh flowers on their markers for me, then find a safe place to hide the breast plate."

Paula nodded. "I'll do it, if you say so. But why not give it to the government? Let scientists study it."

"It may come in handy some day," Rodney grinned. "If those spacemen show up again, you'll know where it is. Now go home and let me get some sleep."

Paula rose to her feet as her grandfather closed his eyes, the old man instantly drifting into slumber. Her footsteps echoed down the hallway as she departed, the tears flowing unrestrained from her eyes.

PEST CONTROL

JOHN GROVER

Lorne entered the backyard to get more firewood for the house. He scooped a few logs into his arms, paused, and looked around. He tilted his head up and sniffed the air. He smelled something bad in it; something rotten, something filth-ridden and decayed.

He glared into the woods at the edge of the yard and started toward them. He made his way swiftly through skeletal trees and thorn-filled bushes.

A withered trail snaked off into the thick of the woods.

In a clearing, he came upon a graveyard. The half moon cast milky illumination over a dozen etched stones. In the light, he spotted a grave defiled, its earth broken and bones scattered around it. The bones were littered with bite marks. Something had been gnawing on them. The logs tumbled from his arms as he moved closer to the grave, and read the etching on the stone.

Louis Castelle. Loving father.

Lorne's eyes grew enflamed. His hands clenched into fists. A cracking noise resounded and his bones shifted, his muscles ripped. His entire body sprouted fur, his hands twisted into claws and his mouth stretched into a snout filled with rows of razor-sharp teeth. His breath frosted the air as a roar, starting low in his chest, to then escape his lips.

Rustling in the thicket beside him sent the werewolf off. He sprung from the graveyard and barreled back into the woods. Something scurried off in a flash of pale white. Lorne bolted on all fours before launching through the treetops and scaling the gnarled, twisted trunks.

He smelled the foul creature just ahead of him. He also smelled carrion and death but it remained just out of his grasp. Ultimately, he lost the thing's trail at the edge of a river. It may have plunged into the water and covered its scent, but Lorne saw no sign of disturbance in the river. However it escaped, he was too close to human territory for comfort and abandoned his hunt. A frustrated howl tore through the night as he turned back home to warn the rest of his family.

* * *

"A ghoul has fed in our burial ground," Lorne told the others between panting breaths.

The Castelle family was one of the more formidable packs inhabiting the wooded lands, and since the death of their father, Louis, leadership of the pack belonged to Heather, the matriarch of the family. Lorne and his wife Willa shared their home with her and his two brothers, Seth and Cain.

Heather struck a match, the flame chasing the shadows from her lined face, and lit a tobacco pipe. The smoke encircled her gray hair. She shook out the match and pushed herself in her rocking chair. "This can't be allowed," she said calmly.

"Vermin," Seth said. "They're worse than the human scum out there."

"Are you sure?" Cain asked. "The vampires on top of the hill haven't mentioned any trouble."

"Idiot," Lorne snarled. "Vampires turn to ashes when they die. There are no bodies to bury."

"And the humans stopped burying their dead when they abandoned their homes and cities," Seth added. "They burn them now so they don't become one of us, or the one of the vamps."

"Boys, enough." Heather took another drag from her pipe and stopped her chair. "We need to stop this now. Where there's one ghoul, others will follow. Before we know it, we'll have an infestation on our hands. They're scavengers, worse than jackals and vultures. They take on characteristics of the dead they eat. We can't let our flesh digest in their system. If they gain the power of shape-shifting, no telling what damage they could do."

"It dug up father," Lorne said.

Heather went silent. Lorne felt the anger coursing through her. The air around her grew thick.

A low growl echoed in her chest. "It's not enough the humans trapped and slaughtered him like a dog. Now his remains are defiled? I want this ghoul scourge crushed. Do you understand me, sons?"

"Yes, mother," the three males answered.

"We'll take turns watching the burial ground every night," Lorne said to his brothers. They nodded in agreement.

Lorne walked over to his wife, Willa, and gave her a gentle kiss on the lips. He looked down at her pregnant belly and rubbed it softly. "Soon our first born will arrive."

"You had me worried," she said to him with a smile. "Fetching firewood should never take that long."

"I made an unexpected detour. It's all right. We're handling it."

"Just be careful. I don't want the new pup to grow up an orphan. He needs his father to teach him how to hunt."

I'll show him. One day he'll be the alpha of the pack."

"Lorne," Heather called across the house. "Don't eat the ghoul. Kill it. It's not like rabbit, deer or human that are living flesh. The ghouls are dead flesh. We don't know what this will do to us. It's filth and abomination. No telling how long it's been dead. Only fresh meat is good for us."

"Yes, mother," Lorne snarled.

"Heed my words," she snapped. "Make your brothers heel and don't eat dead flesh."

The creaking of Heather's rocking chair was the only sound in the entire house.

* * *

Lorne paced around the backyard the next night, anxious for his turn on watch. He cracked his knuckles a few times. He sighed and listened attentively to every sound: the crickets, the bats, the wild dogs miles down the road, the human searching for food in the next valley. With a half hour to go, Lorne shucked his patience and headed into the woods.

He picked up his pace to reach the burial ground, and in moments he saw his brother Seth standing guard, sniffing the perimeter. Lorne smelled the awful stench in the air, both repulsive and attractive. Tracks ran in and out of the burial ground.

Seth turned to him. "Two more graves have been dug up. Our uncles this time."

"It must have come back after I left last night," Lorne said. "The scent isn't fresh. I hate their smell. Their stench is worse than that of those human savages."

"I like the way the humans smell," Seth smiled. "And they taste even better."

"Humans are hit or miss and they're dangerous. I prefer deer or fowl...some nice fat wild turkeys, too."

"Stop, you're making me hungry."

The two brothers laughed until a snapping twig caught their attention. Lorne turned to see a shape dart from one tree to another. His brother growled beside him.

In moments, Seth shed his human flesh like snakeskin. Thick hair spread across his body. His hands stretched into claws as a howl escaped his snout. He lunged for the trees with Lorne racing behind him.

The two stalked the trees when ahead of them a stark white creature appeared, attempting to make a frantic escape. It quivered and zig-zagged through the woods without purpose. The brothers closed in on it and Seth attacked first, leaping through the air.

Lorne's gaze locked on Seth coming down onto the creature and capturing it in his jaws. He shook the thing hard, side to side, up and down, before tossing it to his older brother. Lorne caught it in his right claw and slammed it to the ground.

The ghoul half-laughed and half-squealed under Lorne's grip. The enraged wolf glared down at it as it squirmed, finally getting a good look at its deep sunk eyes, pale almost phosphorescent skin, and long spindly fingers. Lorne noticed a piece of dead flesh still clutched in those fingers and he quickly bit them off.

Seth roared and stomped toward them to help Lorne tear the ghoul apart, when another dropped from the trees. It landed on Seth's back and climbed its way to his right arm. A squeal belted out of its mouth before sinking rows of tiny, jagged teeth into the wolf's arm.

The ghoul gnawed through Seth's limb, then tore it off in a flood of crimson. Seth wailed, a cacophony of howls and cries as he fell to his knees. The ghoul danced around the maimed werewolf with glee, already eating the flesh from the severed arm.

Lorne jerked himself around and snarled. He looked back at the ghoul pinned to the ground, and with a swipe of his free claw, took its head off. The head rolled to the nearest tree and plopped upright—a grin still on its face. He jumped onto all fours and raced to help Seth.

He stared down the dancing ghoul with fury and it fled as fast it came, vanishing into the woods with Seth's arm. Lorne saw something strange in the ghoul before it retreated...its face, its eyes, there were hints of his father in it.

*   *   *

Back in their human forms, Lorne helped his brother back into the family home. Horror washed over both Willa and their mother's face.

"What's happened?" Heather demanded.

"Seth was ambushed. There are two of them now."

"The vermin have multiplied, damn them. No, there are more than two and they will be back. Their defending their feeding grounds now."

"I didn't pick up their scent." Lorne punched the wooden table in the center of the room as Cain helped Seth to a chair. "I couldn't tell they were there. They mess with our sense of smell. We can no longer trust it."

"Yes," Heather realized. "Because their flesh is dead, it doesn't smell fresh to us, it's the live animal that aids us in our hunt. They have us at a disadvantage."

"We're stronger than them!" Cain yelled, his eyes glittering.

"Brute strength alone won't rid us of them," Heather said. "We must be smarter. Their numbers will be great." She walked up to Seth and ran her fingers through his hair. She looked down at his bleeding stump and shifted into a huge gray wolf.

Heather cleaned her son's wound, licking the ripped flesh, soaking up all the blood. When the bleeding stopped, she shifted back to her human form. "Tomorrow night is a full moon. Sit in its light, take in its power and your arm will grow back." She kissed him on the forehead and returned to her chair.

"The one that took Seth's arm," Lorne began, his eyes narrowing. "Is the one that ate from father's grave. I saw father in its face."

Heather looked up at him. "It stole your father's strength by eating his remains. That's how it was able to rip your brother's arm off. A ghoul doesn't normally have that kind of strength. The others will do the same...growing stronger, taking our wolf power." She rubbed her chin with her hand. Troubling thoughts churned within her. Her eyes grew dark. "It's war now. Lorne, Cain, we have the full moon behind us tomorrow. In the morning we'll plan. For now, get some rest."

* * *

In the early morning hours, when the moon had set and the fire in the hearth died, whimpering filled the house. Lorne stirred and woke abruptly. He turned to see Willa curled up in a ball on the floor.

"Willa!" Lorne threw himself from the bed. "What is it? What's wrong? Is it time?"

"Not yet," she grimaced. "It's just been different these last few weeks. It's okay, it's getting close but not yet. Your mother said this was normal. It happened with her."

"Are you sure?" He took her into his arms. "This has been happening for weeks...why didn't you tell me?"

"I didn't want you to worry. It's nothing. A shifter's birth is always unpredictable."

"You shouldn't be in pain all the time."

"It's not all the time. You're worrying too much." Willa pulled herself to her feet and cradled her belly. "Let me do the worrying. You have other things to tend to. Like protecting our home and land."

"You tell me the moment it's time. I don't want any of those things to know a pup is here. They'll hunt it down for its newborn flesh."

"I promise."

Lorne helped her back to bed and gave her a kiss. He stepped out of the bedroom and went outside. The air was cool and the sky cascaded with deep orange and hints of red. A breeze sighed through the trees. He listened to the sound of the rustling leaves. He picked up tobacco in it.

He turned to see his mother walking out of the woods, her pipe clinched between her teeth. Their eyes met.

"I've been surveying the burial ground and the damage," she said. "That's where our plan will unfold. Wake your brothers." She stopped before entering the house and placed a hand on Lorne's shoulder. "I see the distraction in your eyes. Don't worry, I'll protect your wife. They won't touch her. They mustn't. Willa isn't carrying your pup, she's carrying your litter."

Lorne stood speechless as Heather vanished into the house.

*　*　*

The darkness was a thick impenetrable wall and the air was thin. In his human form, Lorne felt vulnerable. The walls of the grave closed in around him, the soil smelled rancid, and the cold bit him with harsh teeth.

In his silence and solitude, Lorne's thoughts drifted to Willa. He was more worried about her than ever. It was extremely difficult to carry and give birth to a litter. Not even his mother had done it. Feelings of joy and fear mingled inside him, confusing him, distracting him. Lorne imagined the worst and it drove him mad. He had never felt this helpless before. He was used to solving everything with a tooth or a claw.

He heard something trample the ground above him, and it pulled him from his reverie. Scratching followed it, resounding all around him. Dirt poured down on his face as the earth breeched and the light of the full moon spilled upon him. In the light, he spotted a ghost-white arm, clawing its way down, searching for the contents of the grave.

Lorne shifted into a wolf immediately.

The black-furred Lorne exploded out of the grave of his ancestor and clamped his jaws around the ghoul's throat. He bit as hard as he could, blood and saliva flooding his mouth. The ghoul squirmed and squealed briefly before going limp. Lorne looked down on it and barked. *"Try eating our corpses without a throat, asshole."*

His brother, auburn-furred Cain, burst out of his grave also, catching a ghoul with his claws and crushing its head. He flung the body over his shoulder as another raced toward him, and another.

Seth also clawed his way out of the grave, using his jaws to take down the ghoul running by him. He pinned it the ground and ripped into its face, spitting eyeballs into the air. His lost arm had grown back halfway, reforming in the slivers of the full moon's light streaming through the trees.

Lorne swung at a ghoul to his left and ripped open its chest, pus and dried organs spilling to the ground. He looked up to see one more rushing at him.

The three brothers howled at the moon, but their calls were met with shrieks as hordes of gaunt, pallid ghouls poured out of the woods and into the burial ground. The hulking wolves met the gangly corpse-eaters head on in a fury of slashing claws, gnashing teeth and monstrous carnage.

Throats tore and heads lobbed as Seth and Cain played tug-o-war with several ghouls until the monsters split in two, spilling swollen stomachs and half-eaten body parts. Seth threw ghouls over his shoulder and into the jaws of Lorne as he struck down any ghoul that tried to get past him.

The ghouls' numbers increased and soon they swarmed over the brothers like rats, scaling their bodies, biting their ears, their heads, scratching at their eyes. They came randomly, running erratically and confusing the brothers. Seth, still fighting with a handicap, fell to his knees as they clamored over him.

Lorne fought his way to his brother's side, tearing ghouls off him as if they were roaches. He ripped the spine out of the one locked around Seth's head as two ghouls dashed by him.

A distraction. They're heading for the house. Willa! Lorne thought.

A howl rocked the woods as Lorne abandoned his brothers and raced back to his home, hot on the heels of his quarry. He thrashed through thorn patches and over enormous deadfalls until the house came into view.

The ghouls were nearly there.

The backdoor opened to his horror and his mother appeared at the threshold.

Heather transformed just as the ghouls reached her and she seized both of them by the throat. She smashed their heads together, reducing them to a cloud of ash and dust.

She dropped the limp bodies and growled at Lorne, "*I told you I would protect Willa. Go back to the fight. Your brothers need you.*"

Lorne snapped and howled, his eyes glinting in the moonlight. "*Yes, mother.*"

He turned and leapt back into the woods. When he reached the burial ground, he heard Willa scream…her labor had begun! He hesitated, listening to Willa wince and set his gaze back on his bothers, who were nearly overwhelmed by the encroaching ghouls.

Cain and Seth battled side by side, slashing and biting, losing ground, backing away from the advancing hordes. Lorne roared as loud as he could, causing a flock of bats to evacuate the surrounding trees. He dove into the air and soared over his brothers, spreading his arms and taking down a wave of filth-ridden ghouls. He thrashed them with dagger-like claws and ripped into them with jaws of steel.

Cain and Seth celebrated, cackling like jackals and stomping their clawed feet. Breaking free of the crowd, a ghoul stormed toward Cain with a femur bone riddled with bite marks in his grip. It used the bone like a weapon and swung hard at Cain's head.

Lorne turned to see his brother take the blow square between the eyes—and become enraged—a gash cutting across his forehead. Cain's temper sent him into a frenzy. He lunged for the ghoul and attacked it mercilessly. In his blind fury, he did the unthinkable, he devoured the creature, eating the dead flesh with gluttony and glee.

"*Cain! No!*" Lorne was aghast. "*Never eat them….never! Cain!*"

Lorne ran to him, bashing ghouls out of his way, but reached his brother too late. Rotting flesh hung from Cain's lips, and black pus stained his muzzle. His nostrils flared and his eyes widened.

Lorne saw something awful happen.

Cain's fur dimmed, the color faded from it. The skin beneath it took on an ashen color. His eyes became sunken. He croaked, unable to howl in protest to his new transformation. He looked down at the other lifeless bodies of the ghouls and ripped a limb off one of them. He began to eat the dead flesh again.

"You've crossed species, Cain." Lorne's heart sank. *"You're like one of them...you crave the flesh of the dead yet retain your powers... you're an abomination. You've tainted our bloodline."*

Seth stopped his attack and looked to Lorne and Cain. *"You know what you must do. He can't be allowed to exist."*

Lorne wailed as tears filled his eyes. He did know what he had to do. Cain turned to him and bristled. He arched on all fours, ready to attack Lorne, but Seth came up behind him and slashed him across the back.

Lorne took his chance as Cain stumbled and leapt onto his chest. The two wolves went down in a crash and the oldest brother tore into Cain's throat, ending his misery.

The agony of it burned inside of Lorne. He stood up and stared down at his brother. His grief nearly caused him to miss the silence that permeated the burial ground.

In the distance, Willa screamed, *"The ghouls! They've gone to the house!"*

Lorne and Seth raced back home and found the ghouls covering it like locusts. The creatures ran across the roof, climbed the chimney, danced in the yard, climbed through shattered windows, and were thrown back out by a furious Heather.

The two brothers stormed toward the house. Dozens of ghouls dropped from the roof on top of Seth as Lorne slipped inside. There he found Heather fending off attack after attack as Willa lay weakened on the bed, seven infants suckling at her breasts.

Lorne raged on, striking everything in his path, cutting a blood bath to his wife's side. He smashed the vermin into walls, stomped them underfoot, and threw them out of the house.

For each one that died, more entered the house. Heather did her best to stand her ground, but there were too many. They climbed up the great gray wolf and toppled into the hearth.

Her fur ignited instantly as did the creatures clinging to her. Engulfed in a fireball, the lot of them stumbled from the house, screeching all the way.

Lorne positioned himself in front of Willa's bed, listening to the sound of his children suckling. He set his piercing eyes on the doorway and watched the ghouls, the smell of rot blowing with them and flooding into the room.

"Come on, you bastards...I'm waiting for you!" he growled.

Lorne prepared for the end when he heard a chorus of howls behind him. He turned to see that his children had all shifted, turning to wolf pups, young but fierce, full of new energy and glistening teeth.

They soared over their father, protecting their parents from danger, and attacked the carrion eaters invading their den. The pups struck terror into the ghouls, who didn't expect such a voracious litter.

Almost laughing, Lorne led his pups in a final attack on the ghouls, ripping out throat after throat, until the last of them ran scared into the night, vanishing back into the woods.

Outside, Lorne saw the body of his brother Seth, his innards splayed all over the ground.

Lorne pushed the image out of his mind and guided his pups back to their mother. He bent to Willa and licked her face.

She lifted her hand to his muzzle and stroked his fur. Moments later, his wolf form melted back into human. "We've lost almost all of our family..." Tears streamed his cheeks, he looked down at his children who returned to their mother as human infants. "But we have a whole new one now."

"Our children saved our lives," Willa said. "It's a wonderful miracle. A litter this strong, and so young."

"No, it's no miracle. It's us. The power of the pack." He kissed his wife deeply.

* * *

In the dawn, as the sun glowed in the trees and the dew captured the light, two figures emerged at the edge of the woods and surveyed the house. They were human, doused in mud and grave-yard dirt to mask their scent.

"You're plan worked," Lana whispered to her companion. "Letting the ghouls know where the wolves' burial ground was has weakened the pack."

"I told you it would," Ron said. "Now is the time. Let's take our homes back from those monsters. After them we hit the vampires."

They loaded silver-tipped arrows into their crossbows and motioned for the rest of their group to come out of hiding.

HOSPITAL OF HORRORS

LORRAINE HORRELL

"Well, kiddo, what are you doing in here? You look the picture of health!" Mr. Alf Byrnes asked a little boy lying in the opposite bed to his in the large ward. Right now, Alf was in his wheelchair.

The boy hadn't taken his nose out of his comic book all night but he now raised his head up curiously and smiled at Alf.

"I'm not sure, but my mom says I'm pretty sick," the boy replied.

"Well, son, what's your name? I'm Alf." He edged his wheelchair over to the boy's bed.

As he got closer, he noticed the boy had large black bags under his eyes and his skin was the shade of worn porcelain.

"I'm Ben," the boy said, shaking Alf's hand.

"Looks like me and you are the only two sane ones in this place." Alf looked over his shoulder and into the hall, to see if anyone was listening to their conversation. He lowered his voice, so it was barely audible. "There's something strange going on in this hospital, the whole town has been taking in with suspected rabies!" He shoved his glasses halfway down his nose, his squinted eyes peering over the top of the frames at Ben. "The doctors and nurses think I'm crazy. They're treating me for senile dementia." He nodded his head as he talked, as if agreeing with himself. "I can tell you now; there ain't a thing wrong with me. I can remember vividly the day I was born."

The other patients lay in their beds, not eating or moving, in a trance.

Ben didn't understand half of what Alf Byrnes was saying, he didn't care either, all he wanted to do was get back to reading his comic book 'Vampire Venom.'

Ben was intrigued by vampires and always had been. "What's that you're reading, sonny?" Alf asked, coming closer again. Ben could smell the mothballs coming off Alf's body.

"It's a vampire magazine," Ben replied, not even lifting his head up.

"Vampires, eh? Deadly creatures they are. Do you know they're all around us?"

Ben looked up now; Alf had caught his interest now. The boy's eyes widened, he looked at Alf as though he was a big blob of candy, with an 'eat me' sign stuck to him.

The old man's eyes bulged in his wrinkly sockets.

"I heard the wail of the banshee earlier. She's been following me around since I moved from Ireland years ago. I will never let her take me," he said taking off his glasses and wiping them with his shirt.

Ben had heard tales of the banshee but he never believed them. "What does she look like?"

"She's wretched, a vile old hag. She can change her appearance, too. Once I saw her hiding in the bushes, she was beautiful, young and fresh. She sat combing her hair, then, once I got closer to her, she turned into an old wench. Her song changed from a nice Irish lilt to an almighty wail!" He took a deep breath and continued. "She took my wife from me that night."

"Mr. Byrnes, don't be filling Ben's head with that nonsense, here let me help you get back to your bed," the old nurse said as she wheeled Mr. Byrnes over to his own bed.

"Goodnight, Ben!" Alf said, waving to him.

The nurse tucked Alf into his bed like a seasoned pro. He argued and pushed her away saying he wasn't an invalid.

The nurse told Ben to put his comic away as she turned off the lights.

Ben and Alf both thought of the other patients in the ward as their heads hit the pillow.

The other men in the ward lay still, they didn't move, just their chests moved in a steady pace up and down as they gasped for air. They all had fever and unexplainable bite marks on their bodies.

Ben and Alf watched as the doctors fussed around them, scratching their heads as they tried to explain it.

*   *   *

Ben woke in a cold sweat. He looked out the window to the left of his bed but there was nothing, only the black clouds cascading over the moon.

Lying back down on his bed, he was about to return to sleep, when he heard a strange sound. It was awful. The high-pitched screech went right through his eardrums, and when he looked around, there was nothing to see.

The sound was getting louder and it sent shivers down his spine. Ben was only ten years old and scared stiff.

"That's her," Alf cried out. "It's the banshee, she's warning us about death, it's on the way Ben."

Ben looked petrified; he sunk into his bed and hid under the blankets.

"Its okay, son, I'll protect you," he promised as he pulled out a massive machine gun from under his blankets. Ben's eyes went wide. How the old man had snuck the gun into the hospital was beyond him.

"Help me into my wheelchair, son," he said.

Ben crawled out of bed. He was still very weak, the treatment wasn't working too well this time. He helped Alf out of bed and into his wheelchair, then they both looked out the window for the banshee.

They could see her now; she was wailing away and looking straight at them, almost mocking them. "I'm going to get her," Alf said, opening the window and pointing the machine gun out of it.

"No, don't." Ben pushed the gun down. "The doctor's and nurses will hear it if you fire that thing in here."

"You're right," Alf agreed. The wailing grew louder and louder, and they both covered their ears in pain.

The bawling got so loud it started to wake the other patients. They rose simultaneously, like a scene from a horror film. The patients' began making sounds, a loud groan that gurgled from the pit of their stomachs like a belch.

Ben looked at Alf. "What's going on here?" he asked.

"I don't know, Ben, but it isn't good, I can tell you that!"

Alf raised his gun into the air, as the patients slid off their beds and stood together, their eyes black and hallow. They smelled the air as they moved towards Ben and Alf, who were backing into the far corner.

"Hi there, folks, can I call the doctor for you?" Alf asked with a slight smile.

The patients acted as if they didn't hear him and continued to walk in a slow but steady pace, their arms out in front of them, feeling the air.

Ben switched on the light, banishing the shadows. The patients weren't human any more, it was apparent by their dull, glassy stares, their wasted flesh. They were an army of zombies, moldy and decapitating zombies, that happened to be heading straight for them.

The zombies shielded their eyes from the light, some of their limbs falling off as they marched towards the man and boy.

Alf fired a few shots at the flesh-eating army. The bullets passed straight through their rotting bodies, but they didn't even flinch. The zombies kept coming for them, slowly, methodically.

"Ben, we have to get out of here, fast," Alf said, breathing hard.

"Yeah, I don't want to be eaten alive," Ben agreed as he grabbed Alf's wheelchair and pushed it as hard as he could towards the door leading to the hallway. He looked back as he ran down the corridor and the zombies were still following them. More and more were joining from the different wards.

"The whole bloody town has turned into zombies!" Alf yelled.

Ben ran to the elevator and pressed the button again and again, frantically. The zombies were nearing, and he could smell their putrid stench a mile away.

"Come on, come on!" Alf shouted at the elevator.

There was a soft ding and the doors opened, the boy pushing the wheelchair inside. The doors closed, and once they were safe and sound in the elevator, Ben asked again, "What's going on?"

"I don't know, son, I really don't know," Alf said. He looked tired and stressed.

"I've been waiting for this day for years, everyone thought I was loopy. I told them they were gonna attack."

"Who?" Ben asked. He was really confused now.

"The monsters, son. I've been watching them for years, you see. I used to hunt vampires when I was younger. I traveled all over Europe and you wouldn't believe the things I've seen."

The elevator grinded to an abrupt halt. The doors opened and Ben pushed Alf out into the reception area; it was all clear.

The hospital was in total darkness, the only sound being the horde of brainless zombies marching around the second floor.

They headed for the exit but were stopped by a group of large red slimy things, they looked like leeches—huge bulky leeches. Alf's tires screeched as he tried to stop the wheelchair.

Ben turned them around and ran. Right behind them, leaving a trail of slithering slime, came the leeches. They were like ravenous vultures as they fought each other to be first. The creatures' eyes were hidden under the slime, but if they moved the right way, they glowed a dull yellow.

"Quick, Ben, get us out of here, they're getting faster!" Alf shouted. He seemed to be enjoying himself, dodging all the monsters and being chauffeured around while barking orders.

Alf fired at the giant leeches, and they exploded all over the white hospital walls leaving, a red pool of blood and slime behind.

"Great shot, Alf."

"Thanks, son," he said, blowing the smoke from his gun. The old man's face lit up. "This is the most fun I've had in ages," he laughed in delight.

Ben, who was now breathless and tired, wasn't having so much fun, and he didn't know if he should laugh or cry.

They made it out of the hospital in one piece, using a side emergency door.

"What are we gonna do now? We can't just leave everyone inside there. What if some people aren't zombies?" Ben asked.

"Well, they will be soon enough!" Alf said. They both looked towards the hospital and in the windows they could see the zombies slowly walking around. The moon was still hidden behind the clouds, and they were in almost total darkness.

"We need to block all the entrances, Ben, can you do that?"

"Yeah, but how?" he asked.

"You need to go back inside and find the control room; there will be a button on one of the panels that says 'lockdown,' press it and then run. You'll have only a few seconds before all the doors close and you'll be trapped inside, too. And for God's sake, be careful!"

Alf patted Ben on his shoulders, and Ben nodded. He ran back towards the monsters, afraid for his life.

After finding a small piece of hose and a few empty buckets, Alf began to siphon all the gas from a large truck's fuel tank in the parking lot. He was planning to throw it into the reception area and then blow the place up once Ben was safe and back outside.

Back inside the hospital, Ben could hear the noise of the zombies scratching and moaning. He went in behind reception. There was a girl lying on the floor, and she was covered in blood. The blood was still oozing from two small holes in her neck. Her face was a ghastly white, and she definitely looked dead. Ben stepped over her and headed out back, he was on a mission and not even the evidence of vampires could stop him in his tracks.

He switched on the light in a room and his eyes went wide. There were dozens of buttons and switches that were lit up in all different colors.

"I'm never gonna find it," he said to himself. He leaned in closer to get a better look.

"Can I help you with something?"

Ben turned around, his heart racing.

The girl from reception area was standing there. She was beautiful, with large captivating brown eyes and shiny long black hair. Ben's cheeks flushed.

Her stare was menacing as it drilled deep into him. "I'm looking for the lockdown button," he said as his eyes searched frantically over the blinking lights.

"Why would you want to do that?" she asked innocently.

"Because the zombies have raided the hospital, and Alf said it would be best to blow all the monsters up," he told her.

She looked intrigued as she glided closer to him. Her head moved from side to side as she glared at him, as if she was choosing a ripe piece of fruit.

Ben became frightened and turned away. Her hands grabbed him and threw him against the wall. She sniffed his neck, her hypnotic eyes drawn to his jugular that was bulging and pulsing. Her fangs appeared; they were sharp and terrifying.

She lunged at his neck at an alarming speed, then stopped.

She threw him down on the floor. "What are you? You're not human."

Ben squirmed on the floor. Out of the corner of his eye, he spotted the button he was searching for. He jumped up and ran to it.

Ben was starting to sweat, his body temperature rising rapidly.

The girl moved towards him, and he pushed her away.

She flew against the wall like a massive wind had tossed her like a feather. He was surprised at his own strength, but there was no time to think about it now. Ben pressed the button.

It was then that he saw the hairs and the nails appear. "Not now, please, not now," he begged.

The moonlight shone through the open door.

"So that's what you are," she said.

Ben's body started to change, as the hairs grew longer all over his body, his nightclothes tearing as the body within morphed.

Ben's eyes changed to a deep red color, and his teeth protruded and grew long, looking sharp and dangerous, the teeth snapping like a vise. He opened his mouth and a loud howl bellowed forth.

The vampire knew she wouldn't stand a chance in a fight against a werewolf, so she turned to leave, but it was too late. Ben ran at her with his claws raised. She was a new vampire and hadn't fed, she was weak and inexperienced.

Ben took full advantage of this. He pounced at her and swung his claws wildly, tearing her flesh as she screamed.

He attacked her until she didn't move anymore, her blood pooled on the floor. The werewolf stopped when her lifeless body was nothing but bloody bits of gore. He then howled and went running off into the corridors.

*　*　*

Alf was finished with his part of the deal. He had seen the hospital doors close, but there was no sign of Ben. He would wait a few minutes more before he blew the building up, the buckets of gas stacked just within the main doors. He would shoot through the doors and the bullets would ignite the fuel. The minutes passed, but there was still nothing. The old man wept. He had sent that poor boy to his death, and he never felt so ashamed of himself.

The minutes felt like hours, and he had one last look around. The moon was gone and he couldn't see much, the lights outside having gone off.

The zombies must have gotten into the electrical wiring of the building. Alf lined up his gun at the door, the smell of gas nearly choking him. Just as he was about to fire, a body crashed out through a window, screaming. It was Ben and he was alive.

"Are you okay, son?" Alf asked as he rolled over to Ben. He saw the boy's nightclothes were torn and there was blood on him, though it didn't appear to be Ben's.

"Yeah, let's get the party started," Ben said.

Alf fired the shot at the doors as Ben ran as fast as he could away from the hospital.

The fire was small at first, and then there was a loud *boom*, and soon the entire building was engulfed in flames.

"Well done, son, we showed those monsters who's boss," Alf said with a large smile.

Ben didn't notice the old man's fangs sticking out. The centuries old vampire had been searching for a home for years and someone to share it with.

Ben was well able to fight off monsters with ease.

The two would make a good team.

THE HALLOWEEN PARTY

DAVID H. DONAGHE

I was down at the office with my feet up on my desk, listening to a Dodger baseball game. It was a cool, fall afternoon and things were slow, so I had some time on my hands. My partner, Roxanne Delaney—I call her Roxy for short—was out running some errands and I had the place to myself. My name is Mike Monroe, and I run Monroe's Paranormal Investigations.

The Dodger at bat just missed his last pitch, ending the game in a loss, and I let out a heavy sigh. Switching the channel to a Country and Western station, my mood lightened when Roxy stepped in the door.

My eyes dropped to her chest and a big grin spread across my face. Roxy was a woman that a man just couldn't keep his eyes off of. She had long flowing blonde hair, large firm breasts, and she never wore a bra. I don't even know if she owns one. She has long, sexy legs, an hourglass figure, a pretty face, and is as smart as a whip. She stood there in the doorway, wearing a black tank top and those damned Daisy Duke shorts that drive me wild. Her large, round nipples pressed up the cotton on her shirt like two, .45 caliber bullets.

She had one hand in her pocket and held a stack of mail in her other one.

"You got eye problems?" she asked, giving me a hard look, but I could see a trace of a smile trying to break forth at the edges of her mouth.

I leaned back in my chair. "No, my dear, I can see just fine."

"Well, why don't you do something besides stare at me," she said, crossing the room, and believe me, when she crossed the room everything jiggled in all the right places. "Here's the mail," she said and placed the stack on my desk. She went to the coffee pot to start a fresh pot, while I went through the mail and kept sneaking looks at her perfect butt.

Most of the mail was just bills, but I paused at a small manila envelope with my name on it. It said, **RSVP Mike Monroe**. There was no return address or any other name on the outside of the envelope. I opened it, pulled out a small card, and read it. On the inside of the card, in bold block letters was, **To Mr. Mike Monroe and guest. You are cordially invited to a Halloween party extravaganza. There will be prizes for best costumes plus food and entertainment. Time: 6:30 p.m. The Devil's Road House, Box 999 Old Route 666, Desolation, New Mexico.**

Underneath this, in almost illegible script, it was signed, Mr. Smith.

Roxy stepped up next to my desk and I handed her the invitation. "What do you think about this?" I asked.

She read the invitation, then her eyes widened and a scowl crossed her face. "I don't know, Mike. This sounds like a trap, and what kind of name for a town is Desolation?"

I laughed. "It sounds like something out of a Stephen King novel. And get the address. The Devil's Road House."

She nodded. "The guy's name is Smith. It's obviously a fake. Maybe we should pass on this." She handed me back the invitation.

I paused, thinking and holding the invitation in my hand. "You know, because of what we do, we have a lot of enemies, but think of what could happen if we don't go? Maybe innocent people could get hurt. I mean the gall of this guy, Smith. If he's some vampire or werewolf out there trying to lure us into a confrontation, don't you want to put him out of business? When we go after a vampire, or respond to a zombie outbreak, don't you enjoy the rush?"

Roxy sighed. "No, Mike, that's a macho guy thing. Most of the time I'm terrified, but I wouldn't want to hear about innocent people being killed because I was afraid to go to a party."

A big grin crossed my face. "That settles it then. We're going to New Mexico, baby."

* * *

We left five days later in my 1984 Mustang, with its 5.0-liter V8 purring along like a kitten. Roxy wore her Daisy Dukes, a white wife beater t-shirt, and as usual, she wasn't wearing a bra. Noticing the direction of my gaze, she rolled her eyes and said, "Keep your eyes on the road, big boy."

Breathing in the smell of her perfume, I chuckled. "But there's so many interesting things to see right here in the car," I said, reaching over, and placing my hand on her sexy thigh. I hoped if I played my cards right, later that night we would fool around.

She gave me an elbow to the ribs, making me jerk the wheel, and I swerved into the other lane. A guy in a Cadillac honked and I pulled back into my lane.

"See? Pay attention to the road," she said.

"Yes, dear," I replied.

We blew through Victorville and Barstow, heading east. The weather was cool, and the sun was setting in the west.

I love the fall.

At Needles, California, we diverted from our route and headed to Laughlin, Nevada. I pulled into the parking lot of the Colorado Bell Hotel and Casino, just after dark. Roxy climbed out of the Mustang, reached her arms over her head and stretched, which caused her breasts to jut forward. Catching me looking, a smile crossed her face; she cupped both of her breasts and gave them a little shake. I stood stroking my chin.

"What?" she asked, dropping her hands and resting them on her hips.

"Did you bring your Saint Christopher medal?"

She nodded. "Of course, Mike. And I brought my wolf bane. I'll be a good little wolf girl."

Roxy had been bitten by a werewolf a few months ago and now, when the moon was full, things got even more interesting than normal.

"Unfortunately, I think that might not help us on this one. You might have to unleash the beast," I said.

"Did you bring our gear?" she asked while taking my arm.

"I never go anywhere without the tools of our trade," I said, enjoying the pressure of her left breast against my arm.

We headed into Colorado Bell, a hotel and casino designed to look like a paddle wheeler on the bank of the Colorado River.

Inside the casino, we checked into our room, unloaded our gear, and headed down to the casino.

Roxy headed to the blackjack table and I went off by myself, looking for a Wheel of Fortune slot machine to waste some of my hard-earned cash. Enjoying the sound of the noisy casino, I found a dollar machine and began to play. Out of the corner of my eye, I saw Roxy sit down at the blackjack table.

I let out a low chuckle. "Those old boys at that table don't know what they're in for," I said to myself. Roxy is good at cards, and knows how to use all her assets. She smiles, giggles and leans forward over her cards so the other players have a bird's eye view down the front of her shirt, and believe me, when she puts those massive mammary glands on display, an old boy can't help but look. Before long, all the male players at the table forget about their cards and have their eyes glued to her, trying to catch a look at her cleavage.

I played The Wheel of Fortune machine for about a half hour. A cocktail waitress came by; I ordered a Bud Light and she headed to the bar. While the waitress was gone, I hit the jackpot and won four hundred dollars. I just love the sound of silver dollars hitting the tray in the bottom of the slot machine.

The waitress returned with my beer, I put two hundred back into the machine and went to the cage to cash out. Finished with my beer, I stepped out the back door onto the boardwalk running along behind the casinos. I leaned over a railing, watching the Colorado River roll by in the dark. Taking a cigar out of my shirt pocket, I fired it up, blew tobacco smoke into the night, and thought about what I would find in Desolation, New Mexico.

A few minutes later, I felt someone's hand on my back and the pressure of a large breast pressed up against my arm. "What are you doing?" Roxy asked.

I took a pull from the cigar, blowing smoke, and said, "I'm just out here having a smoke and enjoying the night."

"How'd you do on the slot machines?"

I smiled. "I won four hundred, but put two back. How did it go at the blackjack table?"

Roxy laughed. "Those old men were such dears. I almost felt bad about taking their money. I won six hundred."

I gazed out at the water, watching a boat cruise by.

"What're you thinkin' about?" she asked.

"I was just thinking about Smith and wondering what his real name is."

"What do you think we'll find when we get to New Mexico?"

I shrugged. "I don't know. It could actually be just a Halloween party."

"Why don't we head back to the room and I'll rock your world. We'll worry about Smith and New Mexico tomorrow," Roxy said, taking my arm.

I snuffed out my cigar on the railing and put it away for later. "That, my dear, is the best offer I've had all night." I let her lead me away.

* * *

I woke up at six a.m., and after we both took a quick shower, Roxy and I ate breakfast at a buffet on the second floor of the casino. We sat by the window, on the backside of the hotel overlooking the majestic Colorado river. While eating our breakfast, I watched a few boaters on jet skis bombing around on the river.

"How long do you think it'll take us to get to New Mexico?" she asked.

I shrugged. "It's about a ten hour drive. We should get there in time to find a room and rest for a bit before we have to get ready for the party."

Roxy nodded in reply. We finished our meal, headed back to our room and packed our gear. After checking out of the hotel, we climbed into the Mustang, headed back to Needles and caught the I-40 east. The freeway snaked its way up into the mountains and we passed through Arizona. Roxy had her feet up on the dash again, showing off those sexy legs as she listened to her MP3 player. I glanced over, taking in her essence.

God she's beautiful, I thought and looked back at the road. We blew through Williams, Arizona, the gateway to The Grand Canyon, and stopped for lunch at Flagstaff. After a quick burger, we got gas and headed east toward the New Mexico state line. At Gallup, New Mexico, we took our exit and headed north on old state Route 666. An hour and a half later, we pulled into Desolation.

Roxy sat up in her seat, looking out the window. "Good Lord. I can see why they call this place Desolation. I don't think I've ever seen such a dreary little town."

I laughed. "We've seen worse. It looks better than Black Rock, Pennsylvania. Remember that place we stopped at on the way back to your grandmother's funeral?"

"How could I forget," she replied.

"This place reminds me of Hinkley," I said, gazing about the dreary little town.

We passed a gas station, a bank, a general store and I noticed an antique shop across the street. It looked different from the rest of the buildings. The rest of the town looked rundown and in a state of disrepair, but the antique shop had a fresh coat of paint, squeaky-clean windows, and a freshly-painted sign on the window facing the street.

The sign said ***Nick's Antiques and Collectibles***. Further down Main Street, I noticed a shabby little motel on the right and we pulled in. The place reminded me of the Bates motel.

We strolled across the gravel parking lot to the office, the springs on the screen door squeaked when I opened it and we stepped into a small, dusty office. A stocky little dark complexioned man wearing a black cowboy hat and a denim jacket looked up. He looked tired and run down by life. "What can I do for you folks?" he asked.

"We'd like to rent a room," I said.

He turned to a key board and handed us a key. "I expect you're here for the Halloween party down at the Road House. Everyone else is. In fact, the place is full up. You just got the last room."

"I guess this Road House must throw good Halloween parties, with everyone coming from out of town and all," I said.

He shook his head. "I wouldn't know about that. The feller that owns the antique shop is throwing the bash. This is the first time they've had a party down there. The whole town is going."

"The man that owns the antique shop, is he a friend of yours?" I asked.

He paused for a second and shook his head. "Nope. He's a creepy fella. He ain't been here long."

"What's his name?" I asked.

"You know, I don't really remember."

"Are you sure it's not Smith? The invitation I got was from someone named Smith."

He shook his head. "No, I ain't never heard anyone call him Smith before."

"Oh, well, I guess we'll find out when we get to the party. Where is this Devil's Road House anyway?" I asked.

"It's on the outskirts of town to the east of here. It's on the right hand side of the road. You can't miss it."

"Thanks for the info. I guess we'll see you at the party," I said and we headed to our room. We stepped into the room and I stopped in my tracks, gazing about. The room was clean, but everything looked old. The brown carpet looked worn out and faded, the blue curtains looked thread bare; at least the bed looked comfortable.

"I've slept in worse," I said.

Roxy brushed up against me on her way to the bathroom. Over her shoulder, she said, "I'm gonna take a quick shower."

"We've only got forty-five minutes until the party starts," I replied.

"I'll be ready in time."

While Roxy showered, I dressed in my costume, putting on a wide brimmed cowboy hat, a pair of denim jeans and a long black coat. Roxy stepped out of the shower in the nude and put on her costume. Forty minutes after we stepped into the room, we stepped back outside. She was dressed up as Elvira, Mistress of the Night, and I was dressed as Wyatt Earp. I climbed behind the wheel of the Mustang, Roxy climbed in the passenger side, and we drove down the street to The Devil's Road House.

I got out of the car, watching a line of people entering the road house; Roxy slid out of the passenger side and took my arm. She felt a bulge underneath my long black coat. "Why don't I get a weapon?" she asked.

I chuckled. "Your whole body is a weapon. You do have your Saint Christopher's medal on, don't you? There's going to be a full moon tonight."

"Yes," she replied.

"Well, depending on how things go, you might have to take it off."

"Let's hope not," she said.

We stepped into the line, entering the road house, and when we reached the head of the line, a tall man wearing a scarecrow costume took our invitation. He studied Roxy; his eyes widened and I saw his nostrils flare. Roxy paused, looking into his eyes, and took a deep breath. I stepped forward urging her on.

"Something's not right about that guy," she whispered, looking back over her shoulder at him. We paused inside the dimly lit bar room and looked around. A band up on a small stage played *Born to be Wild,* while people dressed in costumes of every description milled back and forth. Glancing at the bar, I noticed a couple of empty seats, so I led Roxy over.

"What'll you have?" a man standing behind the bar dressed in a bright-red devil's costume asked.

I glanced at Roxy.

"My usual," she said.

"A Bloody Mary for Elvira, and a Jack and Coke for me."

The bartender brought us our drinks. I turned around to take in the crowd and my eyes widened. "I know some of these people," I said.

Roxy gave me a surprised look. "What? Who?"

I pointed to an older gentleman dressed in a flowing black robe who crossed the bar to join us. "That man right there, he's a priest. Father Murphy. He's from Dallas."

"Mr. Monroe, it's good to see you," Father Murphy said, stepping up to the bar. "And who is this pretty lady?"

"This is my partner. Roxanne Delaney. Call her Roxy. Would you care for a drink, Father?"

He nodded hello to Roxy and said, "Yes, make it a Scotch."

"This is some shindig, huh?" I said, noticing a large man dressed in a Frankenstein monster costume. He had what looked like a flesh-eating zombie on a leash. The zombie had a leather collar and a muzzle over its mouth. "Some of these costumes look pretty realistic."

"Yes, it's quite a crowd," Father Murphy said, turning to face the partygoers. "If you're observant, you'll see three distinct groups of people. There are the townies, then there are the professionals like us, and I think if you look toward the door, you'll recognize the Italian gentleman dressed as Al Capone that just came in the door."

"I'll be damned, if that ain't Vito Giovannelli. He's a PI from Boston," I said.

"And I think you'll recognize the dark-haired young woman standing next to him in the nurse's uniform."

"That's Jan Cunningham from Atlanta. She's a vampire hunter. So we got the town folks and us paranormal types. Who's this third group you're talking about?" I asked.

"Ah, that's the one million dollar question, isn't it?" the priest replied.

"And the two million dollar question is; who is this Smith character?"

Vito and Jan saw us at the bar and headed our way. As they drew closer, I took in Jan's Costume. Her nurse's uniform was short, revealing her long sexy legs, its low cut front revealing an abundance of cleavage. She wore a stethoscope around her neck.

"Yo, Monroe. How you doing?" Vito asked and grabbed me up in a massive bear hug.

"I'm doing fine. How are you, Vito?" I gasped after he turned me loose.

"Forget about it."

"Hello, Mike," Jan said and gave me a hug and a kiss. Roxy stood by my side, scowling, so I introduced her. Jan and Vito said, "Hello" to her and Father Murphy.

"Did you get a look at them boys they got providing security? Them's some big bruisers," Vito said.

"Yeah, and they seem to have all the exits covered. This could be an interesting night," I replied.

"Forget about it. Let's get some food. If those guys want some trouble, we'll give it to them," Vito said.

Roxy took my arm. "I think that guy at the door was a were-wolf," she whispered when we went to the food table. The lights dimmed except for the dance floor and the band started playing a Black Sabbath tune.

"If things get crazy, you take off your medal and deal with him. I have a feeling he's got friends," I told her.

The party wore on. Roxy and I hit the dance floor along with Vito and Jan. Father Murphy sat at the bar watching the crowd. After the song ended, the lights came on and an elder gentleman stepped onto the stage. We returned to the bar to join Father Murphy.

"I think I recognize that face, but I can't place him." I said.

The old man on the stage had long, gray hair. He wore a black suit, and when he stepped up to the microphone, I let out a startled gasp. He looked like Boris Karloff on a bad day.

"Ladies and gentlemen, thank you for coming," the man said. A group joined him on the stage. I saw several vampires, a mummy, and the Frankenstein monster with his pet zombie on the leash.

"Those must be the winners of the contest for the best costumes," someone said.

"I must admit that I have invited you here under false pretences. You people from town, each one of you has slighted me in some way. When I first arrived, did you welcome me with open arms? Heavens no. You came into my store with your noses turned up in the air, but did you buy anything? Hell no. I was an outsider." A murmur went through the crowd. "And you, paranormal investigators, you vampire hunters and zombie slayers; you religious fanatics. You have all done your part to harm—if not myself personally—those of my kind. I sent you an invitation under the name Smith, but you may know me better as Nicolas Von Wolf."

My eyes widened and I let out a sigh of recognition.

"I thought he was dead. He has to be over three hundred years old. He's one of the old school Transylvanian vampires," Jan whispered.

"My colleagues that you see here on this stage are the real guests at this party. They are the winners of the best costume contest, simply because their costumes are real," Von Wolf said.

"A mummy? A real mummy? How do you kill a mummy?" Father Murphy asked.

"I think you just unwrap their bandages, but this should do," Jan said, bringing out a small can of hair spray and a lighter from her purse.

"That Frankenstein monster looks like a real animated corpse constructed from various cadavers. I can't believe this," I said.

"You people are simply the appetizers for *their* party. If the gentleman guarding the door to the storage room will open it and let out the night's entertainment, we'll get the party started," Von Wolf said, motioning to a large man next to the stage.

Another murmur went through the crowd. The man opened the door to the storage room, and ten flesh-eating zombies stumbled out into the room and attacked the crowd. The men standing at the doors convulsed, and course hair sprouted from their bodies, their limbs elongating as the change came over them and they morphed into werewolves. The vampires on stage extended their fangs and launched across the room. The Frankenstein monster jumped off the stage, releasing his pet zombie, and the mummy extended his hands as it stumbled off the platform.

"Here, hold this," Roxy said, handing me her Saint Christopher's medal. She unzipped her dress and let it fall to the floor. Running across the room in the nude toward the beasts near the door, she changed into a werewolf. Father Murphy held up a crucifix. Light burst forth from the cross. I pulled out two small super soakers filled with holy water from under my coat and Jan ran after the mummy. One of the werewolves near the door ripped the head off one of the townies just before Roxy raked her claws across his face. A vamp flew across the room, coming straight at me and I hosed him with holy water. He burst into flames, let out a screech of pain, and crashed into the bar. Another vamp launched himself at me and I broke a pool cue over the bar. Using the broken end, I impaled the vampire through the heart.

A man dressed in a monk's costume threw back his hood and pulled a thirty-thirty from underneath his robe. I recognized the man who worked at the motel. He jacked a round into the chamber and fired a shot into the chest of a werewolf. The beast crumpled to the floor and died. I figured the man must be using silver bullets.

On the dance floor, Jan stopped in front of the mummy, pressed her can of hair spray and ignited it. The spurt of flame hit the mummy's bandages and it burst into flames, its arms flailing as it tried to put out the fire.

People screamed, running for the doors and windows as the zombies attacked them. One zombie grabbed an old woman by her hair. She fell to the floor and the zombie ripped her throat out. Blood gushed from the woman's throat and covered the floor, causing others to slip and fall.

"Father, I need to take out those flesh-eaters! You concentrate on the vamps!" I yelled, tossing the priest the super soakers. I pulled a pair of forty-five automatics from under my coat and charged out onto the dance floor. I shot the zombie—who was kneeling over the old woman and pulling her guts out—in the forehead and it slumped to the floor with half a head. A vampire soared over me, crashed into the wall and dropped to the floor. The man from the motel laid a crucifix on the vamp's cheek and the vile creature burst into flames, the stench of burnt flesh filling the room.

For the next ten minutes, the battle raged, the air filled with the sound of screaming victims and the feral growls of zombies and werewolf's. The Frankenstein monster came at me with hands raised. Vito and I stood back-to-back, taking on the zombies and the Frankenstein monster. I emptied a full clip into the monster's chest. Vito turned and emptied a clip into its face before the creature had fallen to the floor. After we finished off the Frankenstein monster, we concentrated on the zombies.

Head shot after head shot brought them down, spraying brains and bone matter in all directions. The floor became slippery with gore.

When the battle was over, Roxy stood over the last dying werewolf. The man from the motel aimed his gun at her, ready to shoot.

"Don't shoot! She's with us!" I yelled.

Roxy changed back into a human, her body shifting and convulsing as she slumped to the floor. Then the change was complete and she rose to her feet. Standing in the nude, her large breasts rose and fell as she tried to catch her breath. Blood and body parts littered the floor.

"Why? You're one of us," the werewolf at her feet whispered.

"I'm human first," Roxy said.

I crossed the room and put her Saint Christopher medal around her neck. I handed Roxy her clothes. The dead bodies of the zombies, werewolves, and vampires lay everywhere on the floor, many in pieces. The mummy was a pile of ash.

"It looks like you've done this before," I said to the motel clerk.

Jan and Father Murphy stepped up next to us.

"My great grandfather was from Romania. They have their share of vampires and werewolves in the old country," he said.

"Well, we're not done yet. We need to put stakes through the hearts of these vampires. We don't want them coming back."

"That big bastard was hard to kill," Vito said, looking down at the dead Frankenstein monster.

"Thanks for watching my back," I said.

"Yo, forget about it."

Roxy put her clothes back on and took my arm.

"Did anyone kill Von Wolf?" I asked.

"No, we went after him, but he escaped out a window. Some party, huh?" Father Murphy asked.

"Yeah, happy Halloween," I replied.

Outside, a full moon looked down over the town of Desolation, New Mexico. On Route 666, Nicolas Von Wolf stuck out his thumb. An old man in a beat-up pickup truck pulled over, Von Wolf climbed in the passenger side, and they headed south.

THE QUALITY OF MERCY

JASON ANDREW

The quality of mercy is not strain'd,
It droppeth as the gentle rain from heaven
Upon the place beneath: it is twice blest;
It blesseth him that gives and him that takes
The Merchant of Venice, Act IV Scene 1,
William Shakespeare

The old nag that Jebbidah Heller rode across the desert died just outside the Devil's Gulch. It had been a dusty, uncomfortable ride, but he was glad he had made the trip. The sun burned down upon the desert landscape with the subtlety of a blacksmith's hammer. He was nearly forty and felt twice as old, as though death was creeping into his bones.

He wasn't afraid of death. He had spent far too many years killing and expecting that his time would come when he least expected it. His first taste of killing came during the last legs of the Battle of Gettysburg. He had barely been a man before the cannons started blasting. The smell of blood and the clash of gunpowder overwhelmed everything. He had been a first year cadet at West Point, barely a year away from his weeping mother. Back then, he had been more interested in maps and history than fighting, but it was family tradition to serve at West Point.

His father, Joshua Heller, had been a Major in the Army for decades before retiring as a Colonel in Boston. Joshua Heller had been responsible for taming the land of savages as the papers described it. As a child, Jebbidah only knew that his father had been a hero. Looking back, Jebbidah knew that the wars weighed upon him and that when he told the stories of monsters in the world, it was a warning about the family curse.

Jebbidah Heller slipped the rifle and worn saddle bags over his shoulders, slipped the machete under his belt, and then retrieved the canteen. It was almost empty, but the town, such as it was, was in sight. Limping along the trail, he could see that the Devil's Gulch didn't have that many visitors. From the stories he'd heard, you had to be crazy or desperate to willingly come to this town.

The dusty road curved north, along the bank of the river. There was a small dam at the north end of town built to divert the river so residents could live on the comfortable flatlands. Jebbidah stopped near the river to refill his canteen and then took several small gulps. He was careful to drink a little at a time. He knew he was suffering from the heat and too much could make him sick.

Children waved at him down the street in front of the school yard. Heller politely tipped his hat, knowing that as soon as he got closer, their greetings wouldn't be as gregarious. Feeling a bit stronger, Heller continued towards the town. The excited children were huddled en mass, waiting for the stranger to pass them by. As he grew closer, he could sense their nervousness. Jebbidah Heller had lived a life of war, and like old General Sherman once said, war was Hell. As they caught a glimpse of his pock-marked, scarred face, most ran for the safety of the schoolhouse walls.

He was a tall, gaunt man, having never recovered the weight lost during the battle at Castle Pickney. His large Germanic nose had been broken and reset several times. A small flap of the left nostril was torn from a bar fight some years past. The jagged scar across his cheek marked a train robbery in Mississippi that just barely had gone his way. Clad in the long brown, patchwork duster and worn floppy brown hat, Heller grinned at the remaining children, showing off his hideous, yellow square teeth.

He had caught the pox in the camps after the Battle of Gettysburg. General Sherman had flanked the Johnny Rebs and made a decisive strike, but that left a small battalion on the edge of nowhere vulnerable. Jebbidah didn't recall the battle very well and none of them knew that their attack was a feint. They had expected reinforcements that never arrived. The guards of Castle Pickney found harassing their battalion especially entertaining. As the war worsened, their attention became more painful and exacting. After the camp was freed, he fought with General Sherman in the infamous march to the sea; burning everything in his path.

Before the war, Jebbidah had been a handsome boy. More than one young girl giggled at him in church. His mother, Chastity, had vainly thrown an array of dinner parties, inviting every couple with a daughter in Boston. She spent the entire week in a flurry of activity around the house while Joshua Heller smoked his pipe bitterly and hid in his study.

During the war, Jebbidah sometimes received as many as six letters a week from hopeful young girls wanting to marry a handsome officer. Jebbidah did not return home until a year after the South surrendered. By then, his boyish good looks had degraded to a swollen, skeletal face. His father embraced him weeping. Surprised, Jebbidah stood upon their porch, and listened to his father repeatedly apologize to him.

Undaunted, Chastity insisted upon throwing her son a celebration. Families from three counties attended. The young women wore their Sunday's best and arrived at the Heller household joyful and expectant. Jebbidah's entrance in the party was met with a murmur of disappointment. Slowly, as soon as it was proper and polite, each of the families slinked out of the party as quietly as they could. The sole exception was the Harrington family. Wayne and Sarah Harrington chatted with his parents, while Lucinda patiently waited in the parlor for Jebbidah. Lucinda was three years his junior and had loved him since he was old enough to be out of short pants.

Lucinda's love remained resolute. She continued to write to Jebbidah when he left home to join the Pinkertons, as she had done while he had left for the war. As he traveled the railroads tracking outlaws, she waited for him. They married ten years ago and had a son named Jonathon, which was why he was here. At eight years old, Jonathon was already showing signs of the curse. Jebbidah couldn't bear the thought that his son would have to suffer through the darkness. There were dozens of strange whispers about this town, and if they were half right, the Black Duck could save his son.

Lost in thought and delirious from the sun, Heller continued along the street passing by the church. There was a flock of women chatting, surrounding a smiling, debonair but lanky man. He politely tipped his bowler to excuse himself from the company and unabashedly ran to catch up with Heller. "You look like you could use a hand, friend," he said, in a friendly tone.

It had been a few days since Heller had spoken to other people and the sound of another person was refreshing. "Been out in the bush a spell. This is Devil's Gulch, right?"

"It sure is. We don't get a lot of visitors around here. I expect it's because of our fancy name and reputation," the deputy replied. "I'm Bill Watkins. I'm the deputy around here. And you, friend, look like you need some help. You look like you just crawled out of the grave."

"I hear that happens sometimes around these parts," Heller said casually. He knew that the deputy was sizing him up. That suited Heller just fine since he was doing the same. "I'm Jebbidah Heller and I could really use a room and a bath."

"Well, the Lone Star Hotel is just up the street. I'd be glad to walk you over and introduce you about town," Bill offered.

"I won't be around long. Just finishing up some business and then I'm going home to my family," Heller replied.

"What business is that? If you don't mind my asking," Deputy Bill inquired. "We're a bit away from the railroads so I trust that the Pinkertons don't have any business in the area."

The deputy's smile never wavered, but the glint in his eye faded, replaced with a cool gaze. Deputy Bill's mention of the Pinkertons was an unsubtle hint that he knew the name Jebbidah Heller and wasn't afraid. That meant that this small town deputy was either a moron or everything that Heller had heard about this town was true. "The Pinkertons don't have nothing to do with it. I need to speak to the Black Duck about a personal problem," Heller answered, evenly.

As they progressed into town, Heller noticed that his presence was drawing quite a bit of attention. Men and women stared through dusty windows of Caine's General Store and the Stage office. The man that caught Heller's attention was the older fellow relaxing in a rocking chair on the jailhouse front porch while reading the paper. He figured that was Sheriff Randal Stockbridge.

One of the reasons the Pinkertons never visited this town was the low crime rate, and management figured that had a lot to do with the town's sheriff. The home office sent two agents to recruit him, but both returned slightly uneasy and reported that the good sheriff was happy where he was.

"The Black Duck don't get a lot of visitors. Tends to be a bit anti-social. Mostly keeps away from town and things are quiet," Deputy Bill explained. "We like it mostly that way."

"I ain't intending to disrupt the peace, Deputy. You and yours have nothing to fear from me," Heller answered the unasked question.

"There was once a mess of trouble in these parts years ago. Maybe you heard about it. We won't tolerate a repeat," Deputy Bill warned.

"You could ease a bit of that trouble if you could arrange a pow-wow. All I want is to talk," Heller stated. "And I have something he wants."

"The way I hear it, you and yours said the same thing to Jesse James," Deputy Bill replied.

"The way I hear it is that the Black Duck ain't broken any laws or robbed any trains. I only kill a man that needs killin'," Heller explained. "I give you my word I won't cause any trouble."

Deputy Bill nodded, satisfied. "That's good enough for me," he said. "I'll ride out this afternoon and see if I can get him to come to town tonight for a drink."

"That's mighty kind of you, Deputy," Heller said.

Bill laughed. Heller envied the power of that laugher. "Hell, you just put up with my jawing at you. And, you're a bona fide war hero."

After a few weeks on the trail, Heller wanted little more than a bath and bed, but he knew he had to make an appearance lest the locals became spooked. He grunted his acceptance and the deputy laughed pleasantly and nodded to the sheriff.

* * *

The Devil's Fiddle would have been at home in a bigger city like Boston or St. Lewis. There was a stage, a piano player, and an elegant giant mural of a thin, beautiful Irish girl singing. He had expected saw-dust, unwashed cow-poke, and dirty glasses. It had taken an hour and several buckets of heated water for Heller to wash away the grime and grit. He almost felt human again, but there were some things soap and water couldn't wash away.

As he stepped into the Devil's Fiddle, a burly man with arms larger than most men's thighs grunted and gestured to a sign next to the bar. ***No spitting, no weapons, and no IOUs***. Heller glanced around the bar and noted that no one else carried weapons, including the deputy. Nodding his compliance, Heller unbuckled his gun belt and handed them across the bar. The bartender grunted his approval and poured him a shot of whiskey. "On the house," he said, grimly.

"Thank you kindly," Heller replied, tipping his hat.

"That's two words more than he's said to anyone else in a dog's age," Bill said, smiling. He gestured to a woman to his right. "Allow me to introduce you to the belle of Devil's Gulch and the owner of the Devil's Fiddle. Luella Miller-Thompson."

Luella had been beautiful as a young girl, as Heller noted from the mural. Through the wrinkles, he could still see the girl she had once been uncorrupted by age or time. She was old enough to be his mother, but her smile could tempt the devil. "Pleased to meet you, ma'am."

To Luella's credit, her smile never wavered or faded when she got a good look at his face. She twirled her boa and curtsied. "It's an honor to have such a respectable sort in my place. We've read about you in the papers," Luella replied, offering her hand.

Heller took the hand and kissed it gently. "The pleasure is mine. My mother and I once saw you sing in New York while visiting relatives."

"Any chance I could tempt you a bit with sampling the local color?" Luella asked, gesturing to the young girls on the balcony. "My doves are clean and kind."

"I'm certain they are, but I'm a family man and here for business," Heller said. "Best to be getting to it straight away, if the deputy found the fellow I'm looking for."

"That I have, Mr. Heller," Deputy Bill reported, pointing to a table in the corner. "He's waiting for you now."

Heller tipped his hat and left them to join the man sitting in the corner. Johnny 'Black Duck' George was a lean, thoughtful looking man with long black hair braided like an Indian. It wasn't hard to notice that the Black Duck was feared, even by the deputy, which was surprising considering his tender age. The Black Duck couldn't have been much older than Heller had been when he left for the war.

"I'm Jebbidah Heller and I've come to these parts looking for you."

Johnny looked up from his drink and nodded. "Deputy Bill said you had something I wanted."

Heller reached into his duster and produced a small metallic bracelet. It was silver, inscribed with skulls and flames, set with turquoise and obsidian stones. Surviving years on the trail hunting men, had honed Heller's ability to read a man's face. From the widening of the eyes and the attention of the body posture, Heller knew he had bargaining power.

"What do you want, Mr. Heller?"

"It's simple really. A cure."

"I can't fix your face, Mr. Heller," Johnny said, not unkindly.

"My face was my own fault. I can live with the consequences," Heller stated. "What I can't abide is the taint inflicted upon my family. I was told that you know the ways of the world. The ways most don't want to look at."

"I've seen more than most," Johnny admitted. "But I ain't a master like my grandpa. He knew things we can't imagine."

"Your grand-daddy's tribe came from deep in old Mexico. Same place as this bracelet. I work with the Pinkertons and a shipment of artifacts is coming in to Boston for the museum," Heller revealed. "The days of this land being a frontier are just about over. All that's really left is memories and bits folks are encasing in glass. I have enough influence to get you inside to study them. Hell, they might even pay you for the effort."

"And in exchange, you wish for me to cure this curse upon your blood?" Johnny asked, interested.

"I've done my share of killing. I've seen dark things in this world that would freeze your blood. Evil things. Maybe I deserve it. My choices led me to it. My son don't need to play a part in it," Heller answered.

"I can feel the weight of those deaths on you, Mr. Heller. Killing leaves a mark upon the soul," Johnny said, grimly.

"My son is a good boy. He reads a lot. He's innocent, pure. He don't deserve this curse," Heller said, pleading.

"What is the nature of the curse?"

"The men of my family are magnets. We draw the dark things in the world to us. It's the darndest thing. If something evil and unnatural is gonna happen, it happens around us," Heller explained. "It's like we have a special kin with the evil."

"I can't promise anything, but there is a ritual I can use to look into your soul," Johnny offered, nervous. "If we use the proper ingredients, we might cleanse the curse. It will be plenty painful. And there's a chance it won't work."

"I'm not asking for a miracle, just for you to do your best."

"The only problem is that I might not have what we need. This sort of deal requires powerful medicine. We're going to need the blood of a beast of darkness," the Black Duck explained.

"I don't understand."

"Normally, I'd try to use the blood of an owl. It would be enough to glance into your soul and advise you," the Black Duck said. "You're talking about a curse few men could devise. And so we're going to have to be crafty. One of the oldest rules of the old ways is that like attracts like. You want the evil from your blood exercised, then we're going to need the blood of an evil beast to power it."

"I don't suppose you have a beast handy?"

The Black Duck glanced around the room, uneasy. "None that would be worth the trouble. But to the south, in the hills, I've heard stories of creatures living in caves."

"And you think their blood will do?" Heller asked.

"They are spawns of creatures beyond this world. Hideous things that can drive a man insane. You sure you want to do this?"

Heller thought of his wife and son and nodded. "How far?"

"About three days ride. I can leave in the morning, if you're willing."

"You do this, and whatever I can give you is yours. As long as this doesn't touch my son."

* * *

Jebbidah Heller paid almost twice the going rate for a fresh horse. He would have rented one, but no one believed he would ever be coming back. The Black Duck and Heller rode out of town, heading west at first light. They rode for hours silently, taking in the surroundings. At dusk, they broke for camp listening to the howls of the coyotes. Although morning came without incident, the sky was gray and overcast, making the sun barely visible.

As they rode away from the valley and the river, the landscape shifted from lush green plant life to a series of browns and yellow. By noon, vultures circled them, waiting. The shrill yelps of the coyotes gave way to the menacing howl of the wolves.

"I'm not accustomed to so many wolves out during the day," Heller replied, a bit nervous.

"The Star-spawn may have infected them. Much in this land has their taint," Johnny explained.

"Is that why you came with me?" Heller asked. "I'm not exactly known as a friend to the Indians."

"You've killed indiscriminately, but you've never tried to take what's mine," the Black Duck answered, after thinking about it. "This taint could creep into my lands, so you're doing me a favor. And if you die, it's no great loss to me."

"Whatever your reasons, you're showing me kindness and I won't forget it," Heller said, earnestly.

"That's the secret, you know," Johnny said. "Kindness and mercy. It keeps you warm and safe in the darkness."

"Don't think to tell me about darkness, boy," Heller retorted bitterly.

"You know about what's in the world, but you ain't so good at withstanding it," Johnny said. "The things that you've done eat at your soul. You've survived by helping others. I do the same and get by the same way."

"You seem to know a lot about me," Heller stated uncomfortably.

"Well, you hear stories after awhile. A man that kills a werewolf in Texas gets noticed, even in the Devil's Gulch," Johnny replied. "And you and the Pinkertons brought back those kids from that cult in St. Lewis."

"There always seems to be more," Heller complained. "Do you know what's in the cave?"

"Evil. Servants of an ancient, dreaming god that passed through the first world long ago," Johnny said. "They prey upon the land, coming out only at night."

"First world?"

"Some believe that there were worlds before this one. And that there will be one more," he said.

"What do we need to do to kill them?" Heller asked.

"These creatures shamble from one world to the next serving their masters. Weapons made purely from this realm can't hurt them. However, with the proper runes inscribed upon a blade, it will wound them enough for my magic to do the deed," the Black Duck said.

"Like a cross and vampires?"

"More or less, I suppose. Some shapes in this world cause reflections in the spirit world. Those spirit shapes can touch these creatures in a way you and I can't," the young shaman said.

"Your grand-daddy must have been busy to teach you so much," Heller said, impressed.

Johnny paused a moment and glared at Heller. "I grew up in a town terrified he'd raise the dead again. I learned the value of study, fairly quick. There are secrets you don't know about the Devil's Gulch."

"Ain't none of my business."

"I thought that the Pinkertons watched everything. What is their motto again?" the Indian asked.

"We never sleep."

The Black Duck laughed. "There are things in this world that never die, but only sleep, waiting for the right time."

* * *

Throughout the day, the howls continued to surround them. At dusk, they found a good camping spot along the side of a rocky cliff. They kept their hands on their weapons huddled next to the fire. Several hours before dawn, the wolves attacked.

They were bloated misshapen wolves with slick fur and gleaming yellow eyes. The lead wolf leapt over the campfire, attempting to claw into Heller. Nonplussed, he chopped the wolf's head clear off with a blow of his machete. For a moment, the other wolves paused, uncertain now that their alpha had been killed. Heller and the Black Duck likewise paused, hoping the wolves would run away, if not attacked. One of the wolves began to growl. Encouraged, the others bared their fangs and growled lowly. Heller raised his weapons; a machete in one hand and a revolver in the other. Johnny George hid behind the rocks, aiming an old, bolt action Remington rifle. "What the hell happened to these wolves?" Heller asked.

"They've been affected by the taint," the Black Duck said. "Can we take them?"

Heller didn't answer. They had picked a defensible position, a place to put their backs against the wall. Taking aim, he shot the closest wolf in the brainpan, killing it instantly. Though his life on occasion crossed with the occult, Heller knew in most aspects he was an amateur. He didn't read Latin and had lost his taste in books as soon as a revolver was put in his hand. All he knew was killing and war.

For hours, the wolves circled the campsite. Heller waited patiently, picking them off one by one. Sometimes, he would snipe them with his rifle, tracking them by their gleaming yellow eyes. Other times, he would hack at them with his machete. Once two of them rallied and tried attacking at once. One of them, the smaller one, savagely bit into his arm, forcing the gun to the ground. The other tried to rip into his throat. Angry, Heller brought his machete down upon the wolf's head, splitting it in twain. Lifting his other arm to give him room to swing, he savagely chopped into the belly of the wolf until it released its bite.

By first light, the wolves retreated. The Black Duck boiled some water and washed out Heller's wound. His arm had begun to take on a slight greenish twinge. "That bite gave you the taint," the shaman replied.

"How long do I have?" Heller asked.

"Well, you should start feeling the fever by noon. Hard to say what will happen after that. There's some moss that grows in the caves that counters some of the poison. I can try to get you some and come back."

"No. I'll be going with you. I can stand a bit of fever. Have before," Heller stated. "Wrap my arm as best you can."

Johnny washed out the wound and stitched it closed. Heller winced and bit into a small pad of leather. The whisky served as a decent cleanser, but in order to dull the pain, it would have to dull the senses. The wolves were gone, but they could return. Heller also doubted they would be the only guardians that stood in the way of them reaching the cave.

By mid morning, they broke camp and continued along the trail. Smelling blood, the vultures continued to circle. On occasion, one swooped low enough to check on them. Tainted, they were malformed with twisted beaks and oily wings. During a low dive, Heller trained his gun upon them with his non-wounded limb and killed them. The vultures dropped like stones, plunging to the ground. The rest of the flock scattered and waited upon the edge of gunfire range.

"I'm not so sure we should be firing so many rounds," Heller said after killing the third vulture.

"I expect that animals with the taint have already notified them we're here," Johnny said, afraid. "It is too late now. We've already lost the element of surprise. Maybe we should turn back. I have medicine that can help your arm back home."

"We turn back, the creatures might move. Or fortify themselves. Its best that we kill them now," Heller stated, wincing a bit. "It's not just for my boy. If their taint is spreading to the animals like this, it might spread to people. Most ain't equipped to fight this."

"You're not what I expected."

Heller laughed in spite of the pain. They stopped a few hours before dusk and gathered stones and wood for a large bonfire. When the wolves returned, Heller and the Black Duck were protected within a circle of fire. Frustrated, a few tried to slip close to the flames and leap over, but Heller sniped them in midair. The Black Duck used his obsidian dagger to etch arcane symbols into Heller's machete blade.

The third day was mostly uneventful. The wolves trailed them, but made no effort to catch them. Likewise, the vultures continue to circle overhead, but remained content to watch them along with the crows. "Seems like they surrendered," Johnny said, hopefully.

They were being herded, Heller thought uneasily. The dull ache in his arm had made sleep uncomfortable. Johnny washed his arm three times during the day, but the infection continued to turn his pale flesh a slightly grayish green. "If we don't treat that arm, we might lose it," Johnny warned.

Heller thought of the war and nodded. Infection cost quite a few limbs after Gettysburg and in the camps. "Of course, it could be that we'll both be killed shortly and it won't matter," he said, mustering as much humor as he could.

They reached the base of the hills by mid-afternoon. Sweltering heat and a cloudless, windless sky sapped their strength. Leading the horses on foot, they hiked up the trail, armed and cautious of an ambush.

They reached the plateau near the cave entrance early in the evening.

"Bullets will likely stun them. Fire and our blades are the only sure way to kill them," Johnny said. "Even then, we'll need to remove their heads."

"Best to do this while we still have a bit of light out," Heller added. "Looks like we'll have maybe an hour. No more."

The mouth of the cave smelled like an unattended slaughterhouse. In the center of the entrance was a small pile of severed human feet, carefully arranged into a pyramid. Most of the flesh had long been rotted and picked away by carrion eaters, but Heller noted that the apex of the pyramid had a foot that looked relatively fresh, still oozing fluids. Determined, they lit their torches and prepared their weapons. The Black Duck wielded a wicked looking hatchet; the blade bore the same markings he had added to Heller's machete. Armed with torches, they entered the cave.

The rank air inside of the cave was infused with the scent of sulfur. The light from the torches cast flickering shadows along the walls of the cave. It quickly became apparent that the caves were deeper and far more complex than Johnny had expected. "It's too late to go back," Heller insisted. "We'd have nowhere to go before the creatures could attack us. Best to press our advantage now."

At odd moments, it sounded as though other footsteps and wet, raspy breathing noses could be heard. Each time, they would freeze and listen carefully, but it would disappear. Lost, despite their careful efforts, they began to grow desperate, and thereby more bold. Heller began to mark the sides of the tunnels by etching arrows into them. They might have given up and tried to find the way out, if they hadn't discovered the crystals.

At a crossroads and uncertain which direction to take, Heller pointed his torch into three tunnels. The first two tunnels revealed nothing but more tunnel. The third tunnel sparkled with hundreds of tiny reflections. Curious, Heller and Johnny crept into the tunnel to examine the light sources, and discovered a strange emerald crystal.

The light from the torches energized the crystals, causing a low-pitch hum. Gradually, the hum seemed to feed upon itself, growing louder and louder with each passing second. As the sound increased, the glow from the crystals intensified and increased their output by a thousand times.

The blare from the crystals cascaded down the tunnel into a central large cavern. Blinded, they shielded their eyes and waited for them to adjust. As the spots faded from their vision, a gruesome, furious bellow echoed throughout the tunnels.

Shambling creatures crawled into the tunnel, lusting for their blood.

The abominable monsters were humanoid in basic shape, but appeared more bat than man. Their heads were marked with two giant, hairy ears, a smashed nose, and a gaping maw with three rows of ragged fangs. Their arms had the range and motion of a human, but their bone structure and the skin membrane of a wing allowed them to glide effortlessly. Their slimy skin was pocked with short, matted fur.

Dropping their torches between the creatures and themselves, Heller and Johnny readied themselves. Using his weak arm, Heller fired his gun into the crowd to weaken them, then used his machete to finish the job. The sound of gunfire seemed to wound them more than the actual bullets. In retaliation, the creatures rallied against the two men, closing in for another attack.

Johnny wasn't a war veteran like Heller; he solved most of his fights with dark magic from the shadows. Steeled by Heller's resolve, he fired and hacked as best he could. By the end of the fight, his ears pulsed and bled, but he was alive, as was Heller. The black ooze that served as the creatures' blood sizzled in the open air and seemed to eat at the metal of their blades.

"There must be a nest in the main cavern!" Johnny yelled, barely able to hear himself.

Heller nodded.

They retrieved their torches and hurried through to the end of the tunnel. The cavern was dome-shaped with hundreds of crystal stalactites reaching from the ceiling to the ground. There were several exit tunnels honeycombing throughout the cavern. In the center, there was a nest made from human bones, living flesh sewn together, and animal hide. It seemed to breathe as though a living entity.

Cautiously, Heller reloaded his six shooters while Johnny examined the walls. Putrid pestilence dripped from the nest. Along the top of the walls were smaller, webbed sacs made from flesh. "They're breeding. I don't think I brought enough dynamite," Heller said.

Johnny nodded, horrified. He continued his search around the base of the walls, near the pools of water, hoping the creatures would give him enough time. Hidden behind some bones, there was a small patch of lichen. "I found what I need."

"Keep watch, I need to place this very carefully," Heller said.

Although the cavern was large, Heller hoped the blast would cause a collapse in the tunnel. He had brought a slow burning fuse, but there was no way they could exit the tunnels before the blast would collapse everything. Undaunted, he continued to lay the dynamite in optimum positions. He had learned how to blast a tunnel from his time in the railroads and had gotten decent at pitching in when needed.

"We can't blast this cavern and get out," Johnny complained. "We'll have to come back."

The nest started pulsing. The horrid bellow returned. "You have ten minutes to get out," Heller said calmly. "I'll blast it from inside."

"You won't survive."

"There are worse things than surviving," Heller said. "Find my son and give him the cure for the curse."

Johnny blushed, ashamed. "There isn't a cure. You ain't cursed."

"Of course we are. I've told you our history!" Heller yelled, fighting the urge to shoot the shaman.

"You have a taint of magic on you because of your travels. Some of that gets passed on," Johnny explained. "But that's not a curse. All your son needs to do is not chase after shadows. Same as you. You had a choice."

"You lied to me," Heller growled.

The nest began to twist and tear, and tiny claws began to tear through. "I needed someone to help me. The others don't trust me."

"I can see why," Heller replied. He glanced at the shaman, then to the bulging, tearing nest. "Get out. You've got ten minutes."

"You should go, I'll stay," Johnny argued. "I don't deserve this. You have a son."

"I'm gonna lose my arm soon. And I have a bad heart. I only have a few years left anyway," Heller said. "I should kill you where you stand. I've killed for less. But maybe you were right after all. There is a choice. Make sure my son knows that choice and I figure that we're even. Now git or I'll put a bullet between your eyes."

Johnny nodded and scrambled out of the cavern. He had a vague sense of the proper direction of the exit, but the exact route was lost when they entered. Desperate, he started looking for Heller's markers and finally found one at the edge of the light from the crystals. Frantic, he rushed through the tunnels and ran out into the darkness of the night, relieved to see the moon and stars.

Heller leaned against the wall, counting the time on his pocket watch. The claws and fangs began to consume the flesh and bones of the nest. Dozens of heads, mouths, and wings fluttered, struggling to break free like a butterfly escaping a cocoon. He figured there must be almost two dozen creatures contained in the nest. Again, the loud bellow shook the cavern, urging the creatures to move quicker.

A colossal wing burst through the cocoon. It was much larger than the others.

That must be the queen, he thought, horrified. Once free, she would easily overcome him and escape. Terrified, he lit the fuse.

He thought of the horrors he had experienced after the war and wondered how many of them he had caused. He'd done some good in his life, but missed the quiet moments. He had been hunting Jesse James when his son took his first steps. There was a lot of darkness, but also light. Had he ignored the good?

He should have killed the Black Duck for lying to him and damning him, but he couldn't find it in his heart to regret it. His father once told him that an act of mercy does as much for the giver as the taker. Wasn't it an act of mercy that made him fall for his wife?

Jebbidah Heller thought of his beautiful wife and son.

He was crying when the fuse reached its end and ignited the dynamite.

NEED

DANE T. HATCHELL

Susan Richards spent most of the first twenty years of her life alone.

Not like she was on an island somewhere void of human contact. She was alone in the world of normal.

The world of normal walked in step to the same beat: fashions of the season, tunes on the radio, slang language of the day. Her accent into puberty was a stairway straight to isolation. The girls around her were changing, becoming creatures of beauty, passion, and mirth, while she stood on the outskirts of notoriety, hidden in plain sight as boys looked past her as if she wasn't there.

The four walls of her room became her refuge and the only friends she had were the books on the shelf. The emptiness she felt inside was filled with food. Anything in plastic wrap or a can would do. It was the void she was trying to satisfy, not the palate.

Her life came to a defining moment in the summer between high school and college, when she took a stroll down one of the less-traveled hiking paths at the state park.

She was walking with her mind lost in a dull gray world of her creation, on a path at the bottom of a small hill. She heard screams of agony from nearby and froze in mid-step. It almost sounded animal-like, and the skin on the back of her neck tingled. As the cries of anguish faded, she distinctly heard, "Help me," from a withering voice. She was unsure whether to run away or go up on the hill above where it came from. Her sense of obligation won over her fears, and she made the slow trek up the hill.

A handsome young boy she deduced to be a little older than her, was in the middle of a spray-painted pentagram. He was clean, well-dressed, and not even a hair was out of place on his head. It was as if he had laid down on his back to take a nap. An odd looking ceramic pitcher sat to his left and a small fire was burning to his right. A tattered leather bound book was on the ground, open to a page with yellow-highlighted passages.

Susan could tell just by looking at him that he was dead. His body was no longer surrounded by the aura of life. She had never been around a dead body before, and was surprised she wasn't more afraid.

The wind blew her hair across her face and she brushed it out of the way. She gingerly stepped toward him until she was standing by his side, then knelt down between the book and his body.

The wind kicked up again, causing the pages in the book to flip as if an unseen force was rapidly turning them. She picked the book off the ground, and opened it where a thin red ribbon was sandwiched between the pages.

The words looked familiar and foreign at the same time. Scanning them quickly, she guessed it was written in Latin. The passages highlighted in yellow intrigued her. She placed her index finger under the first word, and began to read out loud. *"Atrum sol solis orior oriri ortus, incendia est frigus, orbis terrarum inter mihi nex, ortus est totus."*

The foul smell of sulfur bit at her nostrils, causing acid to well up in her throat. She felt herself become short of breath and forcefully breathed in to fill her lungs. A sense of power flooded through her. It was as if her brain had been fractured all her life and something inside of her now was shoving everything into place.

Susan placed her hand on the boy's left cheek; the coolness of his skin moved her in an unnatural way. Something unknown to her conscious mind was drawing her nearer to him. As her face got closer to his, she realized it was the unique smell of death pulling her.

With her face just inches from his, she closed her eyes and breathed in slowly and deeply. She opened her eyes and marveled at the hue of his pale cheeks and red-blue lips. She had never been with a boy before. None had ever attempted to kiss her. She licked her lips and felt her warm breath bounce off his cheek and back into her nostrils. It filled her with want and desire.

She gave him a gentle kiss. Her eyes swelled with tears as a longing in her soul was fulfilled.

She kissed him again, harder this time. First on his lips, then on his cheek. She dragged her open mouth and tongue across his face until her face was sliding in wetness against his.

In exhilaration, she bit his lower lip and severed it in a bloody strip. She chewed the lip slowly, letting the taste of his dead flesh roll over her tongue, savoring the texture and flavor of the raw meat.

What she was doing was one of the greatest taboos in human society, but there was nothing in her mind telling her what she was doing was wrong. Nothing in her mind was screaming that this was madness and to stop.

She swallowed the bloody lip and wiped the red spittle from her chin with the back of her hand. Chewing through his cheek proved to be more difficult. Her teeth were unaccustomed to tearing through fresh meat. The cheek had a different texture than the lip, but it was equally as pleasing.

She fed until she could eat no more, and cleaned herself up as best as she could with tissues she kept in her purse. Rationality returned and the fear that someone coming upon her unexpectedly brought creeping feelings of anxiety. She darted her head back and forth, expecting to see someone watching her and finding herself in a world of trouble.

She was alone, at least for now. Susan left with her new desire digesting in her stomach, thinking what it would mean in her life from now on.

The demon that entered Susan during that lazy summer afternoon was comfortably hidden in her subconscious. It relished the experience of inhabiting a host and to walk among the living again. And more importantly, feed on the dead.

Drifting through the eons, the demon had witnessed the advancement of man, and much to its displeasure, the modern day burial practices had made feeding more difficult.

No longer was its host able to raid a remote cemetery under the cover of darkness and pull from a shallow grave a tender, fetid, corpse. Modern security and modern science with all its rank chemicals, made its age old practice of eating cadavers a thing of the past. But its hunger still had to be satisfied.

Susan applied her eyeliner and finished with a coat of lip gloss on her pouty lips. When she looked in the mirror, it no longer reflected the unkempt, self loathing societal reject of two years before. Her radical new diet and exercise regiment brought out the hidden features of her natural beauty. Instead of attending college, she was in a nursing program that allowed her to work off hours in the hospital to support herself until she earned her degree.

A lot of things had changed over the two years. The taste for testosterone rich meat gave way to that of estrogen. Her supply of meat from her last victim was gone. Tonight she hoped to change that. It was Saturday night and all the lesbian bars would be full of adventurous loose women waiting to find solace in another's gentle arms.

She slipped on a pair of her sexiest shoes and checked herself in the full length mirror one last time. She wanted to look as desirable as she could, a ghoul's gotta eat, you know.

Susan met Caroline on the dance floor. The blaring music in the dark bar with the rays of cascading colored lights dulled the senses; that and the alcohol. Susan had been careful not to drink too much and had been nursing her beer since she arrived. She had put on her most extroverted party face and danced alone, looking like an unattached carefree girl that was easy to meet.

Caroline danced her way toward Susan. Despite the darkness, Susan was mesmerized when Caroline looked at her with those large eyes through her long lashes. Her full face was framed by high cheek bones and her wide mouth made her look...delicious.

The two danced a few songs together until they were dancing close enough for their bodies to touch. The connection was made; Caroline took Susan by the hand and led her to a table away from the distracting music on the dance floor.

The two spent almost an hour talking and were on their second drink together, complements of Susan. She had made the trips to the bar to get herself a Roman coke—minus the rum—and a drink for Caroline, too. She added a little *rohypnol* that she'd stole from the hospital to Caroline's first drink.

Susan had been waiting for the eyelids on those large beautiful eyes of Caroline's to droop. So far, she wasn't showing any effects of the drug. Susan would usually be driving her victim home by now, and was wondering if the drug was past its expiration date.

The bar was packed with plenty of available women, partying and have a good time, which made a petite young blonde two table's away stand out from the rest. She was alone, looking out of place. Susan could feel the blonde staring at her and Caroline with more than a common interest.

"What is it with that girl over there?" Susan tipped her head to the left.

Caroline took a sip of her drink, and darted her eyes in that direction. "Oh, I've seen her before. Her name's Rachel *somethingorother*. In the past, she and another couple of guys would protest in front of the bar carrying signs. Just a bunch of holy rollers trying to stir up trouble. She's been coming here alone recently. She doesn't mingle and she doesn't drink. I think she's just confused about her sexuality and doesn't know how to deal with it."

Susan smiled and took Caroline by the hand. "So, my lovely, do you think she's stalking you?" Susan let go of Caroline's hand. "Wow, your hand is like ice."

"Sorry, I've been holding my drink with that hand," Caroline said, looking down at the table. She closed one eye and thought for a moment. "You know, I have been seeing that girl out a lot lately. Not just here either. I thought it was just a coincidence, but now I'm not so sure. Maybe she is a stalker."

Susan shot a stern glance at the blonde. "I don't know, but she's starting to creep me out."

"Then why don't we go back to my place? I have locks on my door," Caroline said, smiling. Susan smiled back; everything but the drug taking effect was going according to plan.

Caroline parked her car in her garage, opened the car door for Susan, and then the door leading into her house. "Won't you please come in?"

There was something in the tone of Caroline's voice that made Susan hesitate for a moment. Caroline gave her a questioning look.

Susan stepped over the threshold hurriedly, fearing she might be perceived as being rude.

The door opened into the living room. It was tastefully decorated with dark woods and leather furniture. It gave Susan the feeling of stepping back in time, a place where old British men would go to sip after-dinner drinks and smoke cigars.

Susan heard the jingle of keys, the mechanical sounds of cylinders turning, and bolts sliding into place. There was something final in the way the locks clicked. It was a hollow sound, as if a vault had been slammed shut. Susan started to feel vulnerable, unlike the predator she had become.

"What's the matter, Susan, you're not having second thoughts are you?" Caroline asked as she removed her shoes. She walked in bare feet slowly toward Susan, and held her with the embrace of her penetrating gaze.

Susan's wide eyes softened as she relaxed "No..."

Caroline kissed her gently, feeling warm lips pressed against hers. Susan stood with her eyes closed and her mouth open as Caroline pulled away, and let her dress drop off her shoulders and then onto the floor. Caroline stood naked, her face, arms and legs, darker than the rest of her body. Makeup had hidden the porcelain whiteness of the skin now exposed with the dress off. Susan's will was now under the control of Caroline, and she didn't notice the pale, lifeless skin.

In silence, Caroline took Susan into the bedroom and removed her clothing. The bed was covered in clear plastic. The plastic crinkled and pulled at Susan's skin as Caroline laid her down.

"Here, let me go down on you first," Caroline grinned malevolently. Her canine teeth grew down out of her mouth. She slid her face down to the junction of Susan's thighs, and pulled them apart. Caroline placed her mouth between her legs, and punctured a femoral artery. She drank deeply.

Three loud banging sounds followed a crash coming from the back door of the house. Caroline was fixated on her primordial need to feed and reluctantly forced herself away from her nightly meal.

The sounds of feet pounding the wooden floor of the hallway sent Caroline springing up from her bed. The light in the bedroom clicked on and she was face to face with three intruders, all dressed in black military camouflage.

Caroline stood naked before them, and gave them a hiss while flashing her blood-stained fangs. Susan awoke from her trance and cried out in fear.

Rachel, the blonde from the bar, was standing behind two men. One of the men took three steps forward, carrying a neon-green plastic Super-Soaker water gun. He emptied it contents over Caroline.

She stood there dripping wet, wiped the water from her face with her hand, and crossed her arms. "Let me guess; holy water, right? And you added garlic juice? Now that is some stinking ass shit."

The man with the Super-Soaker took a step back, and looked at the other man beside him.

"Look what you've done to my floors. This is real ebony wood. Do you have any idea how much that will cost to fix?" Caroline argued.

The man threw the water gun aside and charged Caroline, with the other man following closely on his heels. Caroline brushed the rushing man aside like he was a fly, slamming him against the wall. But the other man surprised her when he pulled out a long silver spear with a sharp wooden tip. He drove the spear into her chest, and pinned her to the wall.

"Are we too late? Is the girl dead?" Rachel asked.

"She looks alive, go see about her. Looks like the vamp is still alive, too," the second man said. The spear had missed Caroline's heart, entering too high. She stood impaled against the wall. She was still conscious, but unable to free herself.

Rachel went to Susan's side, who was sitting up in bed and looking at Caroline with confusion.

"That's a nasty looking bite you have on your leg. Did she feed for very long?" Rachel asked.

Susan looked at her wound, "No...not long."

"We had to be sure about her before we broke in. There's a night vision camera set up outside that window," Rachel said, pointing. "When we saw the fangs come out, we decided to go in.

You're safe now. Thanks to God's grace you're safe." Rachel gathered Susan's clothes and handed them to her.

"Bill, you okay? You hit the wall kind of hard," Rachel said.

Bill rubbed the back of his head. "I'll live. But she shouldn't." He nodded Caroline's way.

Caroline's eyes blazed with anger. She grabbed the silver portion of the spear and her hands started smoldering on contact. With a cry of anguish, she had to let go.

"Whew, what a stench," Jeremy said. He was the one who had driven the spear through her.

"So, what do you do now? Call the police?" Susan asked.

"No, that's not the way it works. We're going to take care of the vampire and dispose of it. This is a war between good and evil, between God and the Devil. You don't have to be part of this, although we would like you to join us. God could use more soldiers in his army." Rachel reached out and held Susan by the hand.

Susan looked again at Caroline. The anger from her had subsided and she started to look like a scared little girl. Susan looked back at Rachel and said, "I'd like to stay and help."

"That's wonderful! A new world is going to open up to you. Just wait and see. You'll learn things that will answer all of your questions and erase all your doubts," Rachel said happily.

"Let's get this over with. Where are the stakes?" Jeremy asked.

Rachel let go of Susan's hand. "I left them in the truck. I'll go with you. I need to get the body bag and I want to get the medical kit and clean up her bite. Bill can stay here and watch things."

Bill pulled out a 9mm pistol from his side holster, and chambered a round. "I'm ready. Wooden tipped silver bullets. Custom made by yours truly."

Rachel led the way with Jeremy following behind. "All right, cowboy, don't shoot that thing unless your life depends on it."

Bill waited for them to leave the room, and then approached Caroline with the gun in a firing position in front of him. "You're nothing but the spawn of the Devil. Don't worry, we'll be sending you back to your daddy soon enough." Bill pushed the spear deeper into Caroline until the wooden tip passed entirely through and the silver part touched her flesh. Caroline twisted in pain as the wound began to smoke.

Susan moved away from the bed and stood behind Bill.

"Yeah, you'll be smoking even more when you get to Hell, bitch," Bill said, just before a vase hit him on the head, shattering, and he lost consciousness.

Caroline looked at Susan with surprise as Susan grabbed the spear and pulled it out, freeing her from certain doom.

Footsteps were coming from down the hall. With the speed of a jaguar, Caroline was waiting by the bedroom door as Jeremy entered with his bag of killing tools. Her hands went straight to his head. In one smooth motion, she twisted it to the right, breaking his neck.

Rachel stopped at the doorway and gasped. Caroline grabbed her by her collar and dragged her into the middle of the room. Her fangs shot out and she plunged them deeply into Rachel's neck. Rachel made moaning noises indistinguishable from sounds of pleasure or pain. Caroline drank until the body went limp, and no more blood could be sucked out.

She let the body drop to the floor, and stood looking at Susan while wiping the blood from her mouth. "You saved me. Why?"

"I think I did it because I don't see you as being the monster they were making you out to be. You're being just like any other. You have a right to survive, too," Susan said.

"But now you know I'm a vampire. What makes you think I can let you live, knowing that about me?"

Susan bent down next to Rachel and unbuckled her belt of weapons. She removed the survival knife from its sheath and pulled Rachel's pants down to her knees. Caroline watched, not knowing what to expect.

Susan slid the blade into Rachel's thigh and carved out a slab of meat. She stuck it with the end of the blade and took a large bite of it right off the knife. "It's way too fresh for my liking, but now you know a secret about me. Our secrets can be safe with each other."

Bill started to stir and Caroline ended his life quickly. She removed the plastic on her bed and motioned for Susan to join her. The two spent the night together in passion as the bodies cooled on the floor.

* * *

Susan put several grocery bags full of meat in the trunk of Caroline's car. She needed to get home and Caroline wouldn't need her car until tonight anyway.

usan would have it back by the time she awoke from her daytime slumber.

Caroline had some *friends* that were going to take care of Rachel's truck and the bodies of the two men.

Susan had known about chop shops stripping automobiles, but had not known about 'chop shops' that sold human body parts.

The market was larger than she ever imagined.

She had never been in a relationship and was giddy with excitement. She was feeling love for the first time, real love. There were so many things they could do together, so many ways they could help each other.

The arrangement couldn't be more perfect.

Finding food would be less of a chore now. Only one of them had to work at finding a new victim. Once the trap was set, Caroline could drain the blood, and Susan would have the body to eat for later after it began to rot and fester.

It was a perfect match made in Hell.

GOOD BUSINESS

TERRY ALEXANDER

Albert Parker burst through the doors of Jonas Tyler's Emporium of the strange and bizarre. The glass rattled in the double doors in his wake. His face was flushed a deep scarlet, and he clutched at his chest, as his breath wheezed through his open mouth. Weak shafts of light peeked over the roof, highlighting the parking lot, as the new sun slowly devoured the lingering shadows of the night.

"I heard the news," he panted. "Is this on the level? Do you have one? Have your men captured a ghoul?" Parker drew a deep breath.

A smile crossed the bald, pudgy man's face sitting behind the counter. He leaned back in his expensive leather chair, his interlocked fingers resting on his pot belly. "Yes, Mr. Parker, it's quite true. My men are bringing it here even as we speak."

"Are you sure it's a ghoul? It's not a zombie in the early stages of the change?" Parker wiped sweat from his brow and beefy jowls. "I've got enough problems with zombies. Lord knows I don't need any more running around underfoot."

"Mr. Parker, I have a reputation to uphold, the Emporium only deals in guaranteed commodities." Jonas slammed his fist on the antique desk. "Your accusation is an insult to my business. It is indeed a legitimate ghoul. They're very hard to come by. Only a handful of these creatures remain in the entire world."

"You're going to have to prove it. I won't invest my money in anything that might be worthless." Parker's hands twitched. "How are you going to prove it's legitimate?"

"I have something planned." Jonas lifted a leather bound book from a desk drawer, the cover cracked and aged. "A demonstration is scheduled for this evening at 8:00." He gazed up at Parker. "Are you familiar with the creature's abilities? This book describes its powers in great detail."

"You don't need to read anything to me. I know the stories," Parker snapped. "Look, I've got a government contract and crew of men waiting to go to south Texas and work the oil fields. They're going to need protection. If this thing is real, I want it."

"Ah, yes indeed, the precious black gold. There is still a huge demand for petroleum." Jonas glared at him. "However, Mr. Parker, there are other potential buyers. Each one wants to ensure the protection of their workforce, and a ghoul is the perfect tool to ensure they are protected in these dire times." Jonas pulled a bottle of dark liquid from his desk drawer, then filled a long-stemmed glass.

"It needs to sit for a moment, so I can enjoy the fragrance." He held the goblet under his nose. "You'll have an opportunity to bid on the creature this evening at the Pavilion. Now, if you'll excuse me, it's closing time, I've been up all night and I'm tired." The chair creaked under his weight as he rose to his feet, ushering Parker toward the door. "I think you should arrive early for the presentation. All your doubts will be erased once you see this creature in action." He gulped the contents greedily, wiping a red residue from his lips.

"The government needs fuel, to mobilize the military to destroy the zombies. Just tell me how much," Parker demanded.

"Excuse me, Mr. Parker?" The merchant's brow wrinkled. "What did you say?"

"Look, Jonas, I know you enjoy all your bullshit flowery talk, but give me a number, a bottom line. How much for the ghoul? I'll buy it sight unseen." Parker lingered inside the threshold.

Jonas smiled. "Grant me this small indulgence, sir. It's a failing I have. Mr. Parker, it's only good business to allow as many interested parties as possible to have an opportunity to bid on this fantastic creature." He swirled his glass, watching the remaining liquid spin around the interior. "If you need it that desperately, I'll expect to see you at the Pavilion tonight." Jonas patted his back.

Parker's lips thinned to a firm white line, contrasting with his flushed cheeks. Jonas only sold his most highly treasured items at the Pavilion. "I'll be there." He turned, storming through the doors and into the sunlight. The glass doors slowly closed behind him.

Jonas turned the bolt, locking the doors and closing the shades. He stood straight, and the pot belly and stooped shoulders vanished. "People are like rabbits, dashing in every direction and getting nowhere," he mumbled, striding toward the rear of the store.

The large room buzzed with whispered voices. A small crowd of thirty, well-dressed men and women sat anxiously in the plush seats. They sipped champagne and cocktails, staring at the tall Plexiglas enclosure, waiting for the excitement to begin.

Jonas slowly made his way through the audience. His antique ivory cane, made from an elephant's tusk, tapped on the tile floor. He shook hands with old acquaintances and business associates. He embraced all the women, complimenting each on their fashionable attire, beautiful hairstyles and flawless cheekbones.

He waddled to the center dais, reserved for the master of ceremonies. He banged the cane on the oak desk top, signaling the voices to silence. Jonas relished the spotlight, embraced it at every opportunity. The thought of this crowd of millionaires, the most powerful, influential people in the world, fawning over his every movement, hanging on his every word, filled him with pride.

Jonas pulled the cork from a long-necked bottle. He sniffed at the stopper. He closed his eyes, enjoying the moment. He slowly filled the waiting glass, taking a small sip of the reddish liquid.

"Ladies and gentlemen," the small microphone hidden in the framework of his elaborate desk amplified his voice. "Tonight I am offering a rare commodity for sale, one of a truly unusual and exotic species. Only a few of these magnificent creatures are currently surviving in the world."

He paused to let his words take effect. The entire room grew silent for his oratory to continue. "Tonight, the Emporium is offering a ghoul. Yes, ladies and gentlemen, a genuine ghoul. I know many of you are skeptical of this claim, therefore, I've arranged a demonstration to erase any doubts you may harbor." His eyes locked with Parker's for an instant.

A sliding door opened at the snap of his fingers. An odor of rot and decay wafted through the opening. A large zombie, its face shrunken and pasty, a jagged bone protruded through the rotted flesh below the shoulder, shambled through the opening. It stumbled across the floor, salivating at the sight of the seated audience. It collided into the clear barrier.

"I know him, that's Everett Chambers!" A petite blonde woman in the third row jumped to her feet. "He's supposed to get married next week. What happened to him?"

"Yes, Miss Howard, you're correct. However, matrimonial bliss will not be in Mr. Chambers' future. He and his future bride fell victim to an unfortunate attack on Interstate 40 when his car broke down. He was bitten two weeks ago, and as you can see, the zombie genes have achieved dominance. Fortunately for his future wife, she was destroyed during the capture."

Chambers pawed at the thick glass barrier; saliva drained from his open mouth. A series of grunts issued from stiff, unused vocal cords.

"The prize each and every one of you is seeking was apprehended a month ago in Saudi Arabia. He killed three of my men during the apprehension. They succeeded in smuggling him out of the country a week later. He arrived at the Emporium this morning." Jonas paused for a sip, wiping the corners of his mouth with a silk hanky.

His eyes again met Parker's again. "At first glance, he might be mistaken for a zombie in the early stages of the change. But why should I continue to speak, when his actions can speak far louder than my words." He snapped his fingers once more, and a second section of wall slid aside.

A nude, man-sized figure jumped through the opening. It moved slowly to the center of the enclosure, its misshapen head tilted upward, sniffing the air. White thin strands of wispy hair adhered tenaciously to its skull. The ash-gray skin stretched tightly over its bones. A deep set of oversized eyes scanned the enclosure, taking in the audience beyond the protective glass.

The gaunt face wrinkled in a snarl. It squatted on its haunches, the claw-tipped hands held away from its side. A stream of foul, ammonia-tainted urine sprayed from its penis.

"My men nicknamed him Benedict, in honor of one of the men he killed. He's currently marking his new territory." Jonas provided a running commentary. Several patrons turned their heads and coughed, as the foul odor spread throughout the amphitheater.

The ghoul's eyes fastened on the slow moving zombie. It leaped across the space separating the two. Sharp claws buried in the putrid flesh of Chambers' shoulder, ripping through the muscle to the bone. Dagger-like teeth sank into the neck, ripping a mouthful of flesh away.

"Look at the speed. It strikes with the quickness of a cobra." Jonas sounded like a proud father.

Benedict swallowed the fist-sized chunk whole, his hands clamped down on Chambers' skull, squeezing the temples. The zombie pawed at Benedict's face to no avail. Thick, rope-like tendons bulged along the ghoul's pale arms. Its jagged teeth gritted together. Thick, yellow mucus dripped from Chambers' nose; his forehead crunched as his eyes popped from his skull.

"Witness the ferocity of the attack." Jonas paused to sip from the goblet. "Stare in awe at the pure, unadulterated savagery of his actions."

A loud crack echoed through the large room like a gun shot. Chambers' head collapsed inward. A fountain of yellow pus shot into the air, dripping from the ghoul's hands and arms. The zombie quivered in Benedict's grasp. The ghoul ripped the right arm from the shoulder and let the body fall to the floor. Sharp teeth tore the meat from the bone, swallowing the pieces.

Jonas again sought out Parker, staring at him. "For those of you who may still have doubts, I'll raise the ante." He again snapped his fingers. Immediately the door that Chambers passed through opened. Two more of the walking dead shuffled into the arena.

"Meet Gregory Miles and Sergeant Joseph Conrad. These two have been languishing in my cages for the last week, without any sustenance. They're starving for the taste of blood and flesh," Jonas said.

Benedict attacked swiftly, his claws disemboweling Miles. The dried entrails dropped to the floor around his shuffling feet, and the zombie dragged the length of intestine behind it like a tail. Benedict ripped the top from the monster's head, sucking out the brains in one gulp. The second zombie, wearing the tattered rags of a military uniform, sank its teeth into Benedict's forearm. A chorus of gasps rose from the enthralled audience.

"Ladies and gentlemen, there is no cause for alarm." Jonas motioned for silence. "The ghoul is unharmed. Benedict is not human and is therefore immune to the zombie's putrid, germ-filled bite."

In an act of retribution, Benedict took his time with Conrad. The ghoul enjoyed toying with the slow-witted zombie. It slashed at the walking corpse with its sharp fingernails, clawing and biting at the creature, and then dancing away from the zombie's slow, clumsy attacks.

Conrad fell to the floor, his Achilles tendon severed. He continued to snarl, reaching for Benedict. The ghoul stepped on the zombie's head, grinding his foot into the flesh and bone. It pressed downward with all its strength and weight. The soldier's head was smashed to pulp in a geyser of yellow gore. The thick mucus covered Benedict's foot.

"Now you'll witness the unique abilities of my prize," Jonas gloated.

The creature returned to its first victim. It dropped to all fours, eating at the zombie's stomach and intestines. The claw-tipped fingers ripped the liver and heart free. Benedict's jagged yellow teeth sank into the organs, tearing away large chunks. He devoured them rapidly.

The ghoul's form wavered. The face morphed, fatty tissues plumped the cheeks, the nose and ears reshaped, muscles and tendons grew and thickened. The dry dead skin turned a robust, healthy hue. A shock of dark hair grew from its head. It stood, now wearing the human form of Everett Chambers.

"Benedict can assume the form of anyone he's eaten. The memory is locked within the flesh. He becomes that person for a short time. He's now a combination of Sergeant Conrad and Mr. Chambers. All their personality traits and habits are transferred to the ghoul." Jonas pulled a small box from his suit. "And now a final touch. My tech staff contrived this interesting piece of equipment."

He held it up for the crowd to inspect. "This is a control box. With this the new owner will have complete control of Benedict." He pressed the red button in the center of the device. "Stop, return to your holding area. You will receive additional instructions shortly.”

The ghoul turned. Thick, repugnant gore dripped from its body, splattering the floor. With stiff, robotic movements, it strolled past the ravaged zombies and departed the arena.

Jonas stuffed the device into his pocket, flinging his arms open. “Ladies and gentlemen, you have witnessed the perfect defense against the zombie horde affecting us all. This one creature can kill an average of ten to fifteen of the walking dead each day. Couple that with your own security forces, and your workmen can perform any task in complete safety.”

Jonas sought out Parker, his eye’s locking with the oil man’s. “Please, keep in mind the endangered status of this creature. The opening bid of one million dollars is from Mr. Parker. Do I hear a million-five?”

A well-dressed man wearing a thousand dollar suit waved his paddle in the air. Jonas recognized him as Lyle Barton, a famous commodities trader from the United Kingdom. A plume of smoke rose to the ceiling from the large, Cuban cigar jammed between his teeth.

“Thank you,” Jonas said, acknowledging the bid. “Now, one million-seven?”

Parker waved his paddle, attracting the merchant’s attention.

“Mr. Parker’s bid is one million-seven. Do I hear two million?” Jonas smiled. “Two million, looking for two million dollars for this magnificent creature. Do I hear two million?”

Three paddles shot into the air simultaneously.

“I have three bids of two million dollars. One of you must bid two million-five.”

Parker sat alone in the empty amphitheater after the auction. The place reeked of stale cigar smoke and strong urine. His head rested in his hands. He stared down at his shoes, so self-absorbed in his own thoughts that he failed to hear Jonas approach.

“Quite an affair, wasn’t it, Mr. Parker?” Jonas tapped the floor with his cane, the ever-present wine glass gripped tightly in his hand.

"Yeah, well you and Barton just ruined my business." Parker glared at the merchant. "I'll never get a work crew in south Texas now. The zombies are thick down there."

"I have men scouring the globe at this very moment," Jonas said. "Perhaps they'll find another ghoul."

"What difference would it make?" Parker shook his head in disgust. "You'll just have another circus like today and double the price."

"Mr. Parker, it's just good business." Jonas sipped from the wine glass. "In these difficult times, everyone has to make a profit when the opportunity is present."

"That gadget of yours, how well does it work?" Parker ran his hand over his five o'clock stubble.

"This?" Jonas pulled the control device from his pocket. "This little marvel will keep the ghoul under complete control. My scientists attached a computer chip to Benedict's spine and hard-wired it to his brain. It can control his every move." He laughed. "After all, I can't have the ghoul killing its new owner and assuming his form."

"So you mean with this, you can sic the ghoul on the dead and ignore the workmen?" Parker stared up at Jonas. "He's like an attack dog?"

"Exactly, Mr. Parker, that's exactly what he is." Jonas said. "A ten million dollar attack dog, and completely in the handler's control."

"I really could have used Benedict in Texas." Parker slowly climbed to his feet. He slumped against the back of the chair, looking like a weary, bone-tired man. "Still, I may manage to pull a crew together. I'll have to pay triple wages. And there's always some joker who wants to take his family along. Can you imagine taking the wife and kids into a war zone?"

"I shudder to think about such things." Jonas quivered, shaking his head. "My existence revolves around the finer things in life. I have fifty men on staff to see to my safety. They patrol my estate twenty-four hours a day, searching out any interloper, whether human or zombie that manages to get inside the walls. They have orders to deal with all intruders in a most callous manner."

"Then why not keep Benedict for yourself?" Parker shrugged. "He could provide security at far less cost than all those men."

Jonas smiled. "Profit, profit is my motivation, and even after my expenses I'll clear over five million on this enterprise." He tipped the wine glass to his lips. "With that I can hire a lot of security."

"That must be some good stuff. I never see you without that glass." Parker said.

"It's my own special blend, made just for me, to my exact specifications, by an old gentleman in France. I receive a shipment weekly." Jonas turned toward the exit. "Time to go, Mr. Parker, and try not to look so glum. I'm sure things aren't as dour as you let on. You'll find a way out of your current difficulty."

"I believe I already have." Parker snatched the ivory cane from the plump man's grasp. He brandished it high above his head.

Jonas swiveled, reaching for a chair to regain his balance. The wine glass fell from his hand, shattering on the polished floor. The dark liquid spread across the mirrored surface. The merchant scowled at Parker, scarlet spreading up his face. "What is the meaning of this?" he shouted.

The heavy white cane smashed into his head and Jonas dropped to the floor. He fell onto his back, resembling a large sea turtle trying to regain its feet.

"Parker, what are you doing? Have you lost your mind?" he gasped.

"I'm losing my company, I'm losing my patience, and I've lost my last bit of restraint!" Spittle flew from Parker's lips. His eyes bulged to the point of bursting. "I'm taking what I want. Do you hear me, you fat bag of guts? I'm taking what I want." The cane whipped through the air, striking Jonas above the left eye, splitting the skin around the brow, blood pouring out of the wound.

The pudgy man folded his arms in front of his face to protect it. "Don't do this, Parker! It's not good business. You can't get away with it!"

"You ignorant bastard! I'm gonna let your pet eat you, and then I'll walk out of here with you as my escort." The cane cracked and shattered under the force of the last blow, littering the floor in a half moon around the merchant's head.

"You can't get away with this," Jonas mumbled around his blood. "You can't get away with this."

"I've already gotten away with it." Parker rummaged through the merchant's pockets. His hand closed on the control box. The suit ripped as he pulled it free. "With this I'll have complete control over your ghoul." A nightmarish smile split Parker's face.

"You're going to regret this," Jonas muttered. "Mark my words. You're going to regret this."

"Shut-up!" Parker screamed. "How do you work this damned thing?" His fingers stabbed the multi-colored buttons, trying to figure the correct sequence. "Come here, damn it, come here."

The hidden door slid open. Benedict walked through the opening, still wearing the guise of Everett Chambers. "That's it," Parker whispered. "Come on over here."

Benedict stopped at the Plexiglas shield.

"Stop," the merchant ordered. "Did you think I'd possess any creature I couldn't control?" Jonas clambered to his feet. The deep cut above his eyebrow stopped bleeding. Parker gazed in astonishment as the slash grew together and sealed within seconds, leaving no mark.

Parker's eye's widened to the size of half dollars. "How are you doing this? Damn it, how are you doing this?"

Jonas brushed the elbows and knees of his expensive suit. "Mr. Parker, things are not always what they seem. My family, due to necessity, has become adept at hiding in plain sight."

He stood straight and tall. The pot belly disappeared, leaving the suit hanging loosely on his frame. His face narrowed and a shock of blonde hair sprouted from his bald head. He towered above Parker. "I come from a long line of successful entrepreneurs. For centuries my family has honed our business savvy, building our empire. We've always managed to show a profit in the most difficult times. The exotic has always been our stock and trade. We barter in the darkest desires that cloud the minds of mere humans and mar their souls."

Parker's hands curled into fists. He swung a clumsy blow at the merchant's face. Jonas caught the hand and squeezed. "Resistance is useless, only a handful of humans can do battle with me. Only they understand the extent of my powers, and you are not among their number."

Parker dropped to his knees, as the bones in his hand cracked and popped. His face wrinkled in agony. "What are you?" he shrieked. "How can you do this?"

"I would think that's obvious." He released Parker's broken hand. His canines elongated, extending below the lower lip.

Parker clutched the injured limb to his chest. "I've got to know, what are you?"

"Mr. Parker, I am one of the undead. "The wine that concerned you so is blood, harvested for me weekly by a trusted associate. I demand only the finest liquid refreshments." His hands closed on Parker's jacket and he lifted him above his head as if he were weightless.

"Now it appears I own an oil company." He tossed Parker over the transparent wall. The oil man fell in a heap with the snap of bones. "Feed, Benedict," Jonas said. "Your meal is waiting."

Parker scrambled to his feet, his right arm hanging uselessly at his side. He raced around the enclosure, cradling the wounded limb. "Jonas, please, don't kill me! I have millions! They're yours if you let me go!" His face pressed against the glass as he begged for his life. "Please don't kill me!"

"Mr. Parker, I have all your millions now. While I'm sure Mr. Barton will be disappointed at the loss of Benedict, I can soothe over any problems that may occur. After all, it's just good business." The light reflected from his prominent fangs.

Benedict's feral eyes fastened on Parker. A line of saliva dripped from the ghoul's open mouth and the lips thinned, displaying a line of jagged teeth with bits of meat dangling from the incisors. Benedict advanced toward the oil man, moving slowly, seemingly taunting his trapped prey. Yellow-crusted hands reached for Parker's throat.

Jonas showed a toothy smile as Benedict grabbed Parker and sank stained teeth into the oil man's neck, the blood squirting out to splash the Plexiglass wall.

Minutes later, with the oil man dead, Benedict began to take on Parker's appearance.

"Yes indeed, it's only good business."

MONSTER DETECTIVES 3: THE NEXT, NEXT CASE

ANTHONY GIANGREGORIO/ REBECCA BESSER

"**D**amn it, Zack, you got blood all over the carpet!" Frankie yelled from outside my office. "This is coming out of your cut of the payroll this month!"

"Sorry, Frankie!" I called as I chomped on my liver and kidney salad. My human liver and kidney salad, if you're curious. Hey, fish gotta swim, birds gotta fly and zombies gotta eat.

"Sorry, nothing," Frankie yelled back. "That's not gonna clean the carpet!"

I sighed. The same old thing over and over again.

Frankie is my partner in our detective agency. We're the Monster Detectives and if it's strange or unusual, it's right up our alley. Frankie is our defacto leader, and though I normally don't mind, sometimes he can be annoying.

My other partner, Vinnie, is at least a little more civilized. He doesn't yell and he usually stays out of my way, well, at least during the day. See, Vinnie is a vampire, and though he can move about in the day with numerous coats of sunscreen, he usually likes to sleep in, at least until the sun goes down.

I was in my office enjoying my lunch when a package arrived in the mail. Frankie dropped it off after yelling at me, his deep frown looking as if it would fall off his green-tinted face. I swear, sometimes he gets so angry I think the bolts in his neck are going to simply pop out.

With a simple, "This came for you." Frankie dropped the package on my desk and stomped out, shaking the pictures on the walls as he left.

I put down my salad and studied the package. It was wrapped in a plain brown wrapper with clear packaging tape. There was no return address. The name on the address was mine, Zack Smithfield.

Curious as to who would send me a package, I opened it slowly, not trusting whatever it might be.

I should give you some background on myself.

I'm a zombie, for one thing, the only one of my kind as far as I know.

It happened over twenty years ago when I was in Haiti on vacation. I would like to tell you more, but to tell you the truth, I really don't know much more than that.

One night I went to bed in my hotel room and when I awoke once more, I found myself buried alive in a coffin.

Like a cliché from a bad movie, I dug myself free of the grave, and spitting dirt, I erupted from the earth as if I was a newborn baby leaving the womb.

I don't know how long I stumbled around in the jungle, but eventually my faculties returned and I still remembered who I was.

Other than a penchant for eating human body parts and having an overripe smell of rotting meat, I'm still pretty much me. I know my way around a computer and have superior strength, but usually I try to downplay my attributes around my two partners. They seem to like me acting dumb...like a zombie, I guess, and so far I haven't felt any reason to try and change their minds to who I truly am.

"I can't believe it," I whispered as I pushed aside the Styrofoam packing peanuts to reveal a framed photograph. Something about the picture seemed familiar, and after staring at it for a moment, I remembered with a jolt what I was looking at.

It was Haiti. More specifically, it was the field and building I'd seen in the moonlight as I'd pulled myself out of my grave.

Why would someone send me this?

Frowning, I searched through the box to see if there was any indication as to who sent it to me, or why. I found nothing else.

"What're you frowning about, meat bag?" Vinnie asked from the doorway in a teasing tone. Ever since we'd come back from our last case he seemed more relaxed and inclined to joke around.

I jumped, knocking the last of my salad onto the floor. I winced as I watched the blood-red juices soak into the carpet.

Well, I thought, *at least it happened before the carpet was cleaned or replaced so Frankie couldn't yell at me again.*

"I...uh," I stammered, trying to focus again on the picture I held in my rotting hands. "Frankie brought me this package and the only thing in it is a framed photograph of where I woke up a zombie."

"Let me see," Vinnie said, stepping into my office and holding his hand out to take the picture.

I handed it to him with a shrug. "There was nothing else in the box, and there's no return address."

"Interesting," Vinnie said, sniffing the picture. "Is this the box?"

I nodded yes, and nudged the box closer to the far side of the desk.

He lifted it and sniffed it too.

Finally, he turned his full attention to what he held in his hands. He studied it and then looked at me sharply. "The people, they're zombies. Didn't you notice?"

"What?" I asked while standing and hitting my leg on the sharp corner of the open top drawer of my desk, slicing off a chunk of flesh and meat. "Damn it," I growled, looking down at what I'd done. "Hold on!"

Opening the offending drawer some more, I reached inside and retrieved my super glue, quickly applying a generous slathering and then wrapping some box tape around my leg to hold it in place until it dried.

When I looked up, I noticed Vinnie was watching me with a bemused expression on his face. I know my physical 'maintenance' sometimes disgusted him, but I'm at least grateful he doesn't say anything about it.

"What do you mean they're zombies?" I asked, taking the photo from him. I squinted and angled the frame to get a better look at it, but the shot was taken too far away for me to see any of the people in it clearly.

Vinnie sighed and rolled his eyes. "Don't you have a magnifying glass or something?"

"Yes," I said. "I think so."

I rummaged about in the drawer that was still open, looking for the magnifying glass.

"Oh!" I exclaimed, reaching deep into the drawer.

"Find one?" Vinnie asked expectantly.

His expression soon turned to a frown of disgust when my hand reappeared from the drawer holding a severed human finger. I grinned and stuck it between my teeth, chewing on it as if it was a large piece of beef jerky while I kept looking for the 'expected' object.

"Here it is," I said, shutting the drawer with the magnifying glass in my hand. "I knew it was in there somewhere, I just wasn't expecting a treat!"

Chewing thoughtfully on the finger, I examined the photo closely. Vinnie was right; every single individual in the photo was a zombie.

"I think we should tell Frankie," Vinnie said, pushing the intercom button on my phone so fast I couldn't even get a word out to stop him. Sometimes his quick movements and enhanced senses piss me off.

"What?" Frankie barked through the intercom. "I'm on the phone with the carpet people...again! This better be good."

"We might have a new case," Vinnie said, holding down the response button. "Zack got something...interesting in the mail."

There was a long pause. "You mean in that package I gave him?"

"Yes."

"Okay, I'll be there in a minute."

I was still magnifying the photo, wondering who would send it to me and why, when I heard Frankie's heavy footfalls coming into my office.

"What's up?" he asked.

Vinnie snatched the photo away from me and handed it to Frankie. "They're all zombies!"

Frankie squinted at the picture, because, of course, he couldn't see the figures in it any better than I could. He stepped around the desk toward me, holding his hand out for the magnifying glass. His foot bumped into the bowl on the floor that was laying on its side, the blood now fully absorbed into the carpet. He frowned, looked down and then up at me with a clenched jaw. It was one of those moments I mentioned earlier. I thought for sure the bolts were going to fly out of his neck. His green face started to turn red.

"Hey," I said with a half smile. "It was an accident, and at least it happened *before* the carpet people came to replace it!"

He didn't say anything, just stood there looking at me like he was ready to rip me into pieces just for the fun of it. Grabbing the magnifying glass from my hand, he instead turned his attention to the picture.

"Do you know where it was taken?" Frankie asked it a stilted voice.

I could tell he was still mad. "Haiti. It's where I woke up as a zombie. I remember the house, even though I'd only seen it once, at night. The symbols painted on it make it very distinct."

Frankie nodded. "Do you know what they mean?"

"No," I said with a sigh. "I just opened it when Vinnie walked in. I haven't had time to do any research."

He stood silently for a moment, examining the markings under magnification. The only sound in the room was the grinding of my teeth on the bone of the finger I was eating. With a slurp that was insanely loud, I removed the last of the skin and flesh from the appendage, and noticed Frankie's jaw tighten again.

"I'll take this back to my office," Frankie growled, not looking at me. "You clean up this mess the best you can, I don't want the carpeting crew to find any parts this time. You do remember how much extra it cost to keep them quiet last time, don't you? You know, normal people ask questions when there's a half gallon of blood on the carpet you want replaced."

With that he stormed out. Vinnie followed him as they discussed the best course of action for this 'case.'

I chewed on the finger bones for a moment, looking down at the carpet. With a shrug, I removed the bones from my mouth, slowly knelt down, and started sucking the blood out of the carpet. It was a bit fuzzy, but still fresh and I hated to let it go to waste.

When I had sucked all I could out of the rug, I sat back down, now regretting what I'd done. Have you ever tasted carpet fresh and blood mixed together? Believe me, it's not that great.

With nothing to do I examined the box the photo came in, but there were no clues that I could find. Finally, I stood up and went to Frankie's office to see what he was doing.

Frankie looked up as I walked in. "Ah, there you are, Zack, I was about to call you."

"Did you find anything?"

"Yes, I did. I did a Web search online for the symbols on the side of the house." He stopped talking as he looked at his laptop screen and I waited for him to continue.

When he didn't I said, "And?"

"Huh? Oh, and I found the same symbols associated to some kind of death cult which has its home in a small village about ten miles from Port au Prince." He searched the page that was on his laptop. "It says this cult believes that death is the eternal freedom and that to see God—or what they think is God—you need to die and then come back. But it gets better. I went to another site where there was a message forum and there's been a lot of chatter this past year about the cult and zombies. They say the leader—a Baron Zemedi—has figured out a way to make real zombies. Not the kind where people are in a trance, but honest-to-God zombies, like you. Of course most people say it's all a joke and there's a lot of fighting back and forth about it."

I felt my legs go weak and I sat down in one of Frankie's extra office chairs. There was no true reason for my legs to feel like that but the mind is a powerful thing. The revelation of what Frankie found was like a blow to my chest by a giant fist. It wasn't a coincidence, this was intentional. Someone wanted me to know this. After all, with just a quick Web search, Frankie had found all the information that would have me going in the right direction.

Still, who was it that sent me that photo and the clue?

I decided it didn't matter. If I could find out how I'd became a zombie, then that was where I was going.

I stood up and began to walk out of the office but Frankie called after me. "Zack, where are you going?"

"To Haiti," I said flatly. "That's where I'll get the answers I want."

"Haiti? Are you nuts? You can't just go..." Frankie began but I cut him off with a wave of my hand, my palm aimed at him.

"I can do what I want and I'm going. I need to find out how I came to be like this and Haiti is the best chance of that."

"But surely this is some kind of trap or something. Be reasonable, Zack. Someone sent you that for just this reason. You can't just got flying halfway around the..."

I cut him off again, "Frankie, I appreciate the sentiment but I'm going, now please, just drop the subject."

As I turned to walk out, I was blocked by Vinnie.

"You're not going alone, meat bag. We're coming too."

"You don't have to do that, Vinnie," I said. "I'll be fine on my own."

I knew with his heightened hearing he'd heard every word between me and Frankie.

Vinnie shrugged. "That may be but we're going anyway. We're a team, meat bag, and like it or not, we look out for one another. If this is something important to you, then we're going. Right, Frankie?"

Frankie looked up from his laptop. "Yeah, I heard you; of course we'll all go." He typed for a moment and then sat up straighter. "While you two were talking, I booked us a private charter. It's going to dig into our expense account but..." He shrugged his wide shoulders. "If it's important to Zack then it's fine."

I suddenly felt my dead heart filling with pride for these two monsters that called me their friend.

"Thanks, guys, this means a lot."

"Oh please," Vinnie said with a wave of his hand, "This isn't all about you. I just want to go to Haiti."

I knew he was just trying to be modest and I nodded, not wanting to make a scene. "I'm going to go pack," I said and slid past Vinnie.

The vampire looked at the Frankenstein monster and his right eyebrow went up in curiosity. "Now what the hell does a zombie need to pack on a trip?"

In no time I was ready to go. I packed a cooler with everything I would need—kidney, liver, bags of human eyeballs, blue and brown. Eyeballs were like M&M candies to me, and each color tasted different. Blue ones are my favorite.

Vinnie walked over when I took everything out to reorganize the cooler to see if I could get a severed hand to fit.

"Where do you get all that stuff anyway?" he asked. "Human parts aren't easy to come by, if you know what I mean."

I shrugged. "I know a guy who knows a guy. I don't ask questions."

Frowning down into the cooler, I was wondering how I was going to get everything in. With a sudden grin, I took out one of the bags of eyes and inserted the hand. It fit—pardon the pun—like a glove. After putting the lid on the cooler, I opened the plastic bag with the eyes and popped one in my mouth, chewing appreciatively. The juices exploded in my mouth and I could have purred with delight, but Vinnie was still in the room so I controlled myself. He was looking at me like I was crazy, so I held out the bag and raised my eyebrows.

"Want one?"

The look of disgust on his face almost made me laugh out loud. I loved to torment him.

"No thank you," he said flatly, glancing back at the cooler. "You know a guy who knows a guy, huh? Sounds complicated."

I tossed another eye into my mouth, biting into it sharply, enjoying the loud squishing/popping noise. "Did you want something? Or were you just checking on my snacks?"

Vinnie shook his head like he'd just remembered what he'd come in for. "The plane will be on the tarmac in a half hour, that's just enough time for us to get there. Are you ready?"

I looked around, shoving the last three eyeballs into my mouth and putting the plastic bag in the trash. I said around a mouthful of slimy juices, "Yeah, I'm ready."

Lifting the cooler easily, I followed Vinnie out to the old limousine we used for transportation. The street lights reflected off the hood of the limo and I saw that Frankie was already waiting in the back.

"You bringing a coffin?" I asked Vinnie as I stowed my cooler in the trunk of the car.

"I shipped it out as soon as Frankie told me he'd chartered the plane," he said. "I didn't want to risk it not making it in time."

"Good idea," I said with a smile. "You driving?"

Vinnie glanced at Frankie in the back. "I guess so."

I clapped like I was a rich, stuck-up politician. "Then get us to the airport 'James,' and make it snappy." Without looking at him, I turned and climbed in with Frankie.

Vinnie frowned, clearly annoyed and not finding my joke amusing, but he got in and started the engine. Seconds later, we were in traffic and on our way.

We reached the small, private airport in silence. I had too much on my mind to make small talk and Frankie was absorbed in his laptop. Vinnie was just Vinnie. He never was much for small talk in normal circumstances and he seemed to want to concentrate on driving.

The plane took off almost immediately after we boarded. The sun was just starting to lighten the horizon, so Vinnie got into his coffin, joking that he could use the extra rest with all the work we'd be doing once we reached Haiti. I knew he was right. It was going to be long nights and days for us.

It always was when we were on a case.

As I sat by the window, looking out over the world, everything felt unreal. Bending down and picking up the small backpack I'd brought with me, I slid my hand inside. Sure enough, the framed photo was still in there, bringing reality to everything. Frankie's constant tapping on his laptop keys soon lulled me into a quiet calm as I tried to clear my head.

Though I didn't sleep, I've learned to meditate to pass the time and I did so now.

Darkness, complete and utter darkness. No air movement at all. Coughing and choking I clawed around me, finding only a tight pine box. Grunting and moaning, trying not to panic, I tried to remember what had happened, how I'd gotten here. Nothing. My thoughts were sluggish and tinged with dread. In a fit of anger, I punched out at the wood that encased me and was rewarded with the distinct sound of splintering. With a glimmer of hope, I struck out again, and was pleased to hear the wood weak-

ening more, but displeased when gritty dirt started trickling through the small cracks.

Buried alive! my brain screamed and the panic I'd kept at bay took over. Violently, I slammed both of my fists against the coffin, pulling the broken wooden pieces inside with me and turning my head to keep from inhaling dirt. I felt slivers of the pine slide into my flesh, but amazingly it didn't hurt. Neither did my fists from punching through.

Curious, I thought, but didn't stop to explore these strange phenomena. I had to get out...get free!

I removed more wood until the hole was large enough for me to wiggle out. I filled the casket with the dirt I dug away, hoping I was going to reach the surface soon. After a while with no light or air, I started to wonder if I'd been buried upside down and was digging myself deeper, but I had been lying on my back, so I had to be facing up

Didn't I?

Another curiosity I didn't stop to contemplate was that my lungs weren't burning and starved for oxygen. But again, I didn't stop to think about it. I needed to get out and fast. I dug with desperation, having strange flash backs of a fire and a man's face. It had been painted with a white skull, surrounded by black. I couldn't tell if the man's skin was that dark, or if it too, had been painted. Every time my mind would project one of these images, my body would start to shake and I had to stop digging for a moment, causing my escape to take even longer, but I was determined to break free.

When I'd almost given up hope of ever getting to the surface— the visions coming more and more frequently, disabling me—my hand finally found the outside world. The breeze against my skin gave me renewed energy, and I thrust my other arm through the small hole in the earth as well, clawing at dry grass clumps, wiggling my body, emerging from the ground as if I was a baby escaping the womb.

I lay panting for what seemed like forever. The air moved in and out of my lungs, but didn't warm me. I could feel the heat of it as it entered, and then left, but around me all was cold. I looked down at myself, and in the light of the full moon, my skin looked pale white. I couldn't tell if it was the lighting or if I'd actually turned this color.

Suddenly, the strongest vision yet assaulted my brain, burning against my skull. I rolled over, thrashing, crying out in pain. The man was there again, chanting, waving something in front of my face, then there was a sharp, stabbing pain, and the coldness came.

As suddenly as the pain began, it stopped. All I could think about was eating. I craved fresh, raw meat. Instinctively I knew that not just any meat would do, it would have to be human.

I tried to stand, but fell repeatedly down onto the dry, hard-packed ground. My body wasn't moving like it used to. Each and every movement seemed to take tremendous effort. I felt like a one-year-old trying to walk for the first time. Eventually, I made it to my feet and shuffled forward.

The moon lit the world around me, allowing me to see clearly for a good distance. Sugar cane fields stretched away from me on both sides. Ahead was a structure, a broken down wooden shack with steel sheeting for a roof and beyond it a house with symbols painted on its side. I slowly stumbled closer. There were strange markings on the house, but my eyes were blurry and I couldn't make them out. Stumbling closer, I tried to focus, hoping I would find help here. While I watched, the door of the small, wooden shack started to open, but it was pitch black inside. I couldn't see anyone or anything, but the deep rumble of a man's laughter drifted out to me.

"It's about time you woke up," the voice said, with amusement.

"Zack, Zack!" an agitated voice barked. "Wake up. Snap out of it!"

"Huh?" I said, sitting forward quickly, opening my eyes. "What? What did you say?"

Frankie stood over me, "It's about time you came to. I've been shaking you for more than a minute. The plane's getting ready to land, buckle up."

Without waiting for a reply, he turned and walked back to his seat, sat down, and quickly buckled his own safety belt.

My hands were trembling as I fastened my belt. Frankie echoing the words in my vision, for some reason, scared me. I didn't understand what was going on. I'd never remembered digging myself out of the grave before. Hell, I've never had such a vivid memory like that since becoming a zombie.

I could still see the man's face and feel the panic of being buried alive. Of course, at that point I hadn't known I was one of the undead. Glancing around, I hoped no one noticed my nervousness. Vinnie was up, I noted with surprise. He was already shrouded in a light-colored long sleeve shirt, tan corduroy pants, heavy brown boots, and a wide brimmed ivory colored hat. I'd asked him once why he didn't wear black or other dark colors when he was out during the day, and he said it was because the dark colors attracted and absorbed the heat of the sun, and the light colors reflected it, which was what he wanted.

I could smell the many layers of sun screen he was wearing. It was slightly different from the usual scent, heavier somehow. I figured he was mixing it with something else to see if he could find something that worked better; he'd done it before.

Having a private plane was great. We didn't have to go through the hullabaloo at the airport. Customs was a simple one-person check and we'd used our contacts to arrange for a previous 'client' who worked at the airport to check us out, so we wouldn't have to answer a lot of questions. It was quick and painless. The man even arranged for Vinnie's coffin to be taken discreetly to our chosen hotel.

A taxi took us to our hotel. The driver kept glancing anxiously at Frankie, who'd donned sunglasses, a thick, hooded sweatshirt and dark sweatpants. We've found it's best if we disguise him as a boxer. With his size and the hoodie, he pulled it off well. He was still busy on his laptop. He'd joined the 'zombie cult' forum and was trying to make some friends and hopefully get some new leads. I don't know if it was working, but he'd been on the computer the entire trip.

The sounds and smells wafting on the air pulled and I felt the urge to get out and wander through the streets. I felt like I was coming home, but knew I wasn't. There was just something here that spoke to me on an instinctive level. It scared me. Mostly because no matter what I did, or thought, I couldn't get the laughing man from my vision out of my head.

"Bingo," Frankie said, grinning widely as we got out of the cab and walked into the hotel, the laptop in one of his ham-sized hands, looking more like a toy.

"What?" Vinnie asked.

"I just got our first contact here," Frankie said, trying to show Vinnie the laptop.

"How about we save that for when we get to our rooms," Vinnie said, nodding to the people crowding the foyer.

Frankie nodded and went back to typing.

Vinnie nudged my arm, drawing my attention back to the present. "Go to the bathroom and see if they have any air freshener spray. You're starting to really reek."

For the first time, I noticed the people around me covering their noses and edging away. I'd remembered my scarf, hat, and gloves, but I'd forgotten the Lysol. I nodded and found a bathroom as fast as I could. They didn't have any spray, but thankfully I'd tucked an unopened small aerosol can into my backpack before we'd left. I doused myself liberally, using the entire can. I hoped it did the trick in this insane heat.

By the time I retuned to the lobby, Vinnie and Frankie were waiting with keys to our rooms. We wove through the crowds of people with care, trying not to attract too much attention, but I knew we had to look strange all bundled up in heavy clothing in such hot weather.

"Once you two get settled," Frankie said urgently, "come and see me. We need to discuss our next move. We have plans tonight."

Vinnie raised one eyebrow, but just nodded and disappeared into the room beside Frankie's. Mine was across the hall. I let myself in and had a quick snack of another bag of eyeballs, realizing I hadn't eaten on the plane. It was the first time I'd gone that long without eating something in a long, long time. Things were really getting to me.

After freshening up with some scented spray I found in the bathroom—courtesy of the hotel—I made sure I looked as good as I could given the circumstances and went to see Frankie.

My two partners were waiting for me when I arrived in Frankie's room, and he started right in.

"I've made friends with someone that goes by the handle Zombie_Culture," Frankie said. "He lives here in Haiti and claims to be able to give people the 'full' zombie experience. It's a high dollar thing, apparently. I've arranged to meet him in a bar in a couple of hours. So, do what you have do to be presentable and we'll go and meet this guy. Hopefully he has the info we need. If not, maybe if we scare the crap out of him, he'll tell us who can."

I smiled at the grin that spread across Frankie's face. We didn't often try to scare people into giving us what we wanted or needed, but when we did, we had a lot of fun with it. I almost laughed out loud thinking about the look on the last man's face when Frankie had picked up a car and threatened to smash him with it. I knew the big green guy had a soft heart and would never seriously hurt someone he didn't have to, but the man we were talking to didn't. We'd gotten what we needed in the end and no one was hurt.

After a bit more briefing on what was going down, we went back to our rooms. I unwrapped and doused myself with the scented spray again, then re-wrapped. In no time, Frankie was pounding on my door, yelling to for me to get my undead ass moving.

The bar was somewhat close to the hotel, but we still took a cab. It was a seedy joint. Most of the patrons were locals who looked at us with only mild curiosity before turning their attention back to their drinks, which was their true interest of the evening.

We'd arrived early so we could get 'the lay of the land' as Frankie liked to say. We didn't wait long; our contact was also early.

"You UndeadMan2c?" a very dark skinned man asked Frankie in extremely accented English.

"Yeah, that would be me," Frankie said, standing and extending his hand. "You must be Zombie_Culture."

The man nodded, letting his eyes briefly travel over Vinnie and me. I noticed he took a double take of me, squinting as if doing so would allow him to see past the scarf and hat I was wearing.

"You want the Zombie Experience?" he asked with an amused, yet polite grin. "I can give it to you, but it will cost a lot of money. You bring the cash?"

Frankie grinned. "Sure, we have the money, but I need more information before I give it to you. It's a lot of money we're talking about here, and I don't want to get conned, if you know what I mean."

"Oh, yes," the man said, almost nervous now. "I won't con you. I'll tell you all you want to know. Please, ask away."

Frankie motioned to the empty seat at the table, directly beside him. After the man sat, Frankie started asking a series of questions that seemed casual, but I knew he'd been working on them from the time we'd left his room until we arrived at the bar. It worked. The man told all, and we went on his little tour. It wasn't an up close tour by any means. We were hauled in wooden carts, pulled by donkeys to the hill overlooking the sugar cane fields from the photo, and the house as well. The man became very nervous when we hopped out of the carts and said we'd find our own way back, but once Frankie paid him, he just took off like demons were chasing him and that was the last we saw of him.

The sun was starting to set as we made our way around the sugar cane fields and closer to the dwelling. A small stand of stunted trees grew beside a small stream behind the house with the symbols on it, the same ones as in the picture I'd received.

We hid in the foliage and talked in low voices as we decided what to do next.

As the last rays of the sun slid behind the purple-painted horizon, Vinnie sighed and stretched a bit in the darkness, taking off his hat. With night falling he was in his element. As he did so, we heard a twig snap off to our right, and that's when we noticed them.

Ten zombies stood behind us in a semi-circle in a small glade, and when we turned the way we'd been facing, we found seven more were there as well. I couldn't believe they'd snuck up on us, I mean, we should have smelled them or something. But then again, we were all used to my smell so probably thought nothing of it. Now we were screwed.

Frankie squeezed his hands into fists. "Vinnie, Zack, you guys take the ones at our rear and I'll take the others."

I nodded that I was ready.

"Will do," Vinnie said as he prepared to jump into action. But before either of us could move, a loud voice cut through the forest, stopping us in our tracks.

"There will be no need for violence, gentlemen."

Frankie, Vinnie and I all turned as one to see a tall man in a dark black suit and hat step out from between the zombies that were behind us. He carried a dark mahogany cane with a lion's head for a handle. His skin was as black as night and though he spoke English clearly, his Haitian ancestry was apparent.

"I don't know who you three are, but you picked the wrong place to come to tonight."

Frankie stepped out of the brush, coming to his full height. "Baron Zemedi, I presume."

"Ah, my fame precedes me I see."

"No, not really, I just recognize you from the pictures on the internet."

"Yes, most unfortunate that. A spy managed to come in here and take some pictures. But though he escaped, I assure you he didn't live long after posting those pictures. But alas, the internet has a long memory and once there, it cannot be erased. Even death can't stop it." He pointed to Vinnie and myself. "You two, come out of there so I can see you better. And be quick or my slaves will deal with you."

"You mean your zombies," Vinnie said as he stepped out into the small glade with me by his side.

The moon was full and the glade was bathed in a dull yellow glow. When the baron saw Vinnie, he did nothing, but as I stepped into the pale light, the baron's face lit up with recognition.

"You!" Baron Zemedi said in surprise. "I don't believe it; you've come back to me."

"You know me?" I asked.

The baron nodded. "Of course I do. I made you what you are. You were one of my first, before I honed my skill. But something went wrong in the potion I gave you. You weren't bound to me like you should have been, and when I returned to your grave to raise you, I found you gone, the grave empty. You were the one that got away, but I see you finally came back to me...your master."

I stepped forward two paces, my hands curled into fists, an anger rising in me I didn't understand. "You're not my master and I'm no one's slave," I hissed. "Someone sent me a photo of this place and I came to find out what it means. What it has to do with me and my past."

"Ah, I see, perhaps one of my minions sent it to you when they discovered you still existed, but I assure you, it wasn't me." He waved to the zombies around him and they moved in closer. Frankie and Vinnie tensed for what would come next. "As you can see, I have perfected my magic and can now raise the dead at will. These souls were tourists, come here to get the 'full zombie experience.' I would say they have, wouldn't you?" He began to laugh, a maniacal laughter that told me and my partners the man was totally mad, despite his well-spoken words.

I knew then this man needed to die for the wholesale murder he'd committed, and his zombies—his creations—destroyed also. For years I'd thought I was the only one, it was time to make sure that belief was fact.

I pointed to the zombies. "Take them down," I said in a low voice so only Frankie and Vinnie could hear. "The baron's mine."

Frankie replied by letting out an animalistic roar and raising his arms into the air, his hands curled into ham-sized fists. He took five steps forward and brought them down on the first zombie, crushing the body as if it was made out of straw. Congealed blood and body parts went flying in all directions.

"You dare!" the baron yelled. "Get them, my slaves! Kill them all!"

As one group, the zombies attacked, swarming in on us. Vinnie was in action before I knew he was moving, a blur amongst the other figures. He zigged and zagged, taking heads off and gutting torsos. Intestines and organs spilled forth to splash on the ground, but the zombies felt no pain and could have cared less. Only the ones he beheaded ceased to fight.

Frankie was more mundane in his methods and he simply tore off arms and used them as bludgeons on the others. He had a severed arm in each hand and he used them like sledgehammers, cracking skulls and whacking heads until the arms were nothing but bloody stumps. When his weapons had been whittled down to the point they were useless, he dropped them and tore off two more from a fresh walking corpse. The armless zombie still tried to attack, biting at Frankie with its yellow teeth, but a few blows to the head with the arms knocked it down. With no arms it was hard for the ghoul to regain its footing, and as it tried to right itself, Frankie brought down one of his large boots on its torso, cracking its ribcage and flattening its spine. With his boot firmly entrenched in the quagmire of bodily tissue, he pulled it out, a sucking sound following it.

"Damn it, these are my good boots!" he yelled as he slammed his fist into the face of another zombie. The head imploded and he found he was now wearing the skull like a glove. He tore off the head from the ghoul's neck and used the skull like it was a brass knuckle. At least until it cracked and fell to the ground in bloody pieces.

Vinnie pulled a knife he'd been carrying and was using to devastating effect. As he dashed past zombies too fast to see, in his wake he left carved bodies and severed body parts.

The zombies didn't attack me and I assumed it was because I was one of the undead...like them. But Vinnie and Frankie weren't so lucky, and for every ghoul they put down, more were arriving.

As more zombies came out of the woods, I knew there was only one way to stop this before my friends were overwhelmed and killed.

I charged Baron Zemedi.

The baron had four zombies as his honor guard and they blocked my path to him. But though they were four to my one, I had an advantage over them.

I could think for myself.

As I charged at the baron, he called out to his four guardians and they moved in close to him and came at me. I dodged the first one's outstretched arms and went in to the next one. Wrapping my hands around its rotting skull, I tore the head clean off its shoulders. The headless body stumbled for a moment and then fell to the ground, the open wound leaking a dark liquid.

"Get him, you fools, stop him!" the baron yelled at his undead slaves, but they were no match for me.

I tore off heads and broke limbs until the four ghouls were lying in a pile, some still active, but with broken legs and arms they were helpless to stop me.

As the baron railed against me for destroying his slaves, I moved up to him much faster than any of his regular zombies.

He raised his cane and tried to bring it down on my head, no doubt wanting to crack open my skull, but I reached up and grabbed the cane in its downward swing. I then let it go and slid my hand down its shaft until I had the baron's wrist in my grip.

"How dare you lay hands on me! I'm your master! Let me go, I command you!" he yelled.

I replied by grabbing his other arm, now firmly trapping him in my grip.

"I'm not one of your slaves, Baron, I don't take orders from you," I snarled as I held on to the man as he fought to escape.

"I made you!" the baron screamed. "You can't hurt me! You are who you are now because of me! You're better than you ever were in life. Now you don't sleep, you're stronger and you will exist forever!"

"No one made me, Baron. I am who I am. I'm still me. I'm my own person." Before the baron could reply, I let his left arm go and I used my free hand to punch the baron's chest. The force of my blow sent my fist into the man's chest and my fingers forced their way through his ribcage until I found his beating heart.

Baron Zemedi gasped in shock and pain as he looked down to see my hand and a quarter of my arm inside his chest. Blood began to drip from his lips as he gasped, "You're nothing without me, you're nothing. Now that you know who you are, you will live to regret this."

"I doubt that very much," I hissed. As my fingers wrapped around his heart, I yanked my arm back, tearing the beating organ from his breast.

The baron stared at his still-beating heart in my bloody hand as his mouth opened and closed like a landed fish. Then his body shut down. His eyes rolled up into the back of his head and he slumped forward, voiding his bowels and bladder at the same time. I let his other arm go and he dropped to the dirt like a rag doll.

I looked at him for only a moment, then turned to see how my friends were doing.

Vinnie and Frankie were back-to-back, trying to hold off a horde of over twenty zombies.

But then, like a switch had been flicked, the zombies all stopped moving and slumped to the ground as if they had fallen asleep. They didn't move and I realized that with their master dead, whatever strange hold he had on them—upon their deaths—was lifted. They had truly returned to the peace of the grave for good.

It was then that I realized if this was so, then why was I still alive...so to speak. I decided one mystery at a time. One had been solved—my origin—I could wonder about the rest later.

Frankie and Vinnie were gathering themselves to leave as I walked over to them. I had to walk in a winding route to avoid stepping on bodies and assorted severed parts.

As I reached them, I took a bite out of the heart in my hand. It was warm and filled with blood and it tasted sweet...like victory.

Frankie frowned at me when he saw me munching on the organ.

"What?" I asked as I took another bite. "Why waste good meat."

My two partners laughed and both shook their heads at me. I grinned, showing my blood-red teeth and continued eating my snack.

Later, with the entire glade bathed in the cleansing heat of a bonfire to destroy the zombies and any other evidence, we headed back to our hotel to get cleaned up and then fly home.

For some unknown reason, I was still alive when the other zombies were dead upon the death of their master, and that bugged me.

But at least I now knew how I came to be and who I was.

And sometimes, that's all a zombie can hope for.

ABOUT THE WRITERS

Terry Alexander and his wife Phyllis live on a small farm in southern Oklahoma. They have three children and nine grandchildren. Terry has been published by Moonstone books, Static movement and Living Dead Press.

Jason Andrew lives in Seattle, Washington with his wife Lisa. By day, he works as a mild-mannered technical writer. By night, he writes stories of the fantastic and occasionally fights crime. As a child, Jason spent his Saturdays watching the Creature Feature classics and furiously scribbling down stories; his first short story, written at age six, titled 'The Wolfman Eats Perry Mason' was rejected and caused his Grandmother to watch him very closely for a few years. His fiction has appeared in dozens of anthologies such as Shine: An Anthology of Optimistic SF, Arkham Tales: Stories of the Legend Haunted City, and Frontier Cthulhu: Ancient Horrors in the New World. In 2007, Jason co-edited the fantasy anthology Into the Dreamlands. You can find out more about Jason at http://jasonbandrew.wordpress.com/

Rebecca Besser is a house wife and mother who lives in Ohio. Her writing has appeared in the Coshocton Tribune, Irish Story Playhouse, Spaceports & Spidersilk, joyful!, Soft Whispers, Illuminata, Common Threads, Golden Visions Magazine, and Stories That Lift. She also has short stories in multiple anthologies by Living Dead Press, where she is currently an editor, and a story in The Undead That Saved Christmas, a charity anthology.

Visit her site to learn more about her and her publications: www.rebeccabesser.com

Brandon Cracraft lives in the historic district of Tucson with his partner and a black cat in a house that predates Arizona's statehood. He has published articles on various subjects including role playing games, health food, and the occult.

David H. Donaghe lives and works in the high desert of southern California. In his spare time, David writes short stories and novels. He has had several short stories published in the past, four of which appear in other, Living Dead Press anthologies. David is currently enjoying life and working on his next novel. He invites you to follow him to Face Book and My Space, to join his reader network at www.authornation.com/MCRIDER and to check out his author web page at http://dhdonaghe.weebly.com/index.html

Anthony Giangregorio is the author and editor of more than 45 novels and anthologies, almost all of them about zombies.

His work has appeared in Dead Science by Coscomentertainment, Dead Worlds: Undead Stories Volumes 1-7, and Wolves of War by Library of the Living Dead Press. He also has stories in End of Days: An Apocalyptic Anthology Vol. 1-4, the Book of the Dead series Vol. 1-5 by LDP, Zombie Zoology by Severed Press, and two anthologies with Pill Hill Press.

He is also the creator of the popular action/zombie series titled Deadwater and his action/ horror novel Dead Rage is being optioned for a movie.

Check out his website at www.undeadpress.com.

John Grover is a dark fiction author residing in Massachusetts. He completed a creative writing course at Boston's Fisher College and is a member of the New England Horror Writers, a chapter of the Horror Writers Association.

Some of his more recent credits include Best New Zombie Tales Vol 1 by Books of the Dead Press, The Book of Cannibals by Living Dead Press, The Vermin Anthology, The Northern Haunts Anthology by Shroud Publishing, The Zombology Series by Library of the Living Dead Press, Morpheus Tales, Wrong World, The Willows, Alien Skin Magazine, Aurora Wolf and more.

He is the author of several collections, including the recently released Feminine Wiles, sixteen tales of wicked women as well as various chapbooks, anthologies, and more. Please visit his website www.shadowtales.com <http://www.shadowtales.com> for more information.

Dane T. Hatchell grew up in Baton Rouge Louisiana and has lived there all his life. In his youth he was a fan of old school horror movies, and a collector of magazines such as Creepy and Eerie. Now in his early fifty's, he is devoting his free time to writing to satisfy a lifelong passion. You can contact Dane at Enadious@gmail.com. Special thanks to Sarah Graves for her contributions as my copy editor.

Lorraine Horrell resides in Ireland. She has had twelve short horror stories published, with Pill Hill Press, Wicked East Press and Static Movement.

Kelly M. Hudson grew up in the wilds of Kentucky and currently resides in California. He has had numerous short stories published in many anthologies and has two novels available: The Turning, a zombie tale, from Living Dead Press, and Men of Perdition, available for download on Amazon.com. If you wish to contact Kelly or find links to other stories he's had published, please visit www.kellymhudson.com for further details.

Colin Maguire lives in Seattle, and is a Monster Kid - raised in the 1970's on Creature Features, Aurora models, Famous Monsters and Creepy and Eerie magazines. Born into this life being a Monster Kid, his parents told him that monsters were the first thing he was ever interested in (aside from commercial jingles, apparently). The first film his Dad took him to was "The Legend of Boggy Creek", which is a life-altering memory for him...but it was the movie "Jaws" which advanced him from solely drawing monster pictures into creative story writing. He has been writing horror ever since. This monster story is his latest.

Wakefield Mahon is a freelance writer, poet, and author of Wakefield-isms: The Writer's Inspiration Blog. His stories have appeared in publications by Folded Press, Softcopy Publishing and Living Dead Press. His latest project is the Way of the Sword fantasy series. The first book, Emerald Dreams, will be published next year."

Alan Spencer has published two novels, entitled, "The Body Cartel" (Damnation Books) and "Inside the Perimeter: Scavengers of the Dead" (Living Dead Press). Look for his work in many of the Living Dead Press anthologies, including "Love is Dead," "The Book of Cannibals," and "Book of the Dead 2," to a name a few. This fall, his story "Mother's Solace" will appear in the anthology "Toe Tags 2."

And check out the new Living Dead Press website,
Living Dead Press Presents
Filled with free fiction to read, movie trailers about our books and zombie pop culture, there's something for everyone, including interviews with LDP authors.

UNITED STATES OF ARMAGEDDON
by Jeffrey Thomas Crooms
THE END OF A COUNTRY!

America's enemies plot a sadistic plan to destroy the population and armed forces so they can swoop in and rule the country.

Terrorists called the Horsemen smuggle in a deadly biological weapon straight to the heart of the United States and release it.

The result is a land covered with corpses, bloated bodies strewn from sea to sea.

A few desperate survivors battle through the blighted landscape on a last ditch mission to save the country from total domination.

But the biological weapon has a side effect, one no one would have ever foreseen, one too unimaginable to even contemplate.

Welcome to the future. Welcome to the Unite States of _Armageddon_

BOOK OF THE DEAD
A ZOMBIE ANTHOLOGY VOL 1
ISBN 978-1-935458-25-8
Edited by Anthony Giangregorio

This is the most faithful, truest zombie anthology ever written, and we invite you along for the ride. Every single story in this book is filled with slack-jawed, eyes glazed, slow moving, shambling zombies set in a world where the dead have risen and only want to eat the flesh of the living. In these pages, the rules are sacrosanct. There is no deviation from what a zombie should be or how they came about. The Dead Walk.

There is no reason, though rumors and suppositions fill the radio and television stations. But the only thing that is fact is that the walking dead are here and they will not go away. So prepare yourself for the ultimate homage to the master of zombie legend. And remember... Aim for the head!

REVOLUTION OF THE DEAD
by Anthony Giangregorio
THE DEAD SHALL RISE AGAIN!

Five years ago, a deadly plague wiped out 97% of the world's population, America suffering tragically. Bodies were everywhere, far too many to bury or burn. But then, through a miracle of medical science, a way is found to reanimate the dead.

With the manpower of the United States depleted, and the remaining survivors not wanting to give up their internet and fast food restaurants, the undead are conscripted as slave labor.

Now they cut the grass, pick up the trash, and walk the dogs of the surviving humans.

But whether alive or dead, no race wants to be controlled, and sooner or later the dead will fight back, wanting the freedom they enjoyed in life.

The revolution has begun!

And when it's over, the dead will rule the land, and the remaining humans will become the slaves...or worse.

KINGDOM OF THE DEAD
by Anthony Giangregorio
THE DEAD HAVE RISEN!

In the dead city of Pittsburgh, two small enclaves struggle to survive, eking out an existence of hand to mouth.

But instead of working together, both groups battle for the last remaining fuel and supplies of a city filled with the living dead.

Six months after the initial outbreak, a lone helicopter arrives bearing two more survivors and a newborn baby. One enclave welcomes them, while the other schemes to steal their helicopter and escape the decaying city.

With no police, fire, or social services existing, the two will battle for dominance in the steel city of the walking dead. But when the dust settles, the question is: will the remaining humans be the winners, or the losers?

When the dead walk, the line between Heaven and Hell is so twisted and bent there is no line at all.

RISE OF THE DEAD
by Anthony Giangregorio
DEATH IS ONLY THE BEGINNING!

In less than forty-eight hours, more than half the globe was infected.

In another forty-eight, the rest would be enveloped.

The reason?

A science experiment gone horribly wrong which enabled the dead to walk, their flesh rotting on their bones even as they seek human prey.

Jeremy was an ordinary nineteen year old slacker. He partied too much and had done poorly in high school. After a night of drinking and drugs, he awoke to find the world a very different place from the one he'd left the night before.

The dead were walking and feeding on the living, and as Jeremy stepped out into a world gone mad, the dead spotting him alone and unarmed in the middle of the street,

he had to wonder if he would live long enough to see his twentieth birthday.

THE CHRONICLES OF JACK PRIMUS
BOOK ONE
by Michael D. Griffiths

Beneath the world of normalcy we all live in lies another world, one where supernatural beings exist.

These creatures of the night hunt us; want to feed on our very souls, though only a few know of their existence.

One such man is Jack Primus, who accidentally pierces the veil between this world and the next. With no other choice if he wants to live, he finds himself on the run, hunted by beings called the Xemmoni, an ancient race that sees humans as nothing but cattle. They want his soul, to feed on his very essence, and they will kill all who stand in their way. But if they thought Jack would just lie down and accept his fate, they were sorely mistaken.   He didn't ask for this battle, but he knew he would fight them with everything at his disposal, for to lose is a fate worse than death.

He would win this war, and he would take down anyone who got in his way.

THE WAR AGAINST THEM: A ZOMBIE NOVEL
by Jose Alfredo Vazquez

Mankind wasn't prepared for the onslaught.

An ancient organism is reanimating the dead bodies of its victims, creating worldwide chaos and panic as the disease spreads to every corner of the globe. As governments struggle to contain the disease, courageous individuals across the planet learn what it truly means to make choices as they struggle to survive.

Geopolitics meet technology in a race to save mankind from the worst threat it has ever faced. Doctors, military and soldiers from all walks of life battle to find a cure. For the dead walk, and if not stopped, they will wipe out all life on Earth. Humanity is fighting a war they cannot win, for who can overcome Death itself? Man versus the walking dead with the winner ruling the planet. Welcome to *The War Against Them*.

DEADTOWN: A DEADWATER STORY
B OOK 8

by Anthony Giangregorio

The world is a very different place now. The dead walk the land and humans hide in small towns with walls of stone and debris for protection, constantly keeping the living dead at bay.

Social law is gone and right and wrong is defined by the size of your gun.

UNWELCOME VISITORS

Henry Watson and his band of warrior survivalists become guests in a fortified town in Michigan. But when the kidnapping of one of the companions goes bad and men die, the group finds themselves on the wrong side of the law, and a town out for blood.

Trapped in a hotel, surrounded on all sides, it will be up to Henry to save the day with a gamble that may not only take his life, but that of his friends as well.

In a dead world, when justice is not enough, there is always vengeance.

END OF DAYS: AN APOCALYPTIC ANTHOLOGY
VOLUMES 1-4

Edited by Anthony Giangregorio

Our world is a fragile place.

Meteors, famine, floods, nuclear war, solar flares, and hundreds of other calamities can plunge our small blue planet into turmoil in an instant.

What would you do if tomorrow the sun went super nova or the world was swallowed by water, submerging the world into the cold darkness of the ocean? This anthology explores some of those scenarios and plunges you into total annihilation.

But remember, it's only a book, and tomorrow will come as it always does.

Or will it?

ETERNAL NIGHT: A VAMPIRE ANTHOLOGY
Edited by Anthony Giangregorio

Blood, fangs, darkness and terror...these are the calling cards of the vampire mythos. Inside this tome are stories that embrace vampire history but seek to introduce a new literary spin on this longstanding fictional monster. Follow a dark journey through cigarette-smoking creatures hunted by rogue angels, vampires that feed off of thoughts instead of blood, immortals presenting the fantastic in a local rock band, to a legendary monster on the far reaches of town.

Forget what you know about vampires; this anthology will destroy historical mythos and embrace incredible new twists on this celebrated, fictional character.

Welcome to a world of the undead, welcome to the world of Eternal Night.

BOOK OF THE DEAD
A ZOMBIE ANTHOLOGY VOL 1
ISBN 978-1-935458-25-8

Edited by Anthony Giangregorio

This is the most faithful, truest zombie anthology ever written, and we invite you along for the ride. Every single story in this book is filled with slack-jawed, eyes glazed, slow moving, shambling zombies set in a world where the dead have risen and only want to eat the flesh of the living. In these pages, the rules are sacrosanct. There is no deviation from what a zombie should be or how they came about. The Dead Walk.

There is no reason, though rumors and suppositions fill the radio and television stations. But the only thing that is fact is that the walking dead are here and they will not go away. So prepare yourself for the ultimate homage to the master of zombie legend. And remember... Aim for the head!

REVOLUTION OF THE DEAD
by Anthony Giangregorio

THE DEAD SHALL RISE AGAIN!

Five years ago, a deadly plague wiped out 97% of the world's population, America suffering tragically. Bodies were everywhere, far too many to bury or burn. But then, through a miracle of medical science, a way is found to reanimate the dead.

With the manpower of the United States depleted, and the remaining survivors not wanting to give up their internet and fast food restaurants, the undead are conscripted as slave labor.

Now they cut the grass, pick up the trash, and walk the dogs of the surviving humans.

But whether alive or dead, no race wants to be controlled, and sooner or later the dead will fight back, wanting the freedom they enjoyed in life.

The revolution has begun!

And when it's over, the dead will rule the land, and the remaining humans will become the slaves...or worse.

Twisted Fish
An Aquatic Anthology
Sturgeon's lotion
PlayFish
Edited by
Anthony Giangregorio

9 781935 458876